Praise for *The Small Stuff*

"Romantic and charming, this book will make you believe in the bumps, twists and turns on the road trip to love."

-Nia Vardalos, NYT best-selling author and Academy Award nominated screenwriter of *My Big Fat Greek Wedding*

"*The Small Stuff* is such a sweet, funny, romantic read. With a brilliant and quirky cast, each charmingly written, this story by Paul Davidson will cling to readers' thoughts days after finishing the final pages."

-Ann Garvin, USA Today best-selling author of *I Thought You Said This Would Work*

"An utterly charming romcom hangout of a book, full of snarky pop culture wit and a languid L.A. vibe that will make fans of P.T. Anderson feel right at home."

-David Yoon, NYT best-selling author of *Frankly In Love*

"*The Small Stuff* is a witty novel with a big heart. Paul Davidson has a clear eye for small details and grand gestures, resulting in a story that would charm even the most hardened cynic. And the repartee between reluctant soulmates Josh and Maggie would make Nora Ephron proud."

-Elizabeth Gonzalez James, author of *Mona at Sea*

"Funny, insightful, and charming as hell, *The Small Stuff* is a meditation on love, fate, and free will that plays out like a classic romantic comedy. It's part Nora Ephron, part Philip K. Dick."

-Melissa Maerz, author of *Alright, Alright Alright: The Oral History of Dazed & Confused*

"A fun, romantic book that reads like putting together a puzzle, *The Small Stuff* is sweet and insightful, full of optimism, wit and surprises. I loved every minute of it."

-Suzy Krause, author of *Sorry I Missed You*

"Davidson does something kind of remarkable here as he turns the romantic comedy on its ear with a wealth of quirky, irresistible charm and clever serendipity. You may never look at the 'meet cute' quite the same again. I defy anyone not to root for Josh and Maggie—and to see a bit of themselves in this adorably self-sabotaging pair."

- Gary Goldstein, author of *The Last Birthday Party*

"*The Small Stuff* dives head first into the machine of life, which must work perfectly if any two people are ever to fall in love. It's crammed with characters so full-blooded and likeable that when you're done you want to send them shiny, nice-smelling gifts. That's because Paul Davidson delivers a genuinely funny book that, if I'm being honest, makes me hate him ... for making it look so easy."

-D.M. Sinclair, author of *A Hundred Billion Ghosts*

"Paul Davidson's *The Small Stuff* traverses space, time, and psyche to render the story of one relationship, insignificant in the grand scheme, at cosmic scale. If God exists, I imagine he is much like the novel's narrator: equal parts lacerating and compassionate, as curious about life's bit players as its stars, possessed of an absurdist wit. Those lucky readers who commit themselves to this other Good Book will find themselves rewarded with hard-won but refreshingly uncynical truths about love, the universe, and everything, as well as a rollicking good time. In our age of revamps, revivals, and resurrections, this is—finally!—an old story, boy meets girl, told in a truly new way. Inventive, hilarious and uncomfortably insightful, *The Small Stuff* is a big deal."

-Luke Geddes, author of *Heart of Junk*

THE SMALL STUFF

PAUL DAVIDSON

HADLEIGH HOUSE
PUBLISHING

Hadleigh House Publishing
Minneapolis, MN
www.hadleighhouse.com

Cover art by Max Dalton
Cover design by Alisha Perkins

ISBN-978-1-7357738-7-2
ISBN-978-1-7357738-8-9 (ebook)
LCCN: 2021923104

For Jen

One

JOSH WAS JUST FOUR years old when his mother shit on his hopes and dreams.

At the time, the "starry sky incident" (as he had come to call it) was nothing more than (what she had come to call) a harmless little anecdote from a fairly normal, trauma-free childhood: A small aside made by his mother as she finished a glass of wine, lounging in a foldout chair on the balcony of their cost-efficient Montauk summer getaway. In the years to follow, as the event would grow (to her dissatisfaction) in importance and prominence, referred to during dinners, in line for the movies, and even on family trips like the one to Niagara Falls in the summer of 1998, she would insist that it was nothing more than her attempt to open up an educated dialogue regarding the vastness of the universe and the current limitations of NASA as an institutional organization. It was, in fact, as Josh would point out multiple times throughout his twenties and thirties, the exact moment when the innocence of his childhood had been taken out behind the shed and put out of its misery.

"Perhaps the shed metaphor had a bit too much *Old Yeller* in it," he would tell a green-shirted co-worker, while they readied the newest exhibits for yet another day of visiting school children.

"I want to go *there*," the four-year-old version of Josh had said, looking through a toy telescope and pointing into the pitch blackness of the universe. It wasn't a desire based on any logic or research or knowledge about how science, math, and technology could make such a thing possible. It was a feeling in the gut of a four-year-old, marveling at something human existence had still yet to wrap its head around, but wanting to make sense of it by inserting himself into the middle of it. He wanted in, he wanted to know more, he wanted to surround himself by its infinite reach … if only someone would give him the chance.

"Yes, but just because you want something," his mother shot back, downing the remaining red wine from her plastic tumbler, "doesn't mean it'll ever happen. You'd be smart to make peace with that now before you go through life with unrealistic expectations."

Josh's father, more than familiar with unrealistic expectations and his wife's history with them, turned to his partner with a look of disdain. *Give the kid a break*, said his face. *Don't ruin the innocence of childhood*, shot forth his unkempt eyebrows. *For God's sake, he's only four*, said his torso, shifting in the least sturdy of the three chairs.

"He's just four," she proclaimed with the faux all-knowing confidence of a lecturer on the TED Talks circuit. "Researchers have proven that children don't even remember anything before the age of five. He'll never remember we had this conversation; I guarantee it."

But he did. And he would. It would rear its ugly head when challenges presented themselves, causing reticence and second-guessing. As he got older, it affected every decision, every desire, sabotaging the high-stakes moments that could have changed his life. It would have been an amazing feat had he been able to get out from under the baggage his mother had thrown onto his plate all on his own. But he couldn't. There would have to be a bigger plan, engineered by forces far more intelligent and powerful than Josh's mother. Somewhere in the midst of it all, the universe would have to step up, marshal others at the periphery of his life, and pull him into the middle of it all. "It takes a village," someone at a wedding once said.

It was at the ripe young age of five that Josh threw caution to the wind and asked his kindergarten desk-mate Tina to go to the movies.

See, Tina was different. She wasn't like the other girls. She shared her 64-pack of crayons (including the built-in sharpener) and often willingly traded packaged snacks for raw vegetables without any noticeable regret. She enthusiastically complimented Josh on his ability to color within the lines, shared her Cheetos without needing to count them out evenly, and helped carry him to the nurse's office that one time he flew head first off the swings into the corner of a metal slide, necessitating fifteen stitches. She didn't smother him like the other grabby, in-your-face kindergarten harlots, who considered a snack-sharing moment as an opening to a future life together.

No, Tina was normal. She wasn't weird or entitled and never tried to evolve their platonic desk-mate relationship into anything more than just that. So, it made sense at the time that Josh would invite her to the opening weekend showing of *Big*, starring none other than *Bosom Buddies* star Tom Hanks in the career-defining role of young Josh Baskin. Yes, it seemed like everything was coming up Joshes, and the universe was clearly trying to tell him something.

But let's be clear. The universe was not telling Josh to share his popcorn with Tina. Not even a person pretending to be the universe would do that. That was a decision thought up, executed, and completed by one Josh and one Josh only. On the surface, it was nothing more than a harmless, little gesture. Insignificant in the larger scheme of things. A decision made by a five-year-old boy, without much thought, except for simply wanting to further a friendship he held in high regard. But at the end of the day, no one person knows how the small stuff in life ultimately affects the bigger moments.

For when Josh walked into Mrs. Diamond's class that next Monday, focused and ready for yet another week of upper and lowercase letters, he was met with a very different Tina. She looked at him excitedly, hovered more closely, and eyed him with a twinkle Josh found foreign and new. It seemed a troubled home life, with a lack of emotional support, encouragement, and (yes) generosity, had left Tina with a black void deep in her heart, making it even easier for a tiny, insignificant moment in the darkness of a suburban movie theater to be the catalyst that would drive her firmly into Josh's spindly, freckled arms.

"Boyfriend and girlfriend," she was said to have announced to the entire class, while leaning in to snatch a Cheetos-laden, saliva-drenched, early-morning smooch.

Josh had let his guard down. He had been bamboozled. Scammed. Ponzi'd. He had become complacent, like most kindergartners his age, focused more on the spoils of Play-Doh molds and naptime Z's rather than matters of the heart. He had taken everything at face value when his five-year-old brain should have spent a little more time identifying the signs and war-gaming the outcomes. The results? A premature relationship proclamation and an overly moist Frito-Lay face-mash would be a visual burned into Josh's head every single time a relationship was at a crossroads. The "normal ones" he'd meet over the years would now automatically come packaged with a "side of Tina," causing him to second-guess every relationship at every turn. It wouldn't stop him from dating and flirting and all the other things that came along with such pastimes, but long-term relationships and the potential of a soulmate never seemed to be in the cards. Eventually Josh would give up all hope in something meaningful, despite his mother's relentless efforts, right about the time hope came rushing back into his life.

As for Tina, "the popcorn incident," as she would often refer to it throughout her twenties and thirties, acted as a catalyst to become a more assured, confident young woman. It would cause her to be more generous to others, take risks she may not have taken before, and become the youngest minority female to ever be hired as CEO of a Fortune 500 company.

But that's a different story altogether.

There was the time when Josh was ten and saw a naked woman for the first time.

"Actually, more like forty-five percent of a naked woman," he'd proclaim, when reminiscing about the moment years later with his friends Cody and Damon. "Maybe it was more like thirty-nine percent. But thirty-nine percent of a naked woman, when you've never seen a naked woman in your entire life, is better than no naked woman at all."

"Zero percent of nothing is *nothing*," Cody, the future money manager, would say, attempting to tie in this abstract conversation about naked bodies with the concept of commissions, the stock market and, let's be honest, him.

The naked woman in question had showed up in the most surprising of places, at the most surprising of times: Out behind the picnic tables of Blydenburgh County Park, left to fend for herself, covered in dirt and discarded like a meaningless, forgotten soul. She had once been glossy, with four distinct corners, sharp and new. But after her twelve-page centerfold had been perused by other, less passionate strangers, only a single layout remained, ripped, covered in dirt, and thrown away with the rest of the day's trash.

It was an object of immeasurable value for three young boys living in an age where there was no Internet porn, swiping left, or search engines that could quell their carnal desires. It was so significant and excitedly gut-churning that as they gazed down at the corner of the woman, side-boob and partial crotch protruding from behind an empty bag of chips, John Williams's *Indiana Jones* score played endlessly (and subconsciously) in their heads.

"Treasure," Cody proclaimed.

"Treasure, indeed," agreed Damon.

It wasn't the first (or last) time that über-composer John Williams would score a significant moment in Josh's life. But it was the first time that he would score two significant moments in one day. Josh often wondered if Mr. Williams had any inkling how often his music made life's major milestones more musical and memorable. At fifteen, he would start to write him a letter on actual paper, with an actual ink-powered writing instrument, outlining how his sex-ual awakening *and* reignited passion for a future career had both been accompanied by Mr. Williams's unmatched talent. But it was a short-lived effort torpedoed by a quickly waning adolescent enthu-siasm. For what sane person cited *Jurassic Park* as the catalyst to a newfound lust for life?

Well, Josh, for one.

The movie had started at 4:55 p.m. Eastern Standard Time. For Cody and Damon, it would exist as a moment of short-lived, sum-mer blockbuster escapism to the *nth* degree. Cody would, like mil-lions of others, be entertained for its full 127 minutes, calling it an "enthralling man-vs.-nature parable" of epic proportions. Damon, on the other hand, would get caught up in the risk-management assessment of it all, wondering how bioengineering company InGen could have greenlit such a project knowing the huge financial risks at play.

And yet, while most people saw it as a cautionary tale about playing God with the building blocks of life, and a slightly small-er contingency viewed it as a warning to employers to pay their IT workers a better living wage, Josh saw it as a clear message about his future.

No, this isn't a story about a young man inspired by the cinema and his meteoric rise through the rank and file of the Hollywood elite. No, this is a story about how math, science, and history hold a meaningful place in society. About how Josh, sitting in a dark audi-torium, could see it taking hold of audiences young and old.

While his earlier passions had been clearly quashed beneath the cynicism of certain parental advisories, that didn't mean his hunger for knowledge needed to stay hidden deep inside. By the time the lights came up, something in Josh had changed.

A naked woman took a back seat to dinosaurs.

And Michael Crichton, author of the original *Jurassic Park* nov-el, would find himself involuntarily selected as the central focus of an enthusiastic, flawed, yet strangely effective UCLA college applica-tion essay entitled "A Mosquito Trapped in Ember (Or, How *Jurassic*

Park Set Me Free from a Childhood in Chains"). It would adhere to the strict University of California application rules. No more than a thousand words, double-spaced, twelve-point font. There could be no fancy titles, colored pictures, or hyperlinks. But there could be quotes.

"Michael Crichton once said that 'If you don't know history, then you don't know anything,'" Josh began the essay. "'You are a leaf that doesn't know it is part of a tree.'

"And I want to be a part of the tree," Josh would write.

When Josh was nineteen and a half, he lost his virginity (clumsily) to Ella Jameson.

When Josh turned twenty, he had slept *un-clumsily* with Ella Jameson over seventy-three times, proceeded to break up with her, and subsequently got punched in the face by Ella's brother Kyle, a well-known superstar on the UCLA Men's Rowing team.

"I walked into a glass doorway that I didn't see," he told the nurse at Student Health.

When Josh turned fifteen and a half, he scored a perfect 100 on his California Driver's test, only to total his car six months later … a mere fifteen minutes after getting his official laminated license in the mail.

At five, Josh's hamster died. At six, it was two goldfish. At seven, Josh's grandmother. At eight, it was his grandfather on his mother's side. At nine, it was John Candy. At fifteen, it was Obi-Wan Kenobi. And at thirty, it was Cody.

The open casket was the worst, sending a wave of unfamiliar tingles into his extremities. It shook him and Damon, standing side-by-side at the edge of the casket, staring down at Cody's made-up face, caked-on whiteness filling in the wrinkles that had formed prematurely over the course of his fast-paced, drug-fueled years. Even his hair, which had started to turn gray in his early twenties, had been reversed back to its original brown.

"It doesn't look like him," Damon said, letting out a heavy breath.

"That's because it isn't," Josh replied, giving his shoulder a squeeze.

"He would have loved it," Damon nodded, smiling.

There were three weddings between the ages of twenty and twenty-two, four weddings between the ages of twenty-two and twenty-eight, and ten more after that. Josh would be best man in three, in the wedding party for four, and responsible for making sure each table's attendees took centered, focused, engaging pictures with their assigned disposable cameras (they didn't). By the time Josh was thirty-five, four would result in divorce, two would be annulled, and one would be Damon's.

"She's my soulmate," he'd tell a thirty-four-year-old Josh over a beer, just five months into the relationship.

"Please."

"Says the non-believer. You know, you'd better not let your father hear you say that."

"It's not that I don't believe in love," said Josh, downing the rest of his jalapeño-infused microbrew. "I just don't believe there's only one perfect person for each of us, and that the universe has engineered all these small moments in our lives to ensure we meet them. Hoping for that seems like ..."

"Like what?"

"Like an unrealistic expectation."

There were the times, over the years, that curiosity would get the better of him. When he'd be walking home from a friend's house on the last night of summer vacation, perched on the edge of a balcony while a party raged on behind him, camping on the side of a mountain, or simply out in his parents' backyard, and he'd look up at the sky, squint past the city lights, and think back to that moment, mere years into his existence, when he was made to place logic over instinct. Cynicism over gut. Practicality over passion. What was so wrong with wanting something and going after it? Why was trusting one's gut so wrong? Why was wanting to go there so dangerous? What was the worst that could happen?

So, it was, at the age of twenty-one, with a math degree from UCLA and the manufactured confidence of a dozen self-help "get the job you were born to have" books, that Josh applied for a staff assistant position in the Engineering department of JPL NASA. He would go through six interviews, spend five hours answering written questions, and wait three days by the phone. Landing the gig would be the Trojan horse that would get him inside one of America's most storied institutions, fulfill a dream he had verbalized at the ripe young age of four, and prove his mother wrong once and for all.

Diana Rowland, the official doppelgänger of actress Annette Bening, replete with bifocals perched on the bridge of her nose and a wavy beehive of auburn hair cradling her face, looked across her messy desk and through the stacks of reference books to Josh. He was wearing a suit, donning a fresh haircut and an optimistic attitude. "I suppose your presence here, in my office, is the answer to the question, what exactly happened with JPL," she said, pursing her lips.

"My mother was right. Unfortunately," replied Josh, embarrassed.

"Well, the world changes constantly," she said, leaning back in her chair and taking a sip of a perfectly elegant looking cup of tea, surrounded by antiques great and small, and framed from behind by posters highlighting black holes, the space shuttle *Endeavor*, butterflies, and dinosaurs. "A person who is right today may not be right tomorrow. Before Bohor, Modreski, Foord, and the Cretaceous-Tertiary boundary, most scientists believed it was falling sea levels and a cooler climate that handed the dinosaurs their fatal walking papers."

"But it was an asteroid," Josh said, matter-of-fact.

"Asteroids, *plural*," she smiled, knowingly. "So, your mother may have been right this year, but after a scant few years of experience under me here at the Center, you may be able to prove her wrong. That is, if you'll accept my impending offer of employment."

Josh straightened up in his chair. It sounded to him like a job offer. A real, official job, with a real, official paycheck. But most importantly? There were *dinosaurs*.

It was 2010. Josh was just twenty-five.

Two

AT FORTY-FIVE, MEL ALLEN tried to put his finger on just how he was feeling.

After spending four years at the New York Institute of Technology getting his Electrical Engineering degree, and twenty years working his way from an entry-level position at Hume Technologies all the way up to his role as Chief Technology Officer, he found himself bored, unmotivated, overworked, and generally …

"… in a rut," he'd tell his wife, Barbara, one night after their son had been excused from the dinner table. He'd been thinking about his feelings for some time. At first, it would be for a split second, while waiting for his coffee or for the elevator doors to open. Then, it would be for the duration of lunch or while taking a shower. Here and there he'd find a respite. Usually, he stopped thinking about them when the show came back from commercials. But lately, even the tongue-in-cheek detectives and the plucky sitcom parents weren't distracting him from the mental thread unravelling right before his eyes. "Maybe it's time to think about changing jobs," he'd tell Barbara. "A change might be good for the whole family."

"But you're the CTO," she would remind him. "What's better than being a CTO at Hume where you're the top dog? The big cheese?

The third name down on the stationary? And you're forty-six, Mel. At forty-six you're doing your career a disservice to acknowledge any feelings of discontent. People don't change careers or get new jobs at forty-six. That's just nine years away from retirement. That's you, Mel. You're *that* guy. The guy who's nine years shy of finishing a career. And besides, who throws themselves into the job market after being somewhere for twenty years? After twenty years you either get downsized, retire, or die getting sucked into the jaws of heavy machinery."

She had a way with words, despite there being a lot of them. Mel let the phrases that annoyed him the most wash over him, taking time to remind himself that at Hume there hadn't been an on-site machinery accident involving an employee in over 317 days. *Maybe you should tell her that*, he thought to himself, thinking twice, as his desire to argue sometimes brought less pleasure than the actual act of not talking at all.

"And don't tell me this would be for the family. It would be for you."

"A family is only as happy as its most unhappy family member," he proclaimed.

"Well, if you were to get a new job and it required us to move to a new city, I would be the most unhappy member in this family," she spit back, throwing down her napkin.

While they weren't soulmates in the googly-eyed sense of the word, they still respected each other. They'd been through a lot over the stretch of nineteen years. They had brought one glorious child into this world, got stung in unison by a school of jellyfish in the Bahamas, been robbed at gunpoint on their way to see *The Starlight Express*, rushed their son to St. Catherine's once to get fifteen stitches, and twice to get his stomach pumped. They had gotten stranded on a cruise ship, snowed in for a week in Tahoe, and bonded over a shared food poisoning experience thanks to Rhonda Eisenberg's learn-to-cook-Indian-food-in-the-privacy-of-your-own-home night. They had fought with each other, refused to speak to one another, and laughed with one another. Once, they sprayed cans of whipped cream at each other, giving chase around the room with reckless abandon, exuding such uncharacteristic joy that it would be a family story repeated throughout the years any time there was a pumpkin pie, apple cobbler, or homemade sundae at the ready. But he'd been letting her drive their life for so many years that he was starting to get motion sickness from living his life in the back seat.

"I've deferred to you more often than not," he began, having rehearsed this many times in front of the TV. Or while eating lunch. Or waiting for the elevator. "There are jobs in education everywhere. Stony Brook isn't the only place that needs English teachers."

"But it's the only place *I* want to teach," she would say, holding on for dear life.

Less than one year later, when Mel was just forty-six, he would make a positive/negative list in an attempt to decide if taking the job offer from ValleyCon was the right thing to do.

"Positive … more money," he'd say, jotting it down on a well-lined piece of graph paper that only electrical engineers like him seemed to keep stocked in full.

"Higher tax bracket," Barbara countered, jamming a bag of apples into the vegetable drawer of the fridge.

"Bigger company, more resources …"

"Bigger company, more politics." Barbara slammed the fridge door, rattling the bottles inside.

"Positive … a fresh start. New town, new schools, new friends."

"New seasons. Just one actually. Seventy-five degrees *all the time*." Barbara threw out a perfectly good, brand-new box of cereal, clearly not paying attention. "Are we really talking about moving to Los Angeles?" she said, eyes pleading. "A move like that can't be good for any of us."

Mel moved to the other side of the island, so he could stand face to face with Barbara. He looked up at her, serious. "I already gave Hume my notice."

There are looks, and there are *looks*. And then there was the look that Barbara Allen gave Mel Allen on the evening of March 28, 2001. No amount of apple jamming, fridge door slamming, and perfectly-good-box-of-cereal throwing would give her the ability to find peace in that one moment. All she could do is stare. Flummoxed. Stunned. Insulted.

"I took the job. I told them this morning."

"You took the job without talking to me? Without talking to us?"

He had. Tim Reingart, the owner of Woodland Hills-based telecommunications success story ValleyCon, had given him the hard sell. Phrases like "company car" and "expense account" and "*carte blanche*" had been peppered throughout what had been their third conversation and first in-person meeting. Mel had come highly recommended, his CTO background perfect for the growing upstart, and it had made Mel feel wanted in a way he hadn't felt for years. He had even convinced his sixteen-year-old son that it would be great for him too, with phrases like "skate parks" and "beaches" and "*carte blanche*."

"You're the only one who doesn't want to go," Mel told her.

"Tell them you changed your mind. Tell them you made a mistake. Pretend you never said anything."

"I can't," he said, unemotional.

"You mean you won't."

"It's true. I won't."

"Even if I ask you to do it for me?"

There was the wind-up. Then the pitch. Then a 95-mile-per-hour fastball smacking Barbara square in the face. "I've been doing things for you for most of our life," Mel said, moving his way out of the kitchen before stopping and turning back. "Isn't it about time I get to do something for me instead?"

And it was. Not only would Mel follow through on his own personal fulfillment, but he would single-handedly introduce a new automation workflow into ValleyCon's manufacturing process in the years to come, which would continue to reduce costs and the need for human workers even after he'd retire in 2018. It was big for the bottom line, but not for lower-wage workers like Hector Alvarez, who would find himself without a job within eighteen months of Mel walking out the door.

Barbara stood silently as Mel turned on his heels and walked out of the room.

At the age of twenty-one, Barbara wasn't quite sure how to answer the question.

"I said … will you marry me?"

Barbara angled her head back down, staring at Mel on his knees. His (then) full head of hair blew wildly with Manhattan and the Twin Towers rising high in the distance behind him.

"Are you sure?" she asked, pulling him up from the ground and gazing at the ring in the black velvet box. Her eyes twinkled with excitement as she stared at the twenty-two-year-old version of Mel, standing tall with a confidence that was infectious.

"This was meant to be," he said, pulling the ring out of the box and placing it gingerly in her open palm. She held the ring up to the sun, watching the colors sparkle in each facet of the gem. "If my parents hadn't moved from Texas to New York, and my mother's sister hadn't moved to the Island, I would have never ended up in the city for college. And if your father hadn't lost his job in Virginia, you wouldn't have ended up here either. And if Leah hadn't dragged you out of your apartment to Odie's that night …"

Barbara looked back to Mel, satisfied that the ring was as amazing as she had originally suggested it could be months prior, in exhaustive detail and with multiple locations where he could find one. "You got a point, Mel?" she smiled, still perfecting her edge that would punctuate much of their later years together.

"The point?" he said, taking the ring out of her hands and sliding it on her ring finger. "The point is that too many things had to happen for us to meet each other. This wasn't random. This was exactly how it was supposed to be. *Fate,* Barbara. You can't turn your back on fate. Which is why you have to say yes."

"Oh, I have to, do I?"

"You don't want to piss off the universe."

"Well, when you put it that way." Barbara wrapped her arms around Mel's neck, pulling him close and kissing him hard. There was nothing else beside them in that moment; nothing else mattered.

"Just don't ever piss me off," she said, eyeing Mel, pulling out of the embrace.

"Never."

"Promise?"

Mel looked back at her and nodded. It was all she needed to feel ready to take the plunge.

Barbara was just twenty when her roommate Leah Devins gave her the choice.

"Odie's or Malcolm's?" she yelled over her shoulder, still finishing her hair in the small studio apartment's bathroom/kitchen/living room mirror.

"Which one is Odie's?" Barbara asked, already good to go, pacing in the space often referred to as the bathroom/kitchen/living room.

"Odie's has dollar drafts and karaoke. Malcolm's has Ladies' Night. That's where the guys buy girls drinks. The bartenders won't even let you buy one if you wanted."

"I'm no charity case," Barbara said, downing the remainder of her red wine. "I say Odie's. Do you care?"

"Nope. It's all up to you."

At the age of twenty-two, Mel and Barbara would get married.

Barbara's father would accompany her down the aisle. She would be wearing the dress her mother had worn decades prior. She would look up, see Mel standing at the front, next to his best man and the officiant, and lose herself in his eyes, his face, his smile. *This is the beginning of something great*, she would think to herself.

At the age of twenty-eight, Barbara would give birth to their first child.

She would be in labor for nine hours, wanting to give up every time the contractions came, and held onto Mel's hand through it all. When her son was born, she would be handed her newborn almost immediately, pulling him close and feeling his tiny little heartbeat against her naked chest. The nurses would take the baby from her and hand him to Mel so they could clean her up. She would look up and see Mel standing there with the baby in his arms, smiling wide. *They really should let the mother hold the baby longer before handing it over to the father*, she would whisper, but not loud enough for anyone to hear.

At the age of thirty-three, Barbara would tell Mel she wanted to enroll in the local junior college so she could get her teaching credentials.

"If it's something I excel at," she told him, dropping pamphlets on the table in front of him, "then I may be able to get a job teaching full-time. It'll be great for all of us." Mel picked up the paperwork, staring at them with fatigued eyes after a day at work. She would look up and see Mel mustering a supportive smile as best he could. *Well, I'll do it for me, then*, she would say to herself.

And at the age of forty-five, after a year-long job search and a particularly contentious kitchen-counter argument not altogether surprising for any marriage that's lasted more than ten years, Mel and Barbara would pick up their lives and the life of their son and relocate to the other side of the country, into their beautiful new house in sunny Tarzana, California.

"Edgar Rice Burroughs, the author of *Tarzan?* He lived in Tarzana. They named the place after him," Mel would tell Barbara on the airplane to Los Angeles. "And now we're gonna be living there, too."

Barbara would hear him. It was just that she didn't have the stomach to respond. The "unrealistic expectations" she'd been warning everyone else to keep an eye on all these years had jumped up and bit her right in the butt after it was too late to do something about it herself.

The moving truck would be three days late, leaving them to buy sleeping bags and camping stoves at the local Big 5 and eat beans out of cans and fruit out of syrup. When the truck finally arrived, she would rush outside to greet them only to find Mel already monopolizing the conversation, giving them pointers for the safest passage up to the house. As she sidled up, Mel turned and smiled, pointing to the truck as if to say *the day you have been waiting for has finally come!*

But Barbara just stared at him. And that damn smile.

For some reason, at that moment, she had a mental flash of Leah Devins's face. Her apartment. That night, as they got ready to go out on the town, after Barbara had made the call to go to Odie's, and Leah had told her: "It's all up to you."

What if I'd chosen to go to Malcolm's instead? Then what?

Would she be standing here now wondering how the bed was going to make it through the two front doors?

The small stuff, it seemed after the fact, wasn't so small after all.

Three

WHEN MAGGIE WAS JUST two minutes old, she downed an entire bottle of formula in six seconds flat. When she was twenty-three minutes old, she'd do it again.

Both were ingested quickly and without pause, setting off a debate among the labor and delivery nurses at Edward Hospital in Naperville, Illinois, about whether previous newborns had ever surpassed such a land speed record. Or had gripped the bottle with such force that it would take two hands to snatch it back once she was done. Or had ignored their newfound respiratory abilities and held their breath throughout it all. None had, except for Maggie. She had come into the world guns blazing, stomach growling, determined to experience her first meal in her own time and on her own terms. The head-scratching doctors, attempting to find some modicum of order and expertise in the chaos of the unknown, spouted hypotheses big and small as to the rhyme and reason around Maggie's edge-case activities. Despite her perfectly average birth weight, some suggested in utero malnutrition, others doubled down on anemia, while the fringe outside-the-box thinkers put their money on lupus. But not Dr. Elgin Taylor. He'd seen this many times before. He knew exactly what it was.

"My money's on dehydration," Dr. Taylor would say without pause. Dr. Taylor, who fancied himself an amateur linguist, had often "put his money" on a variety of medically-inspired bets, including "hurling his greenbacks" at a burst appendix, "laying his lolly" on a norovirus, and tossing his "wad of wonga" into the column appropriately labeled irritable bowel syndrome. Sometimes he was right. More often than not, his confidence outperformed his accuracy. And on this particular day in question, accuracy was not his strong suit.

Now, had her personality been fully formed at that moment (and some say it already was), Maggie might have wondered why eating necessitated an entire room of doctors to justify such hunger as a medical malady. She might have worried that this new, bright place she'd just dropped into was filled with judgment, opinion, and entitlement at her own expense. She might have thought about turning right back around and leaping into the safety of her mother's birth canal. But instead, she looked up at her mother, seemingly happy and oblivious, and her father, relieved, face red and exhausted, which would just be the beginning in a long life of Maggie-inspired fatigue. She realized if they were good, she could be too. At least, after fulfilling one simple, instinctive urge to eat. After all, she was ...

"... just hungry," one of the nurses would proclaim, clearly in tune with Maggie and much more in-the-know than the men stumbling over themselves to be the experts in the room. "Let's not give this one body dysmorphia on the first day of her life on Earth. She'll have so many more years to develop that on her own."

Maggie smiled. It may have been because she appreciated the support. It could have been because a third bottle of formula was making its way into her belly. It was probably because she was filling her first earthly diaper with a puddle of liquid so warm it made her feel awake and alive.

If rumor serves, it wouldn't be the last time. No, that would occur at the age of thirty-three, after a particularly memorable evening involving a TV show, a hip new restaurant, a famous movie, and an argument no two humans should have ever had.

At the age of eight, Maggie's father would give her the first camera she would ever own.

Hailing from 1957, the Nikon SP was the first choice among photojournalists and sports photographers, featuring a single stroke film-wind lever, cloth focal-plane shutter with speeds of 1/1000 a second, and even a self-timer. It had a clean chrome finish, favored an outstanding Nikkor 35mm wide-angle lens, and held a patch on the inside of the case that read, *To Maggie, a student of life, Love Dad.*

As for Maggie? She just loved that it had "a strap so I can wear it like a necklace."

She'd seen her father take pictures before on the construction sites of the suburban monoliths he'd overseen, usually of less-than-exciting inanimate objects made of steel and wood and space-age plastic. He had built churches and community centers and even a floating casino boat that the churches and community centers wished would take the hint and float away to some other town. Years later he'd build a waterslide park called Splashdown, but Maggie would be long gone by then, living in another version of "cold" on the East Coast and pursuing a liberal arts education that would barely give her the experience for a real-world career or the money to rent an apartment somewhere warmer on her own. But that was years later, well before her fascination with her father's own Canon VI-T, and decades before she'd take such fascination and put it to good use.

In the beginning, she replicated the inanimate stylings of her father, taking abstract shots of cluttered closets and misplaced shoes. There was a particularly fascinating series of photos documenting the clogged shower drains of her family's home, followed up by a series contemplating where missing socks went to die and a twenty-two-photograph mosaic each highlighting one of Maggie's finger (or toe) nails. But as Maggie's bulletin board collection of developed photos grew, so too did her appetite for expanding her scope and reach. Inanimate objects segued into dead bugs and plants. Dead bugs and plants evolved into candid shots of living family members, delivery men and gardeners, and self-portraits of Maggie brushing her teeth, eating her breakfast, and sleeping in bed. Eventually, when the sights in and around Maggie's home had been exhausted, she took to joining her father at his downtown office, set in an industrial area of town, nestled between an auto parts exporter and a plumbing warehouse. For most kids, a summer shacked up with their father in his place of work would have been tedious. For Maggie, her father's consistency, heart, and measured affection for her drew her closer to him still. She wanted to impress him. She wanted his approval. For Maggie, that's all that had ever mattered. The camera represented their unique connection; she was going to take care of it and put it to good use if it was the last thing she'd do.

"I'm taking photos of *everything*," she'd proclaim, snapping pictures of the buildings around them, the passing work vans, their license plates, and the men who drove them. "This is way better than home," she'd smile, nudging up against her father.

He'd shrug sheepishly to his fellow tenants, and give her a placating pat on the head as he'd return to his office where blueprints and permits were the concerns of the day. He'd call her in so they could have lunch together at his massive wooden desk piled high with papers, making their way through pickles and chips and Mom's famous tuna fish sandwiches. Then he'd send her back out to do whatever it was she was excited about doing until it was time to jump back in the Caddy and head straight home.

One day, there were gunshots, sirens, and screeching cars.

Maggie's father bolted to the door, only to be met by Maggie and a trio of accompanying men by her side. One stood stoic in a double-breasted suit. Another, draped in a slick blue FBI jacket, was joined by a police officer holding Maggie's camera by the strap, allowing it to hang like an oversized necklace.

"Has something happened?" Maggie's father would ask, pulling Maggie into an embrace. "Is something wrong?"

"The auto parts folks next door," said the slick blue FBI jacket, "are what's *wrong*. We've been watching them for months, and let's just say what we've seen and heard resulted in our presence here today."

"A sting," proclaimed Maggie, proud, then embarrassed by her father's look of horror. "That's what *they* said it was. Is that going to hurt?" the uninformed eight-year-old wondered.

"Your daughter," continued the double-breasted suit, "took a few pictures we suspect could bring a measurable amount of clarity to the investigation currently at hand."

"I actually took a lot of pictures," she'd confirm, proud that her doggedness had a place and value in this great big world.

The pictures would be the prosecution's major exhibit in the case, result in the shuttering of many establishments owned by those involved, and culminate in the sentencing of dozens of individuals whose vehicles, license plates, and faces had accompanying photographic evidence that proved their involvement in illegal activities over the course of many months. There would be serious prison sentences, back-room deals, and the end of an era for one of suburban Chicago's most infamous upstart criminal endeavors.

"And all because of that darn Nikon camera," Maggie's mother would announce at the dinner table weeks after the sentence had been handed down. "If you had never bought her that camera, those horrible people may never have been caught."

Maggie's father, the epitome of calm and collected, would finish his twenty-eighth chew before wiping the corners of his mouth and taking a swig of water. He was the kind of man who thought long and hard before he imparted any wisdom on those around him. That was often why his words were treated as the gospel, so to speak. And this night was no different.

"If I'd put that much thought into buying that camera at the time, I probably wouldn't have bought it at all. You can't live life second guessing every single decision you make," he said, nodding to Maggie and her brother Teddy. "If you did, you'd never move forward at all. You'd always be stuck in the moment. Besides, God has a plan, and he'll make you aware of what that is when he's ready. You've got to be patient."

Maggie had no trouble making quick decisions and worrying about the consequences later. It was the patience thing that got under her skin. She wasn't good at being patient. Not then, not now, and not ever.

At the age of thirteen, during the early summer months of 1998, Maggie learned the truth about false advertising.

"It'll be an experience you'll never forget."

"You'll witness one of the wonders of the world!"

"It'll be like you stepped back into the annals of history!"

As is usually the case with false advertising, there's always a disappointing kernel of truth hidden deep inside each sweeping statement, and that wasn't much different for Maggie over the course of one week, during the month of May, on her way from the Midwest to the East Coast.

In a car.

Not a *plane.*

"Not a plane?" she'd ask, passive-aggressively.

"No. The car," her parents would reply.

The parental advertising was somewhat, partially, annoyingly true. It was an experience she would never forget. A three-day, ten-hour drive from suburban Chicago to Niagara Falls, NY. A car ride that existed in the pre-Internet world, where counting cars, spelling "for fun," and listening to the entire soundtrack of *Jesus Christ Superstar* ad nauseum coexisted with arguments about whose leg crossed over the backseat line of demarcation, how long it would be until they would get there, and the fiery debate over why the trip had to actually happen in the first place. "Because it is an experience," her mother would tell her. "An experience you will never forget."

It was true. And *false.* In the most annoying ways possible.

Maggie would wonder why she wasn't seeing any of the seven wonders of the world, a label reserved for The Great Pyramids of Giza or The Great Wall of China. Or Petra, Jordan. Or Christ the Redeemer. Or Machu Picchu.

"Niagara Falls is the eighth wonder of the world," her mother would shoot back in proclamation-mode, with no Internet available to prove her wrong. "Or maybe the ninth. For sure it's the tenth. Or thirteenth. Is it a wonder of the world at all?"

"If only the Encyclopedia Britannica wasn't so heavy," her father said, "we could walk around with all that information at our fingertips, for situations such as these."

"But we're not even *at* Niagara Falls," Maggie would argue, looking out the window of the car at Newfane, New York, a city forty minutes out from the wonderous waterfalls, which were actually not so wondrous after all.

Newfane: Host of the annual Apple Blossom Festival held once a year on May 19, it was always everyone's second stop after visiting the Falls. For Maggie's family, it just happened to be the first. It was one part county fair, one part Civil War encampment, and one part old-timey 19th-century town recreation. A historical experience with an old-school blacksmith, museum barbershop, food, music, crafters, and even a pitch-perfect refurbished general store. Despite all the parts it did have, Maggie didn't want a part of it at all.

"It's like you stepped back into history," her mother would proclaim excitedly, eyeing Maggie as she slumped down onto a wooden bench in front of the W.G. Hall General Store. "Like *really* stepped back into history," she'd enunciate, covertly motioning to a depressed-looking teenager sitting beside her, dressed in a historically accurate Civil War uniform. "Smile for me, honey," she said, taking out an instant camera and snapping a shot of Maggie wearing her trademark sarcastic smile next to her less-than-amused bench mate. "We'll come back to get you after we watch them churn the apple butter, okay?"

"Have fun with that," she said, throwing her head back in utter fatigue as the rest of her family made their way down a dusty road and off toward another termite-infested structure.

"It's actually completely devoid of fun," said the Civil War soldier, staring straight ahead, stoic.

"I was being sarcastic."

"Besides, it takes a minimum of six hours to churn that apple butter. They're gonna show your family something they churned yesterday afternoon. Day-old apple butter. They're going to *churn back time*," he joked, dryly.

"You work here? Because your lack of enthusiasm for the apple butter really torpedoes the excitement around this place."

"No, I don't work here," he replied, embarrassed.

"So dressing like that is a *choice*?" she shot back, tweaking the corner of his uniform's pocket flap.

"Not *my* choice."

"Then whose?"

Four adult Civil War soldiers, seemingly on their way to a faux skirmish, walked by. They stopped rigidly to salute the young man, only moving along once he reluctantly saluted them back.

"My mother's. She kind of gets carried away. She thinks it's educational. You know, like an …"

"Experience?" they both said in unison.

"Do you always do what your mother says?" Maggie asked, truly curious.

"You clearly don't."

"And neither should you."

The teenaged Civil War soldier straightened out the wrinkles in his uniform, then turned rigidly toward Maggie. He saluted her with some authentic-looking hand motions.

"That for real?" she'd ask.

"No idea. The Civil War really isn't my jam."

He walked off. She watched him go. "More like an experience I'll *forget*," she'd laugh.

There were quieter times, Friday and Saturday nights when Maggie found herself in her room, defending her lack of nighttime activities to concerned parents asking pointed questions through her hollow bedroom door. The real truth, which she wouldn't realize for years to come, was that her extroverted confidence scared off the boys from her school and the surrounding areas. Her lack of swooning made them think she wasn't interested, bordering on aloof. Her ability to give it back to them in a similarly egotistical way made her a wild card in a sea of boring, self-conscious, aim-to-please high school girls.

When Maggie was seventeen, she'd find herself at home alone while the junior prom raged three miles away. When she was eighteen, she'd ask her college-aged neighbor to accompany her to her senior prom, ensuring that as long as she could control the narrative, she'd do just that.

There were the four years between the ages of eighteen and twenty-one, while Maggie attended Boston University, that she would dive head first into a long-term relationship with Caleb Parsons, of the Milwaukee Parsons.

"My family made their money in highway reflector dots," he'd tell her on that first night together in Kilachand Hall, highlighting a yet-to-be-hung shadow box framed around the very first highway dot to incorporate the concept of retroreflection. "Retroreflection," he'd often say, was the "technology of the future" and this generation's "armor of light." Without it, "the world would be plunged into a darkness the likes of which only the Bible could have predicted."

That was usually when he'd quote Joel 2:2 and the days of "darkness and gloom" that would "spread over the mountains." That was also usually when Maggie would tune him out completely.

"He's harmless and committed," Maggie would say in response to people who wondered why she had been with him so long. Why would a girl like her be with an almost forgettable guy like him? Why, when there was clearly interest from myriad men looking to find a way into her heart (or pants), would she continue to settle for someone so dependable, respectable, and normal? Why wasn't she out there, pounding the collegiate pavement, looking for her match? For the Yin to her Yang? For her complete and utter soulmate?

"Because there's no such thing as a soulmate," she'd admit to her junior year roommate Cameron one Friday in April, minutes after downing her third *cervesa* of the afternoon. She'd eye Caleb from across the room as he ordered another round from the bar of a San Felipe, Mexico, spring break staple called Rockadile's. "And if there's no such thing as a soulmate, then why waste my time looking for one?"

Cameron stared at her, then Caleb, then back. She shrugged.

"What I should be looking for is the bathroom," Maggie slurred, pushing herself up from the bar stool. "Maybe I should just start with the small stuff and prioritize that?"

At the age of twenty-eight, Maggie's future unknowingly found her.

The Fisherman and the Whale had been the hottest new Pescatarian place in all of L.A., serving up unique and flavorful dishes for the cross-section of the city who had decided on a whim to add fish to their restrictive vegan lifestyle. Chef D.B. Fenton, the mastermind behind it all, had relocated from Seattle ten months prior, leaving his last five hot spots in the more-than-capable hands of his sous-chefs. He had spent months getting the red velvet menus just right, with an embossed quote stretching across the front and back, bedazzled in such a way that the number of times it was re-grammed during those early days of Instagram's launch could not be enumerated or tracked.

"*Give a man a fish, and you'll feed him for a day,*" the quote began on one side of the folded, furry menu. "*Make a man a fisherman, and he'll serve you up a whale.*"

"Do they serve whale here?" Cameron asked Maggie. "Do they serve whale anywhere?"

"Only in the face of international condemnation," Maggie replied, sipping her drink.

Cameron read the quote on the menu, still determined to crack the code. "Does that make sense to you?" She was really trying to get to the meaning, something her years as a reality TV show producer in Los Angeles couldn't help her with.

"I think it's a *Moby Dick* reference, right?"

"*Moby Dick?* No, it's not from *Moby Dick.*"

"So maybe it means …" Cameron began, pausing to finish her colorful cocktail. "Well, a fish only feeds you for a day. But, man, if you learn to fish, baby, you're not eating little tiny fishes anymore. You're able to go so much bigger!" Cameron was feeling it. Grasping at straws had brought her around to a significant, allegorical outcome.

"It's an inspirational quote, Mags. Think big and life will return the favor. Right?"

"I think they just miscopied the quote," she lamented, as her salmon entrée landed in front of her, and an entire grilled Branzino (eyes and all) with wild Tunisian mountain capers landed in front of Cam.

"I feel like I'm in *Game of Thrones*," Cameron said, picking up the entire fish by its head and posing with it.

Maggie looked down at her plate, adorned by the minimalist salmon filet, lightly seasoned alongside a pile of steamed spinach. She dug in, letting the food hit her palate and rolling over her taste buds. She chewed, taking her time, evaluating the taste. Even now, twenty-eight years after she came into this world, she was still making room for food in her own time and on her own terms.

"Everything tasting amazing?" the sidled-up server asked. Maggie turned, swallowing her bite, letting the flavor dissipate as she took a sip of her drink. She eyed Cameron, who was clearly aware of what was coming next.

"I'm glad you asked," she began, turning her chair toward the server, "because we have been trying to get a reservation here for months, and only did because someone else backed out. Clearly because they transitioned back to meat."

"I understand," said the server. "Well, we are glad we could accommodate you tonight."

"But you kind of didn't," she continued. "Because if you had truly set out to accommodate us, you clearly would not have served me this," she glared, pointing at the salmon filet perched on the edge of her plate.

"Is it not to your satisfaction?" the server asked, concerned.

"Where shall I begin?" she said, lifting up the plate. "What should have been flavorful and moist lands on the side of brackish. There's an inordinate amount of pepper overpowering what should have been a subtle scent of rosemary, based on the description on the menu …"

"Of course, but—"

"… and when a customer asks for fish to be cooked medium-well, that means it's a pink hue, not red. So, when you ask me if everything is tasting amazing, I'm sorry but I have to be honest and tell you it's not. For D.B. Fenton, known to uphold a certain level of quality at his establishments, it is not. For a pair of women with relatively modest salaries, living in an expensive city like L.A., who have been trying to get in here for months, it is not, dear sir. No, it is far from that."

The server was speechless. Perhaps it was Maggie's blunt response. Or her eloquent way of delivering it. Or her vowels, having a slight *Downton Abbey* feel as she gave him the British-sounding smackdown. Embarrassed, he picked up the plate perched in Maggie's hands and turned to walk away. Cameron, impressed yet again, gave Maggie a high-five with the fin of her new friend, the Branzino. One of the two women sitting behind them at another table stood up to make her approach.

"Pardon me," the woman said, coming around to face Maggie, "but I overheard what you said, and the skill in which you said it. And I think there's someone you should meet."

Maggie looked up, deer in headlights.

In the larger scheme, it was small. But its significance in Maggie's life would end up being huge.

Four

TREY KNUDSEN CHANGED HIS last name at the age of ten.

"I'm good with the Trey part," he'd tell his parents, blocking the TV with a handful of paperwork. "But the courts say you guys hafta change it for me cuz I'm not eighteen."

"What the hell is wrong with your last name, boy?" Lanelle would ask, halfway off the couch in a defensive position that often became an offensive one in less than thirty seconds flat. She wasn't a big woman by any means, but her beehive of unkempt hair made her scary, and the proliferation of freckles gathered under her eyes made her intimidating. Thing was, Trey seemed to be the only person (inclusive of his father, Tyrell) who wasn't fazed by her one single bit.

"*Knudsen*? That's like a juice. Like an apple juice. I ain't ever gonna be famous with a last name that makes people think about apple juice. There's no edge to that!"

"You *aren't* ever going to be famous," Ty, ever the stickler for proper grammar, would correct him. There was a reason Trey would be attending Coliseum College Prep Academy next year. Ty knew first impressions were everything, and he wanted his boy to have the best chance at making good ones. And if he was lucky, an opportunity to get out of Havenscourt and experience what a college education could do for a boy like him.

"See, Pops gets it."

"I wasn't agreeing with you, Trey. Besides, Knudsen makes grape juice, too. You love grape juice."

"Now you're just stereotypin' me, Pops."

It had been happening for decades. The younger generation strategically out-thinking and out-planning the older one. All Ty and Lanelle had known was Havenscourt, Oakland. They were born down the street at Highland Hospital, then grew up on 66th just a few doors down from one another. They'd meet in school, fall in love, get pregnant, and set up a home. Ty had bucked the tradition of a blue-collar job by getting his C.P.A. license and setting up a small shingle a few blocks away. In spite of the small steps they'd made for themselves, they couldn't imagine ever leaving this place behind. But they'd imagined a different future for Trey, one that included a college degree.

"I prefer the college of life," he'd tell an unhappy Ty and Lanelle when he turned seventeen, taking the many college pamphlets and applications that Ty had sent for and delivering them straight into the garbage.

That's because Trey always had something else in mind. Something far less scholastic but far more entertaining. Something he'd been dreaming about since he had first stepped out in front of a captive audience.

YouTube was born on February 14, 2005 in San Mateo, California, to parents Steve Chen, Chad Hurley, and Jawed Karim. One year later, by the time Trey was eleven years old, the site would see 48 hours of new videos being uploaded to the site every single minute.

But on July 15, 2006, four minutes and twenty-seven seconds of the videos would be of a young comedy stand-up with the edge-worthy name of Trey *Knight*, a surname inspired by the artistic stylings of one George R.R. Martin and his stories of kings, queens, wizards, and yes, knights.

Trey came out of the womb expressing his opinion, despite the fact that no one else knew what he was saying at the time. He would speak his first words at the age of two, his first sentences at the age of three, and his first stand-up comedy routine about peas at the age of four.

"I hate peas," he'd begin, warming up the very small crowd (Ty and Lanelle) at the dinner table. "It's like an explosion of nasty in your mouth."

The true, genuine, echoing laughter gave Trey the fuel for his fire.

At five, Trey would start to monopolize family gatherings, Thanksgiving dinners, Christmas mornings. The third child in a family of four, there were always three other consistently annoyed siblings, especially when their own birthday parties were hijacked by Trey, desperate to try out his latest material on an unsuspecting group of sugar-enhanced captive school friends. It would evolve into recess sets in first grade, full-on snack-break shows in second, followed by openers and musical accompaniment in third, fourth, and fifth. Trey's engaging personality and ability to make anyone his friend allowed him to marshal a group of followers who encouraged him at every turn.

But he needed to expand his audience past the limitations of Havenscourt.

When his four-minute and twenty-seven-second YouTube premiere video, *Knight Moves,* hit the platform, it would generate close to two hundred and fifty thousand views in the first twenty-four hours. By the time it had been live on the platform for a week, it would hit a million. By the time a month had gone by, Trey had been contacted by a manager, an agent, and the creative minds behind Broadway's *Martin Short: Fame Becomes Me.*

The subject matter wasn't anything special. The set list wasn't anything groundbreaking. But Trey's charisma and confidence at the young age of eleven predicted big things for the future. If he could capture the imagination of millions of people at age eleven, there was no reason to think he couldn't do it at twenty-one.

If anyone was being honest, a rarity in Hollywood, they would have said that *Malibu Mom* was a complete and total rip-off of *The*

Fresh Prince of Bel-Air. Instead of telling the story of a young Philly teen coming to live with his rich aunt and uncle in Bel-Air, it told the ham-fisted story of a crew of brothers and sisters from Detroit coming to live with their rich godmother in Malibu after their parents had died in a tragic public transportation accident. The logic behind how Jeannie Taylor (aka Malibu Mom) had been chosen as the godmother was glossed over in the pilot episode (*"Back on Am-Track"*), despite a short exchange between Jeannie and the eldest of the Green family, Michael (played by Trey Knight, in his first-ever scripted network appearance), illustrating the lazy writing the short six-episode run would be known for.

"I mean, it all makes sense to us. You were kinda like their mom when they went to college here in L.A.," said Michael, sipping a kale-infused green juice across the kitchen table from Jeannie.

"Mom, landlord, same thing."

[Laugh Track]

"Didn't you evict them once?"

"Yes, but I gave them a hug when I did."

[Laugh Track]

"But you taught them how to be adults. You taught them how to be responsible. It's why they made you our godmother. That, and the most important thing of all …"

[Michael takes a sip of the green juice, looking back up.]

"You're all about the Benjamins."

[Jeannie looks confused. Some audience chuckles.]

"What I mean is, you're rich."

[Raucous Laugh Track. Jeannie rolls her eyes.]

The show would bomb. The network would burn off the last four episodes on their new streaming service, free and with ads. An online journalist based in Dayton, provided legitimate credentials by Rotten Tomatoes, would write that "the show was less pleasant than a colonoscopy but more pleasant than having one's wisdom teeth removed."

"Is that good or bad?" Trey would ask his manager, who would simply throw his arms up and shrug.

"I think that's good," Trey would tell his therapist in the months following the crash and burn.

Trey would return to the stand-up circuit, honing his skills and re-building his ego alongside a pile of new, irreverent jokes and a reputation for biting social commentary. He would get up at seven in the morning every day, hit Runyon Canyon for an hour, drink his kale-infused green protein shake and then sit down for five hours of writing. Sometimes it would be good, more often it would suck. But Trey remained determined to whittle down an hour from the chaff, with the eventual goal of securing a huge paycheck from a company flush with cash.

When the offer came, it shook Trey to the bone.

Four months later he'd be sitting in his office, below the *Up All Knight* logo, interviewing producers for his new syndicated night-time talk show. He'd be wearing a tailored suit, with a backwards cap, and showcasing the multiple longswords perched on the wall behind him in a clear homage to his last name, a certain medieval hit novel and a lifetime of obsession. Hanging from the ceiling was a model Amtrak train going in circles, and circles, and circles, all day long.

"I like to think of the team I'm building like the Round Table," he began, running his finger across the length of Sword #1. "Honor. Integrity. Honesty. A group of folks that got everyone else's backs. Traitors will be drawn and quartered." Trey eyed the woman across the table, then looked down at her resume. She was new to town, with a few segment producing credits to her name for reality TV shows whose titles sounded patently made up. But the people she worked with gave her glowing reviews, as evidenced by the scribbles and notes he had taken in the margins, the result of phone calls and feedback.

Her name was Cameron Fitz.

"You kind of fucked up your career with, what was it," began Cameron. "*Malibu Mom?*"

Trey sat back in his chair, at first serious. "That shit was a mistake," his mouth widening to a smile. "It's no one's fault but mine. I chose that piece of steaming garbage, and that failure is going to make *this* show a huge fucking success." He looked up at the Amtrak model, *toot toot tootin'* up by the ceiling lights. "That baby reminds me there's always an impending disaster around the bend, so I gotta be vigilant … *always*."

Cameron eyed Trey with suspicion. She looked down from the train and then up to the swords on the wall.

"Well, 'once you've accepted your flaws, no one can use them against you.'"

Trey's eyes went wide. "That's from *Game of Thrones*? I love me some *Game of Thrones*! The books, I mean. That TV series was jacked." He gave Cameron another once-over, this time feeling like they were cut from the same cloth. "You don't have a lot of credits. You don't have a ton of experience."

"But what I do have," she shot back, "is exactly what you need."

"Sure, but what do *you* need?" Trey asked.

"I'd like to be able to make enough to rent a two-bedroom apartment out here. Twenty-five hundred a month is insanity for a gal like me."

"So, you're hungry," he replied, gauging her expression. "Hungry for opportunity, I mean."

"I'm always hungry," Cameron nodded, then picked a French fry out of Trey's Styrofoam container and took a bite. Someone from Depression-era America might have commented on her moxie.

"You're gonna be my Daenerys, aren't you? You're gonna protect this show like it was your first-born motherfucking dragon baby."

Cameron Fitz grabbed another handful of fries, munching away. When her mouth was clear of distractions, she let out a strange, compelling, high-pitched dragon cry.

Trey sat back, arms crossed. Debating. *Was this crazy-ass cracker too crazy for him?*

At the age of twenty-nine, Cameron Fitz walked out of a job interview that would change her life forever.

There was a spring in her step as she navigated the shaded corridor between massive studio stages, pulling out her cell phone and hitting speed dial. The phone on the other end rang. And rang.

"Hello?" Maggie's voice piped through the tinny speakers of Cam's Motorola.

"Pack your bags, baby," she excitedly chimed into the phone. "Now *you're* comin' to L.A.!"

Five

THE SKY WAS BLUE. And the sun was yellow. *Again.*

Josh lay in his king-sized Slattum, still half-asleep, peeking out from beneath his oversized Hönsbär, unsure that the hues outside his window were actually real. He squinted to get a better look, propping up his disheveled head of brown hair on one of his two Jordröks and widening his eyes. How, indeed, could the most perfect blue sky and warm, inviting yellow sun exist outside the second floor of his townhouse without the CGI often employed to create such flawless views? And in Burbank, California, no less.

Simple answer? They couldn't.

But Josh always looked at the realities of life and often imagined them in a colorful way, perhaps with a more exciting backstory and a sunnier, more fantastical perspective. He was constantly (and subconsciously) taking hold of the childhood innocence his mother hadn't bred out of him and doubling down in an attempt to make up for his oft-proclaimed deficiencies. It was the same old story since the dawn of time. Parents unknowingly ruined their children's lives, those children parented *their* children in the total and complete opposite way, then *those* children countered their baggage by reversing course yet again. It was a never-ending cycle of overcompensation that Josh had perfected over the years, as he tried to insert a sense of wonder into his life that he felt had been stripped from his early years. And it was a game that he was completely committed to.

There was the time Josh spent a month trying to convince his co-workers that the dress was white and gold, not blue and black. There was a particular week when he carried around a laminated drawing of the classic old woman/young woman illusion, attempting to push most of his close friends and family into the "young girl" camp. Every once in a while, after a night of physical intimacy with a newfound friend, he'd point out the townhouse's window to the illusion of the sky and the sun and call it his own personal Penrose stairs.

"What's a Penrose?" said every single girl who ever stayed over at his house.

"Can I call you a Lyft?" was usually his answer back.

"Maybe you should try to meet girls somewhere other than bars," Damon would say, over drinks, with his fiancée Lisa by his side.

Josh pushed the Hönsbär off his body, getting up off his Slattum and moving to the window to survey the day ahead. Outside, dozens of upscale townhouses littered his street, and the one beyond that, and the one beyond that, extending out five blocks to the center of town. What once was farmland stretching out as far as the eye could see, then repurposed for housing as the soldiers of World War II returned home, had now become what every undesirable neighborhood in the United States had also become: a real estate developer's dream. The urban professionals like Josh, with years of a career under his belt and a salary with at least six numbers, came pouring in, bidding up the prices to unfathomable heights. With such lucrative pricing, it only made sense that a similarly pricey commercial district would follow close behind. It was a necessity. For where would such Los Angelenos go at the end of the day when work had come and gone? Unfortunately, everyone who bought a townhouse with the promise of their own Burbank-adjacent "Rodeo Drive" just a few blocks down the street was sorely disappointed.

"But there's a Hooters," his in-the-know neighbor, Antonio, once told him.

"Yeah, you've mentioned that several times," Josh would frown, checking that no one nearby had overheard their conversation.

"Also, a Black Angus." Antonio was a meat and potatoes and breast man, who traded stocks from his bedroom in front of three huge LCD computer screens that were always on. Sometimes it was impressive. Other times it made Josh wonder why he thought it was impressive.

"Those still exist?"

"And don't forget the El Pollo Loco."

But in a sea of such mediocrity, there was a shining beacon of hope. A glorious blue and yellow monolith that was not the sky and not the sun. It was none other than the upper northwest corner of a building. A building that was Scandinavia's ultimate claim to fame, not to mention a flagship record-breaker. A 456,000-square-feet behemoth, consuming 22 acres, providing 1,700 parking spots, and having been officially dubbed the largest one of its kind in the entirety of the United States.

Yes. It was IKEA.

"No furniture, no problem," his real estate agent had told him one night, three and a half years prior, as he handed Josh the key to his first official homestead. "They're supposed to open some amazing new retail shops here soon, so you should have a pretty good variety of choices as you're furnishing your dream home!" All these years later, the Jordrök really illustrated the chasm between Los Angeles' ability to tell you a story and the possibility of actually having it come true.

"Another day in paradise," Josh lamented, staring out the window at the muted blue sky.

Elsewhere in Los Angeles, Hank pushed a shopping cart down the street, dragging a second one behind him via an ingenious pulley system that used multiple carabiners, twine, and duct tape.

Between the two carts, he had more than enough personal belongings to qualify as a resident of the city. There were sleeping bags, canned food, clothing, water, chargers, and electronics. Alongside him, keeping up, was a perky Golden Retriever named Sammy that he had saved from a local shelter just six months prior.

"You're a regular ol' Mister Wizard," his Grandma Maddie once told him, proud as she perused his science fair entry *How Condensation Works*, which would eventually score him second place out of the entire sixth grade at Tulsa South Elementary. Gramma Maddie was always there for him, especially in light of his father picking up and leaving two years prior and his mother working double shifts to put food on the table. When Maddie passed a few years later, the 2nd Place ribbon Henry had given her found its way back into his life, and he immediately pinned it onto the lapel of his clean blue jacket, reserved for Sunday morning's trip to church.

But that was then.

Now, his clothes were tattered, a combination of camouflage cargo pants and a worn white t-shirt with the Pep Boys logo on it, covered mostly by an oversized Member's Only black jacket, with the familiar 2nd Place ribbon barely noticeable, peeking out from his front left pocket. His face, disheveled and donning an unwieldy beard of Gandalf proportions, hid who he was from most of the world. But his eyes still held that childhood curiosity, that obsession with tinkering and constructing. They held the question that he asked himself every morning when Sammy licked his face awake: How did I get here? How did life land him in this place? What small *zigs* could he have made instead of the infamous *zags*? He moved on, eyes diverting outward to the buildings around him and the well-manicured rose gardens across the street. Seemingly having somewhere to be, he pushed his sleeve up to reveal an old-school Casio calculator watch and looked at the time. It was 8:55 a.m.

"Gotta go, gotta go!" he shouted to Sammy, pulling him and the two carts quickly toward the intersection as the red illuminated crosswalk countdown continued. 7 … 6 … 5 … 4 … 3 … 2 …

He increased his speed as the red *DO NOT WALK* hand appeared.

But it was too late. Once the carts were moving there was no stopping them. They flew off the curb and into the crosswalk, pulling Hank via the twine and pulley system into the center of the road. The carts flew over on their side and Hank went down on the concrete hard.

Somewhere nearby, the sound of a screeching car rang out, and Hank looked up.

Maggie had a morning ritual.

It began with the quiet sounds of the French Countryside—mostly birds tweeting and brooks babbling and the soft sound of a spring breeze blowing through the trees. Somewhere, a young child called out in French *à quelle heure est le petit déjeuner*. There were wooden wheels traversing cobblestone streets and the distant sound of motorcycles and automobiles on the roads. The sounds came from the smart hub beside her bed, which could also convert currency and tell knock-knock jokes, and always put Maggie in a wonderful mood. Perhaps that was because these were the sounds that kept her sane during her final trying month in the City of Light, putting a period on the year she'd spent in Paris after college experiencing the culture, the food, and the self-absorbed, egotistical, abhorrent men she never wanted to see again. The sounds, it seemed, were Maggie's way of putting lipstick on a pig; of hanging a little tree air freshener from her car's rear-view mirror.

Except the pig was life. The stench in the car was certain unforgettable events that had happened to her while she was there. The calming, romantic sounds of France obfuscated the memories she didn't want in her head, and covered them up until she felt capable of addressing them. Until then, the allegorical scents of Lemon Grove, Spice Market, and Vanillaroma hanging from the metaphorical rear-view mirror of her life, in the hypothetical car, would have to do.

As for her morning ritual, that was just the beginning.

It continued with the AirPods. Then, the checking of the pony in her modest bathroom mirror. The Boston University tee (or sweat-shirt, depending on the weather), the cut-off shorts, and optional second layer. The neon Nike cross-trainers. Where some would blast pop songs of paper-thin female empowerment, Maggie opted for the classics. Bob Dylan. Or Bruce. Maybe the Eagles. Soulful, lyrical songs that got her engine going as she grabbed the front door key off her well-organized kitchen counter and stopped by the mirror on the way out, picking up a Polaroid and snapping today's photo of herself. Down the hallway, she'd pin it up as the image started to materialize, alongside a wall filled with hundreds of daily shots of herself. They hung alongside photos of food porn, meals before they'd been devoured, shots of her and Cameron Fitz, hiking excursions, family snaps, and more.

The pictures of her boyfriends, baes, S.O.s, and *ships* seemingly didn't exist.

Outside was Studio City, California, a modest town in the San Fernando Valley, along Ventura Boulevard and alongside other Valley cities like Tarzana, Encino, Sherman Oaks, Burbank, and North Hollywood. She'd moved there when the gig came through, after living with Cameron for eighteen months, and had quickly charmed those who worked and lived in the four square blocks around her apartment, making the area her own little town.

"It's like my own quiet little village," she told her mother, weeks into relocating there, in an attempt to lessen the blow of not settling down in Chi-town near her family. She hoped to convince her mother that the metropolis of Los Angeles was not a devil-spawned playground for reprobates like her mother's friends at church had alluded to on hundreds, if not *thousands* of occasions.

Maggie loved doing her morning rounds—like a resident at a hospital, she took the same path every day, at the same time, seeing the same people at every turn. She loved that they knew her, and that they knew what she wanted. For someone who sometimes felt out of place in the big city, miles away from her family, this feeling of belonging gave her the kind of daily boost that she longed for. That is, in addition to the caffeine.

"*Bonjour!*" she'd announce to the barista at Le Pain Quotidien, who always had her espresso noisette ready to go.

"What up?" she'd high-five the clerk at the neighborhood deli, who always had a chocolate croissant ready in a brown paper bag.

"Juice me," she'd tongue-click/point-snap to the owner of the hip, overpriced Juice Den, swinging her plastic bottle of green juice into her side pocket for her 11:15 morning energy boost.

One morning, after the previous evening's party at the opening of a new Silverlake gastropub, Cameron would accompany her best friend on the morning ritual. She'd watch her, horrified, as she skipped from place to place like a Stepford wife, bouncing to a rhythm clearly motivated by some internal soundtrack. She'd stop her after the Juice Den, but before her monthly stop at the Good News newsstand (where she'd snag the latest copy of *Saveur*), grabbing her by the shoulders with a look of fear in her eyes.

"Um, Mags? You do realize this is a little like the opening number from *Beauty and the Beast*."

Maggie laughed uncomfortably, looking away from the piercing blue eyes that stared deep into Maggie's soul, peering into the areas she didn't want anyone poking around. "Don't be ridiculous. This is nothing like the opening number," she shot back in total denial. "I'm not poor or provincial."

"Okaaaaay. But you said *bonjour*. Out loud. And you went to a bakery. Where there was an actual baker *with his tray*. I'm just sayin'."

Maggie gave her a doe-eyed look. "Hey! I lived in France for a year."

"Which you *loathed*."

It was true. She had. So, what was it about the place that she still felt so connected to?

Arman was out in the driveway, hood of the Subaru propped up, when Milena stuck her head out of the front door.

"You're going to be late," she said, looking frazzled, as two young kids emerged behind her, backpacks at the ready. Arman struggled with something beneath the hood, the arms of his suit pushed up slightly to protect them from the dirt.

"We can't be late," worried Ani. "I have a study group first thing!"

Arman re-fastened a tube, tightening it with a wrench, then closed the hood of the car. Hands dirty with grease, he wiped them on a towel and turned back to his family on the doorstep of the single-story modest house. "We're good. At least, I *think* we're good."

"So, we can go now?" urged Alex, sidling up to his father. "It's not gonna make that horrible noise like last time?"

"Have faith, my son," Arman smiled, urging Alex into the back of the car. "Who's got your back?"

"You do?"

"Smart man."

Arman watched as the kids piled in the back, then turned to Milena, still in her fuzzy robe. He shrugged in the way most improvising parents shrug. She smiled, giving him a kiss and patting his behind. "Have a good day," she smiled.

"That's the plan," he smiled back.

Off went the Subaru, backing out of the driveway, still making that noise.

In some parts of the world, this is called walking, Josh thought to himself, regarding his steady (and frustrating) 7 miles per hour driving speed. But how could he complain? This was every single morning on the way to work. The two-mile stretch of road connecting the 110 to Vermont was always the last and most painful part of his morning commute. Especially when he could see the grassy knoll of Exposition Park and the hulking buildings of the California Science Center and nearly reach out and grab the rose garden or the IMAX theater or the Oschin Pavilion. Coming off the freeway he would slow to a crawl, proceed ten minutes down the street at tortoise-level speeds, and then watch it open up at the last minute. That was the only time his car's speedometer saw anything north of thirty-five, so he made sure to fill his need for speed as he rounded the corner of Vermont and put the pedal to the metal for the final fifty seconds of his morning journey … which had begun fifty minutes prior.

The fifty minutes always followed a strict schedule, broken up into phases, then further divided into chapters. The clock always began the minute Josh buckled himself into his BMW 3-Series and always ended the minute the *blurp* of his alarm echoed throughout the multi-leveled parking garage. Had one been witness to the organization he applied to the fifty minutes of his commute, they might have been curious enough to ask just what in the hell was going on.

"What in the heck is going on here?" asked Spencer McCurdy, the twenty-one-year-old Mormon intern that Josh had been forced to carpool with on that one particular day. It hadn't helped that Spencer's dream was to work at none other than JPL NASA, a fact that he'd address at the beginning of every single conversation he'd ever had.

Josh simply pointed to his "set list," clipped up alongside his phone, which laid out each chapter of each phase, divided into different media experiences. There was the *Current Event Catch-Up* which consisted of ten minutes (8:05 a.m. – 8:15 a.m.) of NPR's *Morning Edition* for all the latest news. There was the *Mindfulness Moment* which consisted of ten minutes (8:15 a.m. – 8:25 a.m.) listening to the latest daily affirmation from his meditation app. There were the five minutes denoted simply as *Music* (8:25 a.m. – 8:30 a.m.) followed by the fifteen minutes of *Talk Radio* (8:30 a.m. – 8:45 a.m.) and a final ten minutes of *'80s on Sirius XM* (8:45 a.m. – 8:55 a.m.), always ending with one particular rock n' roll classic bringing up the rear.

Which brings us back to that last fifty seconds of the last fifty minutes.

Josh tapped the security code on his phone, bypassing the lock screen at the current time (8:54 a.m.) and pulling up his playlist that had been created exclusively for this part of the ride. AC/DC's "Back in Black" kicked in, giving him the musical boost to accompany his gasoline-fueled one. The traffic let up and Josh swung the wheel to take the turn as the clock on his phone flipped digits to reveal 8:55 a.m.

It was at that moment that the newest phone gadget, clutching desperately to the fins of his A/C vent, started to lose its grip. It angled, slipping slightly, as the car's tires vibrated against the turn in the road. Josh turned to look just as he rounded the corner toward a crosswalk, reaching out to catch the phone as it dropped off its perch.

"Wagghhhhh" was the sound he made as he lunged for the phone, taking his eyes off the road.

"Gtthhhhh" was the sound he made as he looked back up, noticing a homeless man with two carts collapsing in the middle of the intersection.

"Agggphhhh" was the final and most dramatic guttural sound he made as he swerved with all his might to miss the man in the road, flying up over the curb and crashing his car head first into a cement divider. The front of the car crunched inwards, collapsing the instrument cluster and deploying the air bags. Two of them pummeled Josh as the car came to rest on the side of the road.

The homeless man, back on his feet, surveyed the damage, then grabbed his personal belongings and scuttled away. Various onlookers raced to the driver's side door, pulling it open.

Josh was OK.

He got out and stood up. AC/DC's "Back in Black" continued to play, echoing throughout the intersection. A bleary-eyed Josh shook off the trauma, face free of injury, and moved to the front of the car.

"Paradise," Josh muttered under his breath, as he tried to pull the destroyed front bumper away from the hood.

Maggie sang.

She couldn't sing proficiently, but she sang nonetheless. There was the time she attended Carrie Samuel's twenty-fifth karaoke birthday extravaganza at Koreatown's Brass Monkey and sang Pat Benatar's "Love Is a Battlefield." Despite the accompanying music, she was consistently off-tune, delivering runs of notes from seemingly different songs altogether, and comically rewriting the lyrics despite having them up on a monitor, for all to see.

"We were stung. Art aches my heartache, for Stan. No promises for that man. Love is a battlefield."

"Her art, her music … it makes her ache for Stan. That's such a beautiful sentiment. Wasn't she married to a guy named Stan?" Maggie would ask, three sheets to the wind.

Maggie's commute to *The 818*, the San Fernando Valley print and online magazine for which she was the Senior Food Editor, was only two miles away, but in Los Angeles it might as well have been twenty. Nobody walked anywhere. Especially not to work.

"But you're so close," Brian Epstein, the publisher of *The 818*, once told her. "Why don't you do your part to cut down carbon emissions and just walk?"

"But what if I have a lunch?"

"Then walk home, get your car, and drive to lunch. Or call a Lyft."

"But what if there's an earthquake and I need to quickly escape the city?"

"If there's an earthquake," he sighed, looking up at her from behind his unfashionable bifocals, "no one's quickly escaping this city."

"Ok. Fine. But what if I need somewhere to take a nap?" she wondered, serious.

There was a long pause. Brian, who had been alerted to Maggie's take-no-prisoners style and tell-it-like-it-is 'tude from a publishing friend who had stumbled upon her at the now-shuttered The Fisherman and the Whale, knew when to step off when it came to Maggie. Stepping *T* wasn't wise when her skewed logic was more passionate than yours.

"Good point," he'd responded, eyeing *The 818* open work space bathed in sunlight, with no privacy to speak of. "So, drive then."

So, Maggie drove.

And sang.

Neither of which she was particularly good at.

On this particular Monday morning it happened to be Bruce Springsteen's "Secret Garden," featured prominently in the uber-romantic Cameron Crowe-directed, Tom Cruise-starring classic, *Jerry Maguire*.

Maggie sang along with the lyrics, pulling out onto Ventura Boulevard and down toward Hollywood. The music swelled around her and inside her. *This* was why she sang. It was her only respite during the daily rat race; her only opportunity to take her thoughts inward. Sometimes, it was calming. The sights that passed her by on the city streets seemed typical, *normal*. The meter maids. The dog walkers. The professionals in line at Starbucks trying to get their coffee on. A young mother pushing her baby in a stroller, with her very attractive husband holding the small of her back. In the morning. When there was clearly work to be done. Why was her husband with her?

Maggie's brain did a spit-take.

Sometimes, it seemed, Maggie's brain didn't want calm. It didn't want acceptance. It wanted answers, god dammit. It just wanted answers.

Maggie's mouth was still singing, but her brain was screaming to get out from under the Boss's romantic lyrics. Who the hell was this couple? Were they even from here? It was almost nine in the morning on a weekday and these three looked like they hadn't a care in the world, strolling without purpose to some yoga class that maybe, possibly, was starting sometime in the next eight hours. Who paid their bills? Had they invented something so lucrative that they'd never have to work again?

She crooked her head to keep watching as she passed them by, like an accident she couldn't take her eyes off of.

That was probably why she didn't see the accident waiting to happen in front of her, where a Subaru had stalled, smoke coming from its open hood. As she plowed into the back of it, her attention was split between the yoga family and another not-so-charmed group of blood relatives—a suit-laden father and his two backpack-adorned children sitting on the side of the road. They watched helplessly as Maggie's car slammed into theirs, sending it into the busy intersection, causing cars to come to a screeching halt.

Then the car caught on fire. Something that could have happened when the family had been inside it. But thankfully, and surprisingly, it had happened this way instead.

Shook, Maggie looked up from the wheel, surveying the destruction. The family on the curb. Checked her arms, her body. She brushed a pile of debris and glass off her lap and onto the floor. On the side of the road, the yoga family stopped to look. They stared at Maggie. Maggie stared back.

Maggie turned her attention back to the console in her car, using her skewed elbow to turn off the entertainment system.

Screw you, The Boss, she thought to herself.

Six

THE WINDSHIELD OF OV-105, aka space shuttle *Endeavor*, was clean. It was clear of obstructions and obstacles. And yet, when Josh looked out into the depths of space from behind the controls, there was not a single star to be seen.

He tapped at one of the seven square monitors in front of him, flipped a few overhead lights with determination, then sat back in the Commander's chair, grabbing hold of the joystick on his right. He tweaked it, shifted it upwards, then turned a dial on his left that echoed back with each and every click to ensure the autopilot was locked in. He laid his head back, adjusting his regulation purple-mesh shirt, and stared out into the pitch-blackness of the universe.

Thanks to Josh's security clearance, he was one of three people allowed to be up here alone. And that was a good thing, because the cockpit of *Endeavor* was his happy place. Where he could sit quietly and contemplate life, the universe, and everything. On days like today, when "everything" didn't go exactly as planned, his thoughts would turn to the concept of infinity and just how big it felt. After all, he could pilot the shuttle one direction and keep going, and keep going still, and never find himself back where he started. There were millions and billions of stars, and if one believed in the

Drake equation, then one also had to believe there were millions of other Earth-like planets out there as well. Teeming with life. Teeming with *intelligent* life. What was going on down here, on this little blue marble of a planet, was insignificant in light of everything else. Josh's hopes and dreams and early morning car accidents weren't important. What was out there was the most important thing.

"What *is* out there?" he said aloud, stopping short of verbally wondering what was out there for him. That was too personal. That was too scary.

Almost as if on cue, the sound of screaming children "out there" punctured his quiet bubble of introspection, answering his question. Josh angled his head and looked out the corner of *Endeavor*'s windshield. There, perched atop a metal platform, hovering at the edge of *Endeavor*'s line of sight, stood thirty-five kids and two teachers. A California Science Center tour guide pointed into the cockpit of their most prized exhibit, the space shuttle *Endeavor*, recounting the fascinating story of its four-day-long trip through the streets of Los Angeles from LAX to its new home at the Center. The kids jumped up and down, yelling and screaming.

Someone said in space no one can hear you scream, Josh thought, puncturing his momentary daydream and snapping back to reality.

The California Science Center sat at the center of Exposition Park in Downtown Los Angeles. It was the go-to excursion for students young and old, featuring exhibits that ranged the gamut from the space shuttle to dinosaurs, from air and space to ecosystems large and small. Rotating exhibits focused sometimes on animals, history, science, and sports. There was a rock wall, two restaurants, an IMAX theater, and—

"—a rose garden. It's pretty amazing. It's been there since 1928," said Josh, sitting in a chair opposite his mother and father on the family room couch, four years earlier and sixteen hours *after* having opened his rejection letter from JPL NASA. He was excited. As excited as he could be after being turned down for the job of his dreams.

But the more he talked about it, the more the job at the Center sounded like a great opportunity and not a consolation prize. He was seriously thinking about applying because he wanted to, definitely not because his entire future had crashed upon the rocky shores of failure and uncertainty, crumbling into a thousand pieces of rubble that closely resembled his ego.

"I'm confused," his mother said, not confused at all. "You're going to work in a garden? Like a gardener?" Her passive-aggressive know-it-all nature was getting tiring. For him. She seemed to thrive on the drama of it all.

"The *job*," he began, refocusing, "is a director of exhibits position. I'd be working under the senior vice president. Overseeing the ideation and execution of the exhibits, managing some of the exhibition staff, and it would give me the kind of experience that JPL said I didn't have. Real-world exposure. And maybe after a few years—"

"Now don't have unrealistic ..." she started, but didn't finish.

"It sounds like a good opportunity, kid," said his father. "*We*," he enunciated to his wife firmly, "wholeheartedly support you, whatever you want to do."

"Yes. What he said," his mother threw back.

Josh backed out of the space shuttle, descending to the ground of the Oschin Pavilion, which rose high above *Endeavor*. As he reached the ground, he checked his watch (1:22 p.m.) and flipped out his laminated name tag, repositioning it on the lapel of his purple shirt.

It read *Josh Allen, Vice President, Exhibits.*

The "green shirts" were everywhere. They arranged red velvet stanchions, took admission tickets from students and tourists, and accompanied the local students from L.A. Unified when they visited the Center on their field trips. They emptied the garbage, polished the metal, cleaned up the bathrooms, served food in the restaurants, manned the *Explorastore*, and made sure that the "purple shirts"— the more senior-level staff of the establishment—were happy with the overall operation and presentation of the facility.

"And that's *the* Josh Allen," a female green shirt told her tour group as they passed by Josh, making his way to the second-floor exit doors. "He's one of the main reasons we have *Endeavor* here at the Center today." The youngest of the kids looked up to Josh, eyes wide with wonder. Clearly, he was a celebrity to them. Clearly, he enjoyed it. Clearly, he had been told to remain humble.

"One of *many*," he shot back as he moved past. "It's all about teamwork."

The smile came only after he was out of sight, passing by the Touch Tank, continuing down the corridor past the entrance to the World of Life and stopping to look over the railings down at the Air and Space exhibits. The planets. The stars. Telescopes. Children crowded around the exhibits, eyes wide with fascination and wonder. Their teachers encouraged them to take it all in and dream their biggest dreams. Every once in a while, when Josh's mind turned to that infamous moment in Montauk underneath the stars, he'd remind himself of what he was seeing right now. He may have been blocked at the pass in *his* life, but if he had anything to do with it, these kids would know nothing of that disappointment.

The Belarusian *harbatu* was a caffeine-free blend of golden hand-picked chamomile flowers and freshly harvested bee pollen, said to improve one's energy and creativity. It came infused with Salisbury honey, rose petals, and the subtle scent of sunflower oil. The tea bag, stylish enough to be confused for a tiny Victorian doll house's bedroom pillow, was dunked repeatedly into a large rose-colored ceramic mug that sat at the head of the conference room table, emblazoned with the initials "D.R." in a classy Times New Roman font.

Diana Rowland, the SVP of Exhibits, gingerly lifted the tea bag and placed it on a ceramic slat the size of a matchbook, manufactured somewhere in Istanbul by a company who had apparently come up with a product no one else had determined was a necessity for civilized society. *Still.* "Let's go around the room this afternoon and go through the statuses of our pending projects," she said, taking time for two careful sips between "afternoon" and "go through the statuses."

It was a room of purple and green shirts. Diana addressed them from the head of the conference room table with class and courtesy. While some of the team could appear uneasy around her, it was only because they so desperately wanted her approval. Not only was she smart and strategic, but she had come to the Center with years of admirable experience under her belt. She had, like Josh, attended UCLA for her undergraduate degree, then stayed on multiple years until she'd landed her PhD in Anthropology. While there she'd meet and marry her *second* college sweetheart (the first had been German transfer student Bertram Söhm), have a beautiful daughter, and spend years teaching, conducting research, and taking excursions around the world that would add to her mysterious allure and penchant for international (and unpronounceable) teas. When she was sixty-one, her husband would suddenly pass away, causing her to return to Los Angeles so she could be closer to her only daughter, and securing her current role at the Center. At the end of the day, Diana was a wonderful mentor if one could get past the perception that she was all about herself. The reality was that she just liked to give advice in a soothing, all-knowing, condescendingly sweet way.

To her left sat Annabelle Yancy, the head of communications for the Center. She'd spent years working for companies that were giving back to society. There was her time at Greenpeace. Some years at National Public Radio. She'd done a stint with a nonprofit delivering clean drinking water to children in developing countries. And she'd spent ten years during her thirties working in New York City with the Children's Television Workshop on *Sesame Street*. She was always tired and had a horrible fashion sense, but her heart was in the right place.

Josh sat on the other side of the table, flanked by the only two green shirts in the meeting. There was David Reeves, a recent graduate of UC Berkeley, who had slipped into the Director position when Josh had been promoted to VP; and T Greene, the Director of Events, who was a modern-day marvel of organization, attitude, and ingenuity. She had once coordinated the submerging of an entire mariachi band into the 188,000-gallon kelp forest tank for Cinco de Mayo, engineered life-size holographic dinosaurs on the 65-million-year anniversary of their death, and convinced William Shatner to sing his rendition of "Lucy in the Sky with Diamonds" before a special outdoor screening of *IV: The Voyage Home* on the third Sunday in February.

"That's World Whale Day," she'd remind the staff at a Monday morning staff meeting, which took place the previous November, tying it into the whale sub-plot of the *Star Trek* film. The room would nod, clearly impressed. Yes, even Diana.

"I'll start," began Josh, "because I'm going to have to bolt early."

"He drove his car into a cement divider," chimed in David.

"Why would you do that?" asked Diana.

"It wasn't on purpose, clearly. I drove my car into a cement divider because I was trying to avoid *killing* someone," Josh shot back. He pulled out a folder, flipping through pages. "You want to hear my updates? I have some good news on the Technology Through the Ages exhibit."

"And did you?" Diana asked.

"Did I what?"

"Kill someone," Diana double-checked.

"I didn't kill anything except for my car. And now I've got to deal with that." Josh let out a sigh as Diana's face lit up like she'd solved the equation featured prominently in *Good Will Hunting*.

"I know of a well-regarded auto body facility in Hollywood that my daughter Robyn swears by. I'll give you the number," she said, pulling out a buck-slip emblazoned with her initials.

Thank God. Because the car was fucked. And in desperate need of—

"—a brand-new front bumper. And a new windshield. New air bags. The whole front panel on the driver's side was destroyed," laid out Maggie, perched atop the arm of the couch in Brian Epstein's office, in the middle of their afternoon brainstorm sesh. "And there was glass everywhere. It's amazing I came out of it unscathed."

Maggie held up her hands, clear of any cuts or scratches. "I should be dead. Or bleeding out my eyes or something. Or my neck?"

She twisted her neck back and forth, widening her eyes to ensure all parts were working. Drama was turned up to eleven.

Around her sat a half dozen of the key team. There was Darren, the Entertainment editor and walking *Trivial Pursuit* game. There was Robyn, the Life and Style editor, who never wore the same pair of shoes twice and made sure you were aware of that fact. There was Alyssa, the Manhattan transplant and Books editor who carried her rat dog Chumley wherever she went. There was Curtis, the photographer with a chip on his shoulder; Leo, the head of advertising who seemed to think he should have been the Books editor; and Carly, Brian's assistant editor and right-hand woman who was always angling to chase down an environmental crisis or political scandal for the mag, despite the fact that *this* mag wasn't *that* mag.

Brian got up, seemingly looking for something, then found an old coffee press with liquid and grounds in it sitting behind him on a shelf next to a half-eaten sandwich. "We're glad you're still alive," he began, as he pushed down on the coffee press, then deposited the liquid into a dirty coffee cup on his desk. He walked it over to a microwave that was expertly camouflaged by books and stacks of paper and threw it in for thirty seconds. "Since it was before work," he continued, making sure the rest of the peanut gallery was paying attention, "it wasn't during work hours. *Ergo*, while I'd love to help you out, the paper really isn't responsible for covering any repair damages."

"I've got this thing called insurance," she shot back, flipping through her notepad of story ideas.

The microwave dinged and Brian took out his newly hot, rancid old coffee and brought it back with him to his desk. He tasted it. Nodded like it was decent enough, then turned back to Maggie. "Insurance, huh?" He was surprised. "What, do you have life insurance, too?"

"Of course I have life insurance. Don't you?"

Brian looked away; he clearly didn't. Maggie looked to the rest of the room, who all diverted their eyes, ashamed.

"Just go get your car fixed," he said, waving her off. "You got a place?"

"Yes, sir," she smiled back, sharing a look with Robyn and holding up a colorful buck-slip adorned with the initials "R.R." The name of the place was scribbled on it.

Ah, *The 818*.

In a world where newspapers were shuttering, magazines were going digital, and bloggers were *finally* considered serious journalists, it was amazing that the San Fernando Valley spread still existed. It almost hadn't, when the corporate parent company Huvane, Inc. had decided to divest themselves from any media holdings that were perceived to have an opinion about anything. Brian, who had been rocking the editor-in-chief role for almost ten years, did the one selfless thing he had done in his entire life, which was to ring up the only entrepreneur he knew and see if he'd bankroll the future of the mag.

Dustin Schatz, who was most known for his investments in technology startups and the viral dating app *You're Gonna Hate Me, But ...* was flush with cash and happened to be Brian's college roommate. To him, there was something exciting about getting into publishing, despite the fact that the circulation was much less than *Cigar Aficionado*. Still, he did it anyway, ensuring years of guaranteed funding, job security for Maggie, and a little something Brian had been hoping for ever since he first set foot in the building as a copy editor.

"If you haven't noticed," he told his key team in his office just days after the deal had gone through, "I'm the publisher now." He pointed to a name plate on the edge of his midcentury mahogany desk.

"I'd like to be listed as the sole publisher on the website," Dustin told Brian, days prior to Brian's meeting with his key team.

"But we'll keep it off the online masthead," Brian clarified. "I've decided we'll put Dustin Schatz up there, you know, as kind of a breadcrumb of goodwill for the guy. After all, he is making it possible for us to continue doing what we do."

Brian was a true American hero. He was like the *G.I. Joe* of the left-of-fringe publishing world.

Maggie had landed at *The 818* almost three years to the day. It only took six months and three very specific articles for the majority of Los Angeles' food community to both fear and revere her talents. There was the time she visited the opening of The Lamb Shank, writing that "Kenny Fordham's garlic crusted roast rack of lamb, the restaurant's signature dish, feels old and decrepit like the forty million people currently over the age of sixty-five in the Continental United States." There was the time she sampled the breakfast menu at Emily Davies' Up and Att 'EM, writing that "The eggs were runny like the tears of the customers, having sampled dry cinnamon-swirl pancakes, avocado toast that no one was green with envy of, and a waitstaff whose antagonistic attitude caused one to wonder how water boarding could be any worse." And there was that dinner at Henry Grauman's Basic, that "blew my socks off, shook my soul to the core, and made my taste buds wonder what the hell they'd been rubbing up against all these years." The four out of four forks solidified Basic's future, while the other establishments were not so lucky.

"Well, at least you're making money off your ability to be critical," Maggie's mother would say, after being criticized for not being excited enough about Maggie's first online restaurant review.

"It's called being paid for your passions," she'd defend.

"As long as your passions pay your bills," said her logically-minded, financially-aware father, his voice trailing off on the other end of the phone.

And they were. Maggie practically never had to pay for a meal. They all knew who she was, and knew the power that a well-placed rave could do for their restaurant. Fact was, in Los Angeles, there were more restaurants per block than in any other city west of the Mississippi. Getting three or four forks out of four meant you could afford to stay afloat longer than the less fortunate ones. Maggie loved the influence and the power. It made her feel important. Like she'd made her mark on the city. It didn't matter that some of her other passions hadn't found a home. She was successful! She could pay her bills! She had Cameron! Her best friend! She'd been able to lease her beloved Tesla! She was saving the environment!

The lists often made her feel better. The more she could add to them, the more she felt her life was overflowing with positivity. The more she felt busy. The more she could distract herself from that feeling. You know the one. The one concerning that big black void where something significant was supposed to be.

"Elon Musk is tweeting something insane again on social," Curtis said, snapping her out of her list-making mode as he walked by Maggie's desk after the meeting had ended. "Somethin' about building an interstellar highway with a life-sized Habitrail."

"He should focus his energy on creating a front bumper that can withstand a Subaru," Maggie said, shaking her head, then taking particular note of the camera he was cradling in his hands. "You love your D5?"

"Love," he said, holding up his Nikon D5 affectionately.

Maggie pulled out a relatively modern camera from the side drawer in her desk. It wasn't a hulking piece of technology like Curtis's. It also wasn't the camera her dad had given her. No, it was more like a Best Buy special. "Bow down to what I'm rocking," she tried, knowing she was playing in the amateur league.

"The thirty-four hundred?" he sneered. "Nothing beats the twenty point eight megapixels and 4K thirty frames-per-second video on my beloved here."

"I used to have a Nikon SP that my dad gave me, but it got stolen," she lamented. "Now that was a classic." Curtis nodded, placating. "It would have been worth a lot these days," she said, turning back to Curtis's technological monster. "What'd that baby run you?"

"Lists for six, got it for five," he smiled. "Now if they only compensated me enough in this job to pay it off. Art," he announced, as he started to walk off in the other direction, "is valued far less than the commerce it creates."

"Deep," someone in the bullpen chimed in from the copy machine.

Maggie watched him go, her head in the clouds, thinking of something far more personal. She opened the top left drawer of her desk, placing the camera she did have inside.

"Don't ya got a car to get fixed?" Brian's voice blared across the room.

Seven

TOTO WAS PLAYING.

Western Auto Body was a modest little shop, with a modest little waiting room, featuring three attached rows of plastic-molded chairs, a Keurig that was out of pods, and a slew of magazines whose subscriptions had lapsed at least twelve months prior. A makeshift *Sonos*-like sound system featured speakers on both sides of the room, with a long rectangular bar under the debilitated crack-enhanced flat-screen TV. Off to the side, two metal double doors led to the auto body garage where loud banging and other questionable repair-like sounds continued incessantly as a female clerk juggled receipts, paperwork, and a particularly intense conversation on her cell phone at a messy front desk.

Josh sat reading *Time* magazine, its cover touting *2015: The Year in Review*, drinking out of a steaming plastic cup. He periodically looked up at the sounds coming from the garage, sharing a worrying glance with the clerk.

"They got to evaluate the damage, *then* you gotta sign off on the estimate before you can go," she said, almost scolding him for even looking in her general direction as she turned back to her phone call: "I've gotta call you back, Hector," she said, hanging up.

Josh nodded affirmatively, turning back to his article on the Supreme Court making same-sex marriage legal in all fifty states, as the front door's jingling bell announced another customer on the lookout for mediocre service. He checked his watch (3:25 p.m.), took a sip of his drink, then continued his literary trip back through time while humming along with the final bars of Toto's "Africa."

The music ended and another song began: Toto's "Africa." As far as Josh was concerned, this had been going on for thirty-five minutes now. Someone clearly deficient in the skills of managing music mixes had selected the wrong playlist at the start of the day. But Josh didn't care. After all, it was Toto's "Africa."

"Coffee?" a voice asked, causing Josh to look up. Sitting two seats away, in another plastic-molded chair, was an attractive young woman he'd never seen before, though she had a familiar look that immediately drew his attention. Well-dressed, a cascading head of brunette hair, a fashionable bag, and a cell phone surgically attached to her right hand, she gave Josh a once-over, paying particular attention to his purple shirt. When her eyes diverted to it, so too did Josh's focus.

He held his cup out to her so she could see inside. "No, not coffee. It's just hot water. Apparently they ran out of coffee in 2015 when they stopped renewing their *Time* magazine subscription." He held up the magazine, punctuating his point.

The woman looked into the cup, confused, then approached the Keurig. Like an FBI agent tossing someone's apartment upside down for evidence, she opened containers and drawers looking for anything that might resemble a pod. The cupboards were bare, save for a half-eaten Twinkie. "That's probably okay since over two-thirds of Americans get their news from social media, anyway," she proclaimed as she moved back to the chairs, sitting down directly next to him. She leaned in closer, with no lack of confidence: "So, Josh. Inquiring minds want to know. What's with the outfit?"

He put down the cup, giving himself a once-over, and realized he still had his name tag hanging there for all to see. Embarrassed, he took it off. "This is what I wear to work," he said. "Regulation dress code. At least I don't have to wear the green shirts. They're lime green, which isn't good for anybody's complexion. Anyway, those are for the general employees and more junior staff members."

"What, do you work at an amusement park or something?"

Josh ignored her and her question, reaching back out for his cup of hot water and taking a sip. At some point, the repetition of Toto's "Africa" finally made an impact on her consciousness, snapping her to.

"Didn't they just play this?" she asked, incredulous.

"They sure did."

"It's Toto."

"Oh yes, I know."

"You a big Toto fan?"

"Maybe not this big."

A smile flashed across her face. Josh turned back to her with something else on his mind. "So, you work in news?"

"No, I work in *food*."

"Like, food kiosks at an amusement park?"

Oh, snap.

"You enjoyed making that joke, didn't you?" she shot back.

"Honestly, yes," he said. "Yes, I did."

She took a breath, then made it abundantly clear: "No, not like at an amusement park. I review restaurants. It's real cultured stuff. Don't get me wrong, I don't buy into that whole culture game, I just leverage it to shake things up with the people who do. And for your information, it's for an established publication that is available both online and in print."

"For now," Josh smiled.

A loud crash accompanied by the sound of upset workers echoed from the double doors. The two of them turned to look, cringing at the chaos. The clerk at the front desk noticed their concern, waving their worries off with a casual, unconcerned hand.

"I hope that wasn't your car," the woman said.

"No, my car is already in a hundred pieces," Josh smiled.

"Oof. Someone hit you?"

"No. Someone hit you?"

"No," she frowned.

"So, we both suck at driving," he said, shifting so he could face her more directly. The banter felt familiar, comfortable, right.

"I don't suck at driving," she defended. "I suck at paying attention *while* driving."

He was drawn to her. Maybe she was feeling it, too. When Josh pivoted his body toward her, she moved to close the chasm between them. He made note of her blue eyes, which never wavered or turned away. They sat there for a beat, both saying nothing, yet the noise in Josh's head was thunderous.

She looks a little like Lea Thompson, he thought, focusing on her reddish-brown locks, laid perfectly across her shoulders with small strands barely touching her tanned neckline. *Like, Back to the Future Lea Thompson, not Casual Sex Lea Thompson. I'm not suggesting Casual Sex Lea Thompson wasn't attractive as well, but there was something sweeter and more approachable about Back to the Future Lea Thompson*, his mind reasoned. *Yes, I know she played Michael J. Fox's mother in that movie, but that doesn't mean I want to sleep with mine. My mother can't hold a candle to Lea Thompson. I shouldn't even be mentioning my mother and Lea Thompson in the same breath*, he frowned, growing uneasy with the connective tissue of his monkey mind. He didn't even know her name.

"So, clearly the auto body shop didn't reach out to you before your arrival. There's a strict name-tag policy if you're gonna show your face," he said, holding up his tag and doing his best Vanna White reveal of his name. She looked back at his goofy smile and could barely contain her own.

"It's Maggie," she volunteered. "My name's Maggie."

Maggie? The name bounced around in his head, trying to attach itself to any last name that was recognizable. *Maggie Gyllenhaal. Dame Maggie Smith. Maggie Q.* Josh repeated the name in his head long enough to come to one very adamant conclusion. "That's not your name," he accused. "You're lying."

"Well, if I'm lying, you're certifiable," she shot back.

Clever girl, Josh thought to himself. Lying about her name, then playing the defensive card in an attempt to throw him off the scent. Well, Josh wasn't having it. "I get it. Some guy drinking hot water in an auto body shop asks for your name, of course you tell him it's Maggie. Or Sophie. Maybe Bernadette."

"Bernadette? I don't look like a Bernadette. In fact, I find that personally insulting."

"I know a lot of cool Bernadettes."

"Well, you don't know Bernadette Calder," she said. "Meanest girl in junior high. Poured vinegar into my gym locker and all over my P.E. clothes."

"OK. So, maybe not Bernadette. Lois, then?"

Maggie was clearly getting annoyed. She jerked her head back like an ostrich pulling its head out of the sand.

"The name's Maggie. I'm not messing with you. Why would I do that?"

"Why do women give guys fake phone numbers? So they don't have to worry about getting a call."

Maggie cocked her head. "That would only be pertinent if you were planning on asking me for my phone number. Is that your master plan?"

"That's a little forward, don't you think?"

"Which?" she asked. "You asking me for my number, or me asking if you were going to ask me for my number?"

"Maybe I should have said *premature* instead."

Maggie shrugged with an untranslatable smirk, turning back to her phone. Josh watched her for a moment, then picked his up as well, checking e-mail. There were three e-mails from online retailers and a text from Diana asking when he expected to be back at the office. Josh pursed his lips, eyed his watch, then turned back to Maggie as she scrolled through her Instagram with one hand—a real pro. Every other photo highlighted an item of food or a meal, with filters that made even the most horrific item look delicious.

She clearly knows a lot about the social sphere, he thought. *I wonder if she's one of those needy social tastemakers who lives and dies by how many people like her posts? You know, all those companies have totally fucked with the wiring of our brains. All those badges, those alerts, those sounds? It's like Pavlov's dog all over again.*

Toto's "Africa" ended. Toto's "Africa" started playing.

She recognized it was Toto without Shazam, Josh thought. *That means she knows music. Even from the '80s.* Josh's thoughts turned to the Peter Cetera-fronted Chicago. Toward the classic love song "You're the Inspiration." As an adolescent romantic, Josh had imagined finding the girl of his dreams, then playing the song for her as a way to communicate how he felt. Josh had imagined himself on a beach with a faceless young woman, at the top of a Ferris wheel, chasing each other through a park, on the top of a red rock cliff, obviously somewhere in Sedona, Arizona. Each time, he'd pull out a pair of earphones, hand them over, and then start playing the song. The eyes of the faceless woman-to-be would go wide, then waterworks would ensue. *That's the only way to do it,* he thought to himself.

Although, play a song like that for a girl, and she's bound to go all Tina on you, he worried, backtracking. A quick flash of sharing popcorn with Tina entered his head. He cringed. Ick, the baggage.

"Well, I don't get the sense that you or I are going to be that forward when it comes to our phone numbers," she said, never looking up from her cell, and settling the matter for good.

"Sir?" the woman at the front desk called out. Josh turned to look. She held up his key and paperwork while taking a call on her cell. "Hang *on,* Hector," she whined through the phone, waving for Josh to join her up front where the magic happened.

"I guess that's me," he said, pocketing his phone and throwing his cup into an overflowing wastebasket. Maggie put her phone face down on her lap, hands folded.

"She called you *sir.* I'd say that's pretty impressive, all things considered," she joked, motioning to his purple shirt.

"Good luck with *food* and all the amazing career opportunities that come with *food,*" he said, moving past her toward the front desk. They shared one last look before she turned back around, picking her phone up but holding the scroll.

Josh reached the front desk where the clerk continued to argue into her phone. "Yes, but what did you tell *him*, Hector? They owed you. You put in the time. How could they fire you?" Josh's hand tapped on the countertop. Half out of her mind, she grabbed the first piece of paperwork to her left and threw it up on the counter with his car key. "Just sign here and they'll call you when it's done. Your rental's out front."

Josh grabbed a pen, quickly signing the paperwork and exiting with his copy. The front door's bell rang out, causing Maggie to turn one last time as Josh disappeared from the building.

Josh sat at a red light in his tiny blue metallic Fiat.

The insurance company had been speedy at getting him the rental car, dropping it off at Western Auto Body. They had also been speedy at leaving him without any instructions on how to operate the car. He flipped switches and pressed touchscreens, attempting to stop the blasting heat and salsa music from overwhelming his senses.

The heat turned off, then came the blast of A/C—taking the paperwork from his passenger seat and sucking it up onto the passenger side window. He turned to look, its flapping corner taunting him. But something else really got his attention.

The name on the invoice.

It wasn't his name. It wasn't even his invoice. It was the invoice of one Maggie Mills. With her full address, automobile statistics and, yes, *her phone number.*

Oh, distracted female desk clerk and her recently unemployed boyfriend. It seemed that his firing and the mindlessness it caused had been the culprit in the Case of the Switched Auto Repair Shop Invoices. Josh had solved it inside of three seconds, even before the red light turned green.

So, her name really is Maggie, he thought to himself, adding a fourth name of significance to his internal ledgers.

Maggie sat in the back of a Lyft, looking down at the invoice from the Auto Repair Shop. She'd made the exact same discovery and was now in possession of all the pertinent personal information of one Josh Allen.

She smiled. Then worried. She quickly folded the invoice four times, shoving it in her back pocket. Then opened up Instagram, scrolling with fervor.

Maybe it would help her drown out that little voice in the back of her head that was repeating his name over and over again. *Josh, Josh, Josh, Josh, Josh, Josh Allen.* Despite the repetition, which often sucked all meaning out of any word, this time its meaning held at least a little significance.

In fact, when Maggie thought about it, it actually meant a lot.

Eight

"*PELLUCIDAR*," SAID MEL ALLEN.

The utterance was timed perfectly to the moment when Barbara Allen put her finishing touches on the dinner presentation, laying the final side dish on the edge of the table and taking off her stylish, toile pot holder gloves. These were the ones with the churches and steamboats, not to be confused with the ones picturing the old Western settlers or the lighthouses and octopi. She had been tracking the Milky Way galaxy ones on eBay for years, but the minimum "Buy It Now" price of twelve hundred bucks was too much for the goodwill she thought they'd bring. She stood there, waiting for someone to cue her speech, foot tapping impatiently. But she had walked into a conversation that was already in progress between Mel and a young woman sitting across the table from him.

"What's *peculiar*?" the woman asked, cocking her head, looking to Barbara for some assistance in the matter. Her name was Teresa Gaines, and she'd shown up for dinner at seven o'clock sharp with a handwritten invitation sporting some pretty awful calligraphy, courtesy of Barbara. How they knew each other or where they'd met was a mystery, the kind that Mel seemed doomed to face every time Barbara had returned from a seminar, art class, museum excursion, or extended supermarket conversation. Still, when the teaching thing hadn't materialized upon their relocation to California, her quest to better herself through education and new experiences unfortunately became Mel's cross to bear. At this point in their lives, no one was changing who they were. No one was developing new skills or finding groundbreaking ways to engineer an overall attitude adjustment. She had her baggage and he had his.

"Pel-luce-eh-dar," Mel sounded out for Teresa, "the inner sanctum of our house. It's an homage to the book *Pellucidar*, by Edgar Rice Burroughs. The story was about a fictional hollow Earth and the adventures that took place within it. And get this: in the book they travel over five hundred miles into the center of Earth. And ironically, this room you're sitting in right now? Five hundred feet from the front door. Coincidence or fate?" he marveled, nodding with fascination. "I say *fate*," Mel answered, as Teresa turned to look behind her through the doorway, gazing upon the closed front doors. "And since we live in Tarzana, a place where Mr. Burroughs dreamed up all his magical stories—"

"Some people say grace. Dad says *pellucidar*," said Josh, chiming in from the other end of the table, looking perfectly disinterested in the meal, the conversation, and the strange woman sitting to his right.

"Now, that's a story I'd like to read," exclaimed Teresa, further frustrating an impatient Barbara Allen, clearing her throat for dramatic effect in an attempt to regain the spotlight.

"There's a pending announcement I'd like to tackle if everyone's ready to refocus their attention," said Barbara, in her classic passive-aggressive way.

"Pellucidar!" said Mel again, for effect.

Barbara rolled her eyes and cleared her throat. She pulled a note card out of the front pocket of her apron, a mess with calligraphy that had been scrawled with a leaky pen. "As I am closing in on the final days of my Wolfgang Puck culinary seminar, I am pleased to present the second-to-last class assignment for all of you tonight. As each class assignment must be tested by a minimum of three other individuals, I've invited Teresa here to help fill in the gap."

Now aware of just why she'd been invited over, Teresa shrunk back in her seat as Barbara flipped her note card to the next in line.

"Over here, you'll find a wonderful side dish: A hot broccoli cauliflower salad, making use of cauliflower direct from a locally sourced farm in Portland, Oregon. Next to that, a chopped caprese salad with cherry tomatoes and a subtle mango garnish using fruit flown in from the agriculturally rich island of Maui. And for the pièce de résistance, a rosemary and goat cheese stuffed chicken, with wild mushroom sauce from the Gelsons down the street." She slid the cards back into her apron, then sat down on the other side of the table, opposite from Josh.

"Soooooooo," Josh spoke up, plucking a chicken leg from the serving platter. "How did the two of you meet?" He pointed to Teresa, then looked to his mom.

"Well, since you've asked," Barbara replied, scooping some salad onto her plate, "I met Teresa after that calligraphy class I took a few months ago."

"Oh, so you're artistic-adjacent like Mom?" joked Josh, clearly not to his mother's appreciation.

"No, I didn't take the calligraphy class," Teresa replied. Josh and Mel regarded her with confusion.

"I said *after* calligraphy," Barbara clarified. "At the Applebee's. Teresa was our waitress. She gave us free dessert that day. Mmm. The molten chocolate brownie."

"One of our biggest sellers," Teresa chimed in, appearing comfortable now that she was speaking about a familiar subject. "Did you know that one out of three customers who order dessert order the molten chocolate brownie? And twenty-five percent of those customers come back at least two to three more times in the six months to follow?"

"Is that so," Mel chimed in. Josh turned to look at her. She was cute. She was young. She was clueless as to what she had walked into, here in the pellucidar.

"Teresa was your waitress," Josh laid out slowly, unbelieving.

And then, believing.

"You might not know this," Barbara spoke up, enjoying a bite of her chicken, "but Teresa is just twenty-nine years old, loves science, the beach, skateboarding and …" Barbara stopped, thinking, then pulled another card from her apron, on which she had apparently written the stats of newfound friend Teresa. "Oh!" she realized, her eyes coming into focus. "She can whistle backwards."

"Fantastic," Mel spoke up. "Let's hear it."

"Yes, please," Josh agreed.

"Go ahead, dear," goaded Barbara, proud to know there was a showstopping pre-meal performance about to occur in her presence.

Everyone turned. Teresa wet her lips, then sucked in all the air she could muster, eliciting a pretty convincing D-sharp. Barbara clapped, impressed.

"And she's single," Barbara concluded, finally getting to the real point.

Maggie and Cameron sat across from each other at Le Fleur Wine Bar, each with a sizeable glass of red, staring at the auto body invoice in the center of the table.

"He was wearing a purple shirt, Cam," Maggie cringed. "*Purple.*"

"Bold. At least it wasn't pink, like what's-his-name."

"Brett."

"Right. Wet Brett."

"Why do you have to call him that? You really gave him a complex, you know. He started carrying paper towels with him everywhere we went. Because of you."

"Why are you still defending him, two years later? The guy always looked wet. Like he'd just sprayed himself with a bottle of mist or something."

"It wasn't mist. He wore, like, I don't know, sunscreen of some kind. He cared about his skin. Aren't we, as progressive women, supposed to want our men to care how they look, how they take care of themselves, how they—"

"I just want a man who smells like a man. Screw the rest." Cameron tapped at the wrinkled invoice, which had clearly been folded, un-folded, and folded again many times over. "Focus, Mags. You're carrying around some guy's auto body invoice because, why?"

"Well, if I have *his*, then he clearly has *mine*," she began. "Why should I throw his out if he is possibly holding onto mine? Either we should both have each other's invoices or nobody should."

"Uh huh," Cameron evaluated. "You've really thought this through, haven't you?"

"Shut it, Fitz."

"So, when are you going to call him?" Cameron asked, moving on.

"Oh, no. I'm not going to call him," she shot back, defensively. "I already gave him the no-call vibe. Now, if I were suddenly to call him? Chaos."

"So, you're hoping he calls you?"

Maggie took another swig. "Tell me. How's the show going?"

Cameron rolled her eyes. "Trey is out of his mind, as usual," she said. "But we're clocking like half a million a night and it looks like we should get a fourth season pickup from the network. You know, you haven't been to the show in ages. You should come. You should bring your purple-shirt guy. What's his name?"

Maggie turned the invoice. Cameron let out a huff. "Please. You know his name; you don't have to look."

"I was just making sure, you bitch," she said, slapping at her. "It's Josh Allen," she relented, sitting back and finishing off her glass of wine.

"Is he cute?"

"More annoying than cute," she said.

Cameron gave her a once-over. Maggie turned away from her prying eyes. "He really got under your skin, huh, Mags? When was the last time a guy had that effect on you?"

It was a good question.

There had been Maggie's senior prom date, Fitch Caldwell, her next-door neighbor and bully-savior who had beat the crap out of the neighborhood boys after they had thrown her lunchbox on the roof of a neighbor's home. He had been reluctant at first to accept an invitation from a girl, let alone a girl two years his junior, when he was already into his second year at the local community college. But Maggie had been relentless, promising a good time, but deathly afraid of being unable to engineer a trip to that year's prom, especially after sitting out for the previous one. She had purchased the corsage for him to give to her, she had rented the limousine, she had even given Fitch some talking points about how to tell the story of their subtle, yet mutually appreciated childhood crush. But it had been her insistence that he dance with her to "Hey Ya!" by OutKast with "the kind of enthusiasm" that would convince her friends "he really wanted to be there" that was the final straw.

"I'm gonna sit this one out," he'd said.

"You're refusing to dance?" she'd shot back, adjusting her oversized corsage. "You're refusing to dance … *at a dance*? Where's the logic in that?"

"Yup. Just not feeling it."

It had been stupid. But it hadn't gotten under her skin.

KC refused to try sushi. James didn't believe any singer should be allowed to refer to themselves as The Boss. Carmine came from an Italian family but was adamant that he had never, and would never, try spaghetti. Caleb refused to change lanes on a freeway if it meant he'd drive over the reflector dots for fear of destroying his family's invention. These were strange personality quirks. Things that made no logical sense. Obsessions that clearly required further exploration with a fully licensed therapist. But these weren't things she spent much time thinking about or debating over. They came and went and Maggie let them slide off her back like the baubles of water descending a cold can of Coke.

"Never," she realized, turning to Cam, finally answering the question.

"Don't make me say the G-word, because I will," Cameron eyed her, suspicious. "You seem to forget we were friends when you were living in Paris that year."

Maggie's face dropped. *Oh, Paris.* "Fine," Maggie relented. "Maybe once." But it wasn't a story she wanted to revisit. Her expression made that abundantly clear.

"So, in your entire life only one guy has ever had an effect on you? How come?"

Yes, Maggie, how come? She thought about it as she sat there, staring at the auto body invoice. An invoice that represented a name that represented a person that she couldn't stop thinking about. Why had men so rarely had an effect on her? Was it because she hadn't found the right man, or was it because she had built a protective moat that was keeping all of them out? Whose fault was it? Could she ever reverse the trend?

They waved goodbye to Teresa as she walked out the front doors, taking with her a plastic grocery bag packed with Tupperware containers, filled with leftovers from the night. Barbara waved enthusiastically as Mel and Josh stood behind her in the foyer.

Barbara closed the door, turning to the boys. "Well?" she smiled, looking to Josh.

"No," said Josh, turning and walking out of the room. Barbara looked to Mel.

"I thought she was nice," he said, turning to follow Josh. "What a whistler."

Josh was already sitting at the kitchen counter, making his way through a bowl of ice cream, when Mel walked into the room. He made eye contact with his son as he retrieved his own dish from the cupboard and snatched the open ice cream container from across the counter, leaning onto his elbow as he dug a few scoops out with his spoon.

"How's work?" Mel said, taking a bite.

"It's good."

"Yeah? What are you working on these days?"

Josh finished his bowl, reaching for the container near his father.

Mel pulled it back, out of arm's length. "Tell me about work first."

He shrugged, sitting back, arms behind his head. "It's fine, it's good. About to start working on this Technology Through the Ages exhibit. Some really rare pieces we unearthed, plus a few donated by the trustees of the Center. Also trying to get the University of Witwatersrand to loan the Center this new species of Sauropodomorph they discovered in their vaults after thirty years. Can you believe it? It was laying there, misidentified in Johannesburg, for that long. That would be a big score, if I could make it happen."

"And you're happy? With the job?" he asked, genuinely concerned. "I know it originally wasn't what you wanted. But it seems like you've really taken to it over the years."

"Yeah, Dad," Josh said, "I'm good."

"He's good, he says," Mel said to the air over his left shoulder, then turned back to give his son a judgmental once-over in only the way he could. He slapped the counter, clearly satisfied. "Now, you may have more ice cream." Mel slid the container back toward Josh. He grabbed it, digging in for a few more scoops, nimbly trying to get the good chunks of caramel and chocolate like a skilled excavator. "You've just … been at the Center for a long time," he threw out, clearly wanting to put a period on the debate.

Josh finished his bite, swallowing. "I said it's good. What else do you want me to say?"

"You don't have to convince me," Mel said, retreating from the conflict as he took back the ice cream container and put another scoop in his bowl. "It's Grandpa Harris who needs convincing," he said, motioning to the invisible pocket of air over his shoulder.

"Well, tell Grandpa Harris he's *dead*," Josh shot back, "and that he'll have more than enough time to ask me questions when I join him in the afterlife."

The two of them dug back in, each staring into the bowl looking for something unattainable. While the two never came out and said what they were thinking, there was an unspoken understanding between them. Maybe it was because they both spent their lives contending with Barbara. Maybe it was because there was PTSD there that they both felt. Heck, maybe it was the Stockholm Syndrome of it all.

Josh had a thought, and pulled out the invoice from the auto body shop. Mel watched as he unfolded it and smoothed it out on the counter.

Josh slid it over, raising his eyebrows. Mel scanned the page. "Thirty-five hundred bucks? You must have really hit that divider with a vengeance. Wait, when did you get a Tesla?"

"Look at the name at the top," Josh directed.

Mel scanned to the top. "So, does that mean it's not going to cost you thirty-five hundred? Because that's a lot of—"

"No. I mean, it's going to cost me more. That's not the point, Dad."

"Then what's the point?" Mel wasn't sure.

Josh tapped the name at the top of the invoice. "This girl … *woman*, whatever. I met her today at the auto body shop."

"And you stole her repair invoice?"

"No, they mixed them up," Josh said.

"You got hers and she got yours?" he asked, a wide smile spreading across his face.

"It was an accident, obviously," Josh replied, knowing where Mel was about to go.

"*Puh!* Accident," Mel spat. "There's no such thing as an accident in this infinite universe of possibilities," he grinned. "Accidents are just the universe's way of making sure things happen the way they were supposed to happen in the first place." Mel eyed the name at the top. "Maggie Mills," he verbalized. "I like the sound of it. The alliteration of it. So, what then? You like her?"

"Well, I just met her."

"Maybe you didn't *just* meet her," he argued. "Are you sure?"

"Yes," Josh rolled his eyes. "I'm sure." Josh turned away, futzing with the invoice.

"Did you know I met your mother four times before I, quote unquote, actually met her?" Mel said. "We crossed paths, were in the same restaurant, attended the same concert? It's all about timing. It's all about being ready for it. And it's all about the small, insignificant details that become the huge, meaningful milestones."

"How do you mean?" Josh wondered, still pushing back on the concept.

"Well," Mel said, "if my parents hadn't moved from Texas to New York, for example. What if we never moved to California from New York? What if I never took the job at ValleyCon? We wouldn't even be living here. Would you have ever met the one and only auto shop girl? Think about that."

"Yeah, sure. Getting you and Mom together was job number one for the almighty, infinite universe," Josh shot back, tossing his spoon into his empty bowl. "For what reason would the universe want that?"

Cue the fireworks. Barbara entered the kitchen, carrying two stacked trays of dirty dishes from the dining room. Mel immediately stood at attention, realizing he'd neglected to offer up any help after their guest had left. She glared at Mel, walking around him to the kitchen sink, then letting the dishes drop into it with an ear-shattering crash.

"It's a question I ask the universe every day," Mel whispered, widening his eyes and chasing after Barbara into the other room.

Josh picked up the invoice, looking at it curiously.

Maggie sat in the driveway of her apartment building, inside the perfectly satisfactory, perfectly road legal, perfectly gray Hyundai Sonata.

The good news was that it had seat belts, although they wouldn't automatically tighten around one's body when the ignition came on. It also had cup holders, so Maggie would have a place to store her morning espresso, despite the fact that one of the two was inoperative due to a melted plastic *something* filling up its base. Yes, there was even a CD player, although there was no Bluetooth to speak of, suggesting that playlists on her phone would have to live to fight another day. The bad news was that the car worked. Which meant she would have to drive it to *The 818* where everyone would see her, notice she was driving a Sonata, then spend the day making adolescent jokes about classical music and the generic form of the drug zaleplon. When you worked with writers and editors, people who had spent the majority of years on Earth anally researching random topics and often guilty of hilarious, yet inappropriate, non sequiturs, it was par for the course.

Maggie pulled out a CD with the words "Kick Ass Music Mix" emblazoned around the diameter of the old-school TDK disc. She turned on the car, placing the disc in the slot of the player. It made a grinding sound, sucking in the disc, pushing it back out, then sucking it in for a second time. As the opening guitar chords of The Eagles' "Hotel California" began playing, Maggie threw her bag onto the passenger seat, causing some lipstick, a brush, her cell phone, and the auto body invoice to fall to the floor. She leaned over to pick them all up, pausing on the invoice and paying particular attention to the phone number. *His* phone number. The one she had promised herself, multiple times, to never, *ever* call. No matter what. No, she was known for her unwavering ability to stay strong. She was not a waffler. She was a bad-ass promiser. She could keep promises like the best of them.

"Damn it," she said, grabbing her cell phone.

Damn it, she thought again as she looked at Josh's number.

"Damn it!" she said aloud, as she pressed the green phone icon on her cell.

What if he's another Gabriel, the voice in her head who knew everything about that year in Paris questioned. *You do NOT want another Gabriel Marchand in your life. You gave one man your heart, and the minute you did he abandoned you forever. Do you want to risk that happening again?*

"Oh, relax," she said, attempting to convince herself. "That was a long time ago. You will be fine."

She eyed the phone number, tapping in the seven digits on the keypad. She stared at her finger, hovering above the icon that would connect the call. And she waited. Debated. She pulled back her finger. Outside, a few pedestrians walked by eyeing Maggie, sitting in the car, "Hotel California" blasting. She waved them off, as if they were pressuring her to do the deed. "Fuck it," she said, pressing the button and engaging the call.

A wave of terror shot through every part of her body.

"Are you insane?" she yelled at herself, hanging up before the call could go through. Although the phone, in all its wondrous intelligence, would log the phone number in its call history … *just in case.*

It was 8:17 a.m.

Josh merged the blue metallic Fiat onto the freeway, making his way downtown. Because it was 8:17 a.m, it was smack-dab in the middle of his *Mindfulness Moment* of the day, which on this particular morning involved the soft relaxing sounds of a babbling brook, accompanied by a suite of classical string instruments, playing the familiar notes of an even more familiar symphony. Josh looked around the interior of the car, identifying the dozens of speakers installed around the perimeter. *This isn't so bad*, he thought to himself, taking a deep breath and sinking into the premium leather seats.

It was 8:18 a.m.

Maggie pulled the crappy Sonata onto the main drag of Ventura, causing items in her purse to slide off the cheap vinyl seats and onto the floor. *Again.* Maggie kept her eye on the road this time, not paying much attention to what her fingers were doing as she grabbed her phone off the floor and threw it back into her purse. Had she been looking, she would have noticed that she had hit the circular green phone button, instructing her iPhone to dial the last number she'd called.

"Hotel California" kept playing. Maggie was feeling it. She started singing, head pivoting, body moving with the rhythm. At a stop light she shared a look with the people in the cars on both sides. Her enthusiasm was infectious. She wasn't embarrassed. Why would she be?

Still 8:18 a.m.

Josh's cell phone rang through the Fiat's advanced Bluetooth system, prompting him to hit a button on the dash to take the call.

Unknown caller, he thought to himself, then hit the button on the dash.

"Hotel California" came blasting through his speakers. Not the song, as sung by The Eagles, but as sung by an unfamiliar, yet extremely enthusiastic voice: that of Maggie Mills. "Hello?" Josh yelled back into the Fiat's advanced voice-recognition system. "Can you hear me?"

Maggie powered through the chorus.

"Hello?" Josh yelled at the top of his lungs, timed perfectly to the bridge in the middle of the song. "Who is that?"

It was the bridge. Maggie loved the bridge. Well, up until this moment she did. In subsequent years, the bridge of "Hotel California" would give her real, noticeable, raised red hives.

"WHO IS THAT?" came a voice from somewhere in her car. Maggie lowered the music, confused, as the voice continued to yell. She hit a red light, stopping the car and listening for where it was coming from. "HELLO" came again. She turned, filled with dread, and shook her purse like it had a rattlesnake inside. Her phone slipped out and onto the edge of the seat. A phone call was engaged, and had been for what the phone determined was approximately forty-nine seconds.

She picked up the phone like it had come out of the oven and cleared her throat. "Hello?"

"For god's sake, who is this?" the voice asked. "And why are you singing 'Hotel California'?"

Maggie eyed the invoice from the auto body shop. She knew who was on the other end of the line. With today's modern technology and caller ID, there was no way out of this one. She gripped the steering wheel, angst-ridden.

"It's Maggie Mills."

There was a long pause. Maggie sat there, cringing.
"From the auto body shop?"

Maggie bit her tongue, not sure what to say.

"Maggie Mills from the auto body shop," Josh stated, stifling a chuckle.

"Why are you laughing?"

"Me? I'm not laughing."

"You're *laughing.*"

There was another pause.

"Don't laugh," Maggie lamented, feeling like an idiot.

"I'm sorry," he said. "I'm glad you called."

"I didn't technically call," she began, but then perked up with her follow-up question. "But wait ... you're glad I did?"

There wasn't much more to be said.

Eight and a Half

YOU CAN NEVER TOTALLY trust the village.

Some villages lived in complete and total harmony. Ask them what they wanted to order for dinner, and they'd agree across the board that pepperoni pizza with a side of hot wings and a two-liter bottle of soda was the way to go. Suggest a nice five-day, four-night excursion to Maui for the village's twentieth anniversary, and they'd all jump at the chance to go, not asking where their airline seats were located, what class they were flying, or how many stars the hotel had garnered from the infamous *Fodor's*. And when you asked them to recall if it was Josh who asked Maggie out, or the other way around, they'd circle the wagons and give you a completely aligned, totally-in-agreement short-and-sweet answer. It was a wonderfully, glass-half-full way to imagine the village surrounding Josh and Maggie. It was also exceptionally misguided, if you knew absolutely anything about the people in Josh and Maggie's village.

Because *their* village wasn't harmonious or agreeable like *that* village.

Half of *their* village wanted cheese with black olives, while the other half wanted pineapple and sausage. Ask them to commit to their choice, and they'd change it again. Some thought Maui would be a wonderful trip, as long as they could fly first class and stay in a five-star hotel. Others wondered why they couldn't just book a stay-cation, ordering in from said-referenced pizza place and enjoying the facilities already at home. Mention hot wings and you'd spark a debate about the hot factor, milk versus water as a spice diminisher, and a red-state/blue-state argument about free-range versus hormones. Ask them a question about if it was Josh or if it was Maggie, and the responses were worse than a ten-year-old's game of telephone.

"Like I said, I could hear her singing 'Hotel California' through my window, at the stop light," said Cammie Simpson, the latest nanny to grace the inside of the Kohn family's Mercedes SLK. She had been on her way to taking Pepper to her acapella singing lesson and Sebastian to his Krav Maga hand-to-hand combat class when she noticed the chaos in the next car over. "One minute she was singing her heart out, the next she looked mortified. Then surprised. I saw her lower the music and then she began talking to someone over the speakerphone. She was listening. The person on the other line asked her a question. Then she did one of those fist pumps. She was clearly stoked. And then the light turned green and I never saw her again."

"Mr. Allen asked me a favor," said Freddie Alvarez. "I'm in early, keeping an eye on the Security Office when he walks in with this suspicious, happy smile. Like, I see the guy every day and aside from opening night for the new exhibits, I've never seen this. And he asks me for a favor. The kind of favor that if I cleared it with Ms. Rowland, she'd probably say no to. But Mr. Allen's a solid dude. Made sure we saw a good bonus last holiday. So, I asked him to give me the lowdown and he does. Seems he asked this lady friend out, and now he had to deliver something spectacular for their first date. And he needed my help. What was I gonna say, no? I'm a lover, not a fighter."

"He said *she* called *him*," Damon remembered, enjoying a lava flow by the pool at the Four Seasons Resort in Maui, telling the story to his new wife, Lisa. "I said to L, good for her to not wait for Josh to find the courage to do it himself. And it's a good thing, because if she *hadn't* ... But Josh was very clear: he made sure I knew he asked her out. And remember, I was adamant about this key point ... make sure you pay for the damn date. People remember that shit when they're retelling the story of how you met. It's like first dates, wedding proposals, and the birth of your firstborn, I told him. Those are the milestones people remember."

"She called me at work the same day it happened," said Maggie's brother Teddy, a podiatrist working out of downtown Chicago. "I was in a nasty bunion surgery for at least five hours, so Janice took the message. She wrote it down word-for-word. Like a transcript. It just said 'The Fat Lady is singing.' That meant she was going on a date she actually cared about. It was our secret code. I'm glad it was word-for-word, because if it wasn't, I would have never believed it. Maggie really is that picky."

"I asked him why he looked so happy that day," Josh's co-worker David told Diana, as they did a walk-through on the third floor, through the *Rockets: A Blast from the Past* exhibit. "He said he hadn't been on an actual date in ages, but that this girl made him want to put in the kind of effort he put into the exhibits here at the Center. He couldn't put his finger on why, but it's what he wanted to do."

"Yes, she called and told us," said Maggie's father. "She always has. Always been forthright and transparent and honest with us about what was going on in her life. Of course, he asked her out for dinner. She wouldn't have said yes had it been the other way around. No, I don't just *think* that, I *know* that."

"When you grow up with strong, honest, confident male role models in your life," said Maggie's mother, "that's exactly the type of man you're going to want beside you as your partner."

"The confidence part needed some work, though," Maggie's father added, receiving an "Oh, Frank," from his wife.

"Does it really matter who asked who? Feels extremely insignificant now, all things considered," Mel said, smoking a cigar on the balcony of his Woodland Hills hotel room, wearing the Four Seasons terry cloth robe he would eventually smuggle out in his suitcase. "I mean, we're here, aren't we?"

"Howard Kohn told me once that he heard from his kid Sebastian, who had been in a car with their nanny Katie-something, that there had been a woman singing 'Hotel California' in the car next to him," remembered Irving Azoff, the long-time manager of The Eagles. "Apparently, the young woman singing had surprised some dude on the phone and was asking him out for the first time. Don and Glenn and I always loved to hear stories about how their music became the soundtrack to people's lives. I wish there was a way to monetize those kinds of moments, but what the heck. I think we'll just thank our lucky stars there's such a thing as Spotify streaming residuals."

"I'd prefer to not talk about them at all," said the familiar paperwork-pushing clerk from Western Auto Body. "Don't you think I've already done enough?"

Nine

AT THE AGE OF twenty, Caleb Parsons, heir to the Milwaukee Parsons' highway reflector dot fortune, found himself up at the bar ordering three more beers.

The crowd surge at Rockadile's behind him was easily four people deep, a reasonable crowd for three in the afternoon during the months of February, March, April, or May. Spring break always brought them in droves, and on this particular April afternoon, it was clearly drove-enhanced. The bar sat in the center of the rancid, recently deloused warehouse, flat-screen televisions playing the latest sports and music videos, with bikini-clad barmaids selling shots in test tubes and Jell-O in cups. Around the room, college students flirted, took pictures, and screamed obscenities.

"*Tres más … cervesas!*" Caleb shouted over the noise, waving a stack of cash that in any other setting would have gotten him mugged.

Maggie and Cameron conferred in the back, balancing atop two bar stools at a tall table littered with empties. Maggie was tan, her sun-bleached hair looking blonder than the traditional brown she often rocked. She wore a tank top, beach shorts, and a pair of Nike flip-flops, waving her arms wildly, letting the alcohol already in her system drive her passion for the subject at hand. "And if there's no such thing as a soulmate," she said, grasping onto Cameron's arms like she was holding onto the railing on a rocky ocean cruise, "then why waste time looking for one?"

Cameron stared at her, then Caleb, then back. She shrugged. Maggie's face changed as she clutched her bladder. Clearly, nature was calling.

"What I should be looking for is … the bathroom?" Maggie slurred, pushing herself up from the bar stool. "Maybe I should just start with the small stuff and prioritize that?"

Around the back of Rockadile's, Cody and Damon propped a drunk Josh up against the establishment's wall, slapping his face to try and bring him back into consciousness. "C'mon, bud," Cody said, "We found you a place to drain the snake and purge your guts."

Josh opened his eyes, his narrowed vision only slightly more problematic than the fluorescent yellow flip-flops and neon pink tank top he had mistakenly chosen for the day. He could just make out his two friends by his side as the sun moved behind the clouds. Josh snapped into the present, readying a statement he'd been waiting forty-five minutes to share with the audience that had bought tickets to the show. "No more tequila," he nodded, slurring, trying to pat Cody's chest but missing. "And I mean it."

"C'mon, you lush," Damon said as he rotated Josh toward the back door and opened it wide. A long hallway led to the bathrooms. "Down there. Thirty steps forward and on your right."

Josh peered into the darkness. "Return the map!" he joked to his friends, an inside joke that only the most '80s obsessed would have understood.

There was a *Señor's* door, and there was a *Señorita's* door. The *Señor's* door featured a male frog, wearing a colorful poncho and a sombrero. The *Señorita's* door featured a female frog, wearing a hot pink dress, gaudy eye make-up and pulling up her dress to show off her long, silky-smooth green-hued assets as she danced the salsa.

Maggie stood opposite the women's bathroom door, waiting, head in her hands. Down the hall, a bright light emanated, then disappeared, as a figure began shuffling like a zombie toward Maggie who was waiting her turn. She took a breath, lifted her head, and pushed back into a standing position. Josh stood next to her, his head in his hands, leaning up against the wall opposite the men's bathroom door. He groaned.

Maggie gave him the once over and laughed as he tried to balance himself on the wall. "Somebody can't hold their liquor," she pointed, almost losing balance herself.

Josh groaned again, but this time it seemed like commentary on Maggie's opinion.

"You okay?" Maggie asked, crooking her head to get a closer look. "You look a little gray. Actually, a lot of gray. All gray. Think that's kind of a warning sign of … something."

"No more tequila," he replied, lifting his head to get a better look at the girl beside him.

"Liquor before beer, never fear," she announced, though it seemed to make no sense. "So, you're okay. Now you can have beer … if you want."

Josh squinted, shaking his head no. "Beer before liquor, getting drunk happens quicker," he shot back.

"I don't think that's the real saying," she countered.

"Beer before wine, you'll be fine," he said, almost collapsing onto the floor.

"Wine before beer, all is clear," she said.

Two drunk idiots. In a hallway. Debating the logic behind the old wives' tales of what to drink when. Had any sane person listened in, they would have been completely lost in the gibberish of it all. But for Josh and Maggie, it was a serendipitous moment of being on the same page.

"Tequila first, then you'll have no thirst," Maggie spouted, extra proud of the rhyme.

"Make sure to eat nuts, or you'll throw up your guts," Josh threw out, looking pleased with himself. Maggie giggled; she was pretty partial to that one.

"You guys are so lame, please stop playing this game," said a young dude who had clearly heard the whole conversation, emerging from the men's bathroom and collapsing on the floor as he entered the bar.

"Like I'm gonna take that guy's opinion," Josh said, pointing to the downed fool.

"Now that he's on the floor," Maggie said, "I think you can enter that door," she laughed, referring to the vacant bathroom.

Josh entered the men's bathroom and closed the door. A second later, the women's bathroom door opened and Maggie went inside.

Neither would remember the moment, despite the fact that germs of the memory would sit dormant in the furthest reaches of their cerebellum from that point forward. They wouldn't see each other again that night, although they'd push past each other on their way to get yet another beer, down a Jell-O shot, or ingest yet another beer. Or maybe it was liquor. Or wine. They wouldn't remember which.

But they'd remember the male frog wearing the sombrero. And the female frog wearing the pink dress.

Because in what world would you *not*?

Ten

EVERYONE KNEW WHERE THEY were when JFK was shot. They knew what they had been doing when the space shuttle exploded in the sky. There was no forgetting who they were with when the horrific events of 9/11 occurred. These were significant, heartbreaking, painful memories that were stitched into the fabric of time.

Then there were the memories of a person's smaller, more insular world. The small stuff insignificant to the strangers that flitter about the edges of one's life, yet at times could feel hugely significant to those who were living it themselves. Who could forget where they were when their father broke his leg? Or what they'd been doing when the upstairs bathroom sink overflowed, causing $15,000 of damage to the floor below? Or who was with them when they, as a child, had gotten their head stuck in between the banister at the top of the stairs, necessitating one police cruiser, an ambulance, and a fire truck to be called to the scene? Yes, they were small and insignificant for those without any personal investment in the moment, but big and weighty for those whose lives were smack dab in the middle of it all.

The argument between Curtis and Brian had been one such weighty thing for a good portion of the staff members at *The 818* that Friday afternoon.

At least it had been for Darren, who often used Curtis to take the profile pictures of celebrities whose latest movie, TV show, or streaming special was the talk of the town. It made sense for Robyn, whose features on the latest wellness trend or newly launched fashion label required the kind of photographic poetry that captured the true hues of real life. It was a moment Alyssa wouldn't forget, as Curtis had been integral in setting up the green-screen photo booth, which had completely upped the game for book photos, transitioning from stock shots and two-dimensional snaps into the vibrant, tactile imagery that accompanied her reviews.

"This will single-handedly save the ailing business of published literature," Alyssa was overheard to have said, eyes wide at the finished product, imagining endless possibilities.

Carly, on the other hand, had never been a fan of Curtis since the incident involving him eating her leftover pad Thai from the office fridge, in which he denied that the guy holding the camera *and* eating the pad Thai on the security camera footage was him at all. So, it made sense that she found the moment extremely satisfying, as she ironically ate some of the previous night's leftover pad Thai as she watched it all unfold.

As for Maggie, watching from her desk, her Best Buy special cradled in her arms, it seemed like the moment of opportunity she'd been waiting for. Mostly because, in the seconds following Curtis throwing down his press badge and shouting obscenities at Brian, he was told in no uncertain terms that his services were no longer needed at *The 818*. The staff photographer was being let go, leaving a vacancy for some smart, resourceful, passionate visionary. "I'm a visionary," Maggie whispered as she watched Curtis storm out of Brian's office, rifle through his desk, and shout vulgarities as he made his way to the elevator; once there he pressed the down-button and waited. And waited. And waited some more.

"You've got an Otis HydroFit from oh-eight in here," Maggie recalled the elevator repairman telling Brian eighteen months prior. "Unless you're willing to upgrade to the newest model that incorporates faster recall speeds, you're going to have to be okay with the two to three-minute wait." But Brian was cheap. Brian had chosen to leave things well enough alone.

And so it was … Curtis stood awkwardly, waiting for the elevator. Every time there was a grinding sound or the echoing of the thick cables vibrating from within, he'd turn to the doors, anticipating freedom. But the doors stayed shut.

"It's perfectly reasonable for an individual to decide that it's time to move on from one job and turn their focus toward the next opportunity," Brian said, pacing the room as he ate something questionable out of a dirty brown paper bag. One which, had the U.S. Department of Health and Human Services seen with their own eyes, might have caused an entire office shutdown and subsequent quarantine. The main editors and writers sat around the room, perched on chairs and in the oversized leather couch, listening curiously.

"Sounded to me like you fired him," Leo said, raising a pencil to get Brian's attention.

"While HR would prefer I don't discuss the situation openly, I can tell you that it was a mutual decision," Brian said, plopping down in his dirty red vinyl chair, facing the team.

"You yelled *you're fired*," Alyssa said, always concerned to not rock the boat but desperate to be a part of the conversation.

"But then he agreed with me." Brian waved off the logic of it all, ready to move on. "Look, we have work to do here, people. We have our next monthly issue going to print in two weeks. And many of you still haven't delivered. I want to hear where we're at."

"Who's gonna handle photog?" asked Maggie, especially interested.

"I'll hire a few stringers," Brian replied. "Until I can find a full-timer." Maggie regarded this with interest as Brian flipped his feet up on the coffee table and pointed to Darren. "Your feature on Zack Tolman?"

"I'm calling it 'Man with a Plan,'" Darren perked up. "From commercial actor to the face of the *Sky Spy* trilogy. Did the sit-down for the interview already, just need to get the photo shoot going, but due to your mutual agreement about Curtis's future …"

"*Stringer*," Brian proclaimed, matter-of-fact. He looked to Robyn.

"The growing trend of scarves. Got a lot of celebs on the record, fashion designers, plus a good interview with Josie and Jeanette Baylor who have the go-to shop out here. They're doing three million a year now, and that's just in the two years since they started." Brian nodded, chewing, interested. "Just need to do a shoot of their store in Malibu and I'll be all good. But seeing as though Curtis …"

"*Stringer*, people. We'll get a stringer." He looked to Maggie, eyes wide, prompting. "My inbox is strangely devoid of a new restaurant review."

"Deciding this week, Chief," she said. "It's between that new place that's blowing up … they do nothing but brussels sprouts. Sprouted. Or I may do it on Lucas Harrison's new buffet spot, Spork. Obviously, I'm gonna need someone to get an outside shot of whichever place I land on, and maybe an insert of a dish or two, but I've got a stellar idea on how to handle that sitch."

The rest of the group turned to Maggie, curious. Brian rolled his eyes; he'd seemingly had this painful conversation before.

"I can do this," Maggie pleaded, holding her camera in her hands, opposite Brian. Aside from the two of them, the room was empty, doors closed. Brian looked longingly at the doors to the bullpen; in the event that things got dicey he had a clear escape path already laid out in his head. He'd hurtle over the desk, push Maggie onto the couch to buy himself some time, then hit the back stairwell down to the emergency exit doors on the ground level. He smiled, imagining it play out, then snapped back into the realm of annoyance.

"You already have a job, Mills," Brian lamented, sitting back behind his desk as he chewed what was once a Popsicle stick in between his teeth. "I need you to do that job, not pick up the slack for Curtis."

"But I can do both."

Brian rolled his eyes. "We've been through this before. Many times, in fact. You're a writer, not a photographer. I mean, what professional experience do you even have in photography?" He noticed an excited thought about to escape Maggie's pursed lips. "Besides Instagram," he stopped her. "Digital filters do not make one a professional photographer, and I wish someone would tell the millions of people online who think they do. Just because you use a filter called X-Pro Two doesn't mean you're a *pro*."

She shrugged, shrinking down like a deflating tire. "I've been a photographer since my father gave me my first camera at the age of eight," she said. "Look, I'm good. Give me a chance and I won't let you down. I won't let you down in either job. With all you've got going on, do you really want to deal with finding a stringer right now?"

Brian leaned in to get a better look at her camera. Man, was she persistent. And annoying. Persistently annoying. But the path of least resistance seemed like the prudent way to go with the next issue's deadlines looming.

Brian swallowed the latest geyser of stomach acid. "First priority is the job I pay you for," he said, watching for the affirmative head nod that came a split-second later. "I'll let you handle the shoots for Darren, Robyn, and Alyssa's pieces for this issue *only*. And then it'll be up to me to decide if you're cut out for this. If I say you're not, we will never have this conversation again." Brian extended his hand, still gripping the Popsicle stick. "Swear on the Popsicle stick."

Maggie, smiling, shook his hand instead.

Maggie sat down at her desk, eyes forward, letting out a sigh and a smile. She looked down at the camera in her hands, holding it up and wiping off dust near the lens.

"You convinced him, didn't you?" Carly said, sidling up. "You motherfucking convinced him. They said it would never happen, but here we are."

Maggie turned, quickly wiping the subtle smile off her face when she noticed she was in Brian's eyeline through his opened office doors. "If at first you don't succeed ..." she said, "and then you don't succeed again ... and again? And then Brian gets noise-canceling earphones so he can put them on when he anticipates you trying to succeed one more time? He's giving me a shot at covering a few of the features."

"Drinks. A celebration is in order. We need happy hour drinks. After work?"

"Drinks? Well, totally, I think—" Maggie paused. "I actually can't."

"You can't? Why not?"

Maggie smiled. "If you can believe it, I actually have plans."

"Plans are one thing," Carly began. "Plans on a Friday night? That smells like a date."

Maggie winced. *When was the last time I actually had a date?* she wondered. The fact that she couldn't remember ... that there were visuals of casual meals here and there with faceless men she couldn't put her finger on ... Well, it meant it had been a long time. A *really* long time.

There was the time she took [*insert faceless male date here*] to Sangria, a short-lived hole in the wall that served nothing but tacos and, well, sangria. When the red stuff in huge goblets landed in front of Maggie and [*name starting with an N*], she did her impression of the Kool-Aid man breaking through a wall. His face, had it been in focus in her memories, would have exuded the kind of pop-culture confusion that turned Maggie off completely.

There was the other time she took [*insert second faceless male date here*] to the local miniature golf establishment in the Valley. "The one from *Karate Kid*," she'd tell [*he wore white high-tops*]. But [*his ear lobes were huge*] had no idea what she was talking about.

And there had been that infamous time she took [*insert third faceless male date here, but with clearly attractive, in-focus blue eyes*] to the set of *Up All Knight*, courtesy of Cameron, and despite the attractive features she *did* remember, he was an open, disgusting bigot. "I told [*beautiful blue eyes*] to leave," she remembered telling Cameron, sitting alone in the green room. "He was an a-hole."

So clearly it had been some time. But, yes, it was—

"—a date," she said, embarrassed. And proud. But mostly nervous.

"But you never have dates. You abhor dating. Wasn't it you who said dating is like eating bao? Only you. Why was that, again?"

Maggie shrugged. "Because bao always looks like it's going to deliver, then when you dig in there's nothing of substance on the inside. Yes, I said that. Hell, I don't know. It'll probably be just another waste of my time."

"Then why go?"

"Because what if it isn't." The words bounced around in her head. *What if.* What if it wasn't a waste of time?

"And who's the guy?" Carly asked.

"The illustrious Mr. Allen."

It was lunch time. But only one person brought their lunch to the Science Center weekly status meeting. Diana, the face behind the illustrious comment, gingerly opened numerous compartments on a quaint-looking, wooden puzzle box of sorts, revealing an elaborate collection of fresh sushi and accoutrements. She plucked a pair of granite-looking stone chopsticks, picked up a piece of fresh salmon, dipped it in a small bowl of soy sauce, and lifted it up to her mouth. The team watched her, entranced, as she chewed.

She looked up and noticed everyone watching. "I'm pleased to share," she said, despite never truly wanting anyone to angle for her edamame, kale BLT, or cold tofu salad. Annabelle had started keeping track in the margins of her notebook. To date, Diana had offered to share her chef-prepared gourmet lunches 711 times. Only once did someone take her up on the offer, and he (not surprisingly) didn't work at the Center anymore.

"We're a month away from the opening of our new exhibit, Technology Through the Ages," Josh said, flipping through his papers, which included photos of a variety of technological items: vintage telephones, early video game consoles, the first cell phone, music media players, Morse code machines, and more. "T's been handling the invitations to the gala opening and we're really plugging along, right?" he said, looking over to T.

"Already have a hundred and ten confirmed, thirty-five of which come directly from the Board of Trustees. Bruce Anderson, our Chair Emeritus, confirmed he's coming as well."

"Oh, Bruce," Diana spoke up, putting down her chopsticks. "He was the chair when they hired me. A wonderful man. A smart man. Turned all his investments in technology companies into his firm Andoco, then put all those profits into philanthropies and rare antiquities. He's a true collector."

"He's also a real generous dude," Josh shot back. "He's donated six separate items that we'll be including across the various decades in the exhibit. He filled in a few of the holes we had in the fifties and the seventies. A mint-condition TRS-80." Everyone in the room stared at Josh, face blank, except for David Reeves. He knew everything about the groundbreaking personal computer that took the world by storm in 1977.

"Zork!" David called out, referencing the text-based adventure that was one of the first to be sold alongside the computer's hardware.

Josh continued. "Now that we have the list of all the items that will be featured in the program, we've got our graphics team working up the visuals that will fill out the dioramas and background posters for each. We will ..." Josh looked to Diana, clearly trying to impress, "... stimulate curiosity and inspire science learning by creating yet another fun, memorable experience."

Diana grabbed her chest. No, she wasn't having a heart attack. It wasn't heartburn from the full-sodium soy sauce. She was moved. "Well, somebody memorized the mission statement."

"Six years ago," grinned Josh.

"Did you ask us to memorize the mission statement?" asked Annabelle, concerned, flipping through her notes. "Because I would have written it down if you had."

"I don't ask, darling," Diana said, perfectly sweet and collected. "I assume that each of you are the driven self-starters I hired, with your own goals you'd like to accomplish. If memorizing the mission statement isn't one of those, so be it."

"I'm going to memorize the mission statement," Annabelle said, looking it up on the Science Center's website.

Josh walked Diana through the Special Exhibits Gallery on the third floor of the Center.

There was blue tape everywhere, outlining the pathway that visitors would take as they traveled through time, from the fifties all the way to present day. The plexiglass boxes whose dimensions would be cut perfectly to scale with the rare items they'd house were already stacked in the corner, and the large floor-to-ceiling graphically-enhanced walls were in place, waiting for the visuals to be printed, affixed, and glued.

"And as visitors move past this point," Josh motioned to the notations on the ground that read *End '50s, '60s Start Here*, "the area will open up with a diorama of the music technologies from the sixties, classic album imagery, and …" Josh pointed to five white plexiglass boxes, all empty. "We'll feature some of the rarest record players of the time: A Dynatron, Bush, Kolster-Brandes, Ferguson, and an amazing, mint 1963 Dansette that was donated by Dr. Faber."

"It's coming along," Diana nodded, as they made their way toward the third-floor atrium, with a view of the two floors below. Teachers, parents, children—they all moved through the exhibits, a colorful sea of passion and excitement.

Josh moved alongside her. "Do you think?"

"Do you really want to know what I think?" she said, turning to him. "I think you've done it all," Diana said, putting her hand on his shoulder.

He let the words hit him, confusing as they were. "Well, the goal was to hit all the decades. So, yes. I guess I have."

"I was speaking more figuratively," Diana said, removing her hand. "I'm not blathering on about the exhibit, which is clearly shaping up to be a stellar production, as expected. I'm talking about you. Here. At the Center. I think you've done it all," she said, trying to make her point. "Am I misguided in my assumption?"

"Well, *shit*," he said, drawing Diana's squeaky-clean ire. "Done it all? That's a pretty sweeping statement. I don't know. But I know I love it here. That I still love working here. And besides, I haven't even cracked the Sauropodomorph yet."

"You'll get the Sauropodomorph," she said matter-of-fact, looking down her nose at Josh with the kind of benign motherly judgment he was unfamiliar with.

"Is there an overhead issue? Do you have to cut staff?" Josh asked, concerned.

"There's no overhead issue," she replied, scolding.

"Then what are you trying to say? Because I kind of feel like, you know, you and I? We've done a lot of great stuff here over the years. Like partners in crime or something. We're like a modern-day Vega and Winnfield."

Diana let the reference hang in the air. "Vega and Winnfield. They're both researchers?" she asked. "You mean Dr. Yaireska Collado-Vega of NASA's Space Weather Office?"

"I hear great things, but no," Josh smiled. "I'm talking about Vincent Vega and Jules Winnfield. From *Pulp Fiction*."

Diana stared at Josh, oblivious. After all, she ran her house like an Amish paradise. No music, no video games, and no movies or TV. It was literature, non-fiction research, and the kind of educational toys that grew the regions of the brain that had shrunk in the shadow of the day's new technological wonders. It was just the kind of no-frills upbringing Diana was used to. It was no wonder that the minute her daughter Robyn turned eighteen, she dove head first into the world of celebrity fashion and never looked back.

"It's a Tarantino movie. Quentin Tarantino?"

Diana looked at him, disapprovingly. "Well, now that you've brought it up," she said, "how is this film pertinent to our partnership?"

"Well," he began, trying to explain. "Vincent is a no-nonsense, worldly traveler. Smart, resourceful, and when you really need something done, he's your man. As for Jules? He ended up getting paired with Vincent, who kind of took him under his wing through some pretty wild situations. Vincent was basically his mentor. And together, they really got a lot of sh- ... stuff, done."

"I'm Vincent?" she asked, hopeful.

"Yes, you're Vincent."

She laughed quietly. Despite the distance she tried to keep from her staff, she was closest to Josh; he had been there the longest. She wanted him to succeed, enjoyed his presence at the Center, and at times felt responsible for him being there for as long as he had. "Be honest. Is this your dream job?"

"Not everyone can have their dream job," Josh said. "Kind of an unrealistic expectation."

"So sayeth your mother," she winked. He'd been working with her for almost ten years, so they'd talked about his mother often. "I'll try once more. Is this your dream job?"

Josh stood silent, with cautious determination in his face.

"Yes. Yes, I believe it is."

She furrowed her brow, thinking. "A person who believes something today," she reasoned with Josh, "may not be right tomorrow. You remember? Before Bohor, Modreski, Foord, and the Cretaceous-Tertiary boundary?"

"I'm sure today and I'll be sure tomorrow," Josh replied, attempting to convince Diana and himself all at the same time.

Eleven

MAGGIE HAD PUT HER money on The Gap.

After all, when you met a full-grown, mature man out in public who was rocking a purple mesh collared shirt, a pair of tan pants, and a nametag, one's mind started to wonder where the rest of their wardrobe was sourced from. She had spent a moment considering the flannel stylings of L.L. Bean and scrolled through the latest "fashions" on the Old Navy website, but when push came to shove, it was the all-day pique polo shirt and wrinkle-free pants of The Gap that kept haunting her thoughts. *A person is not how they dress*, she tried to convince herself, as she finished blowing out her hair and slinked into a pair of dark blue jeans and a form-fitting top. *That's the easiest thing to get a guy to change about himself.* Still, when she told the story years later at a big to-do catered by Manhattan's then up-and-coming chef, Maurizio Tallerico, she would admit she was worried she might have another Brett on her hands.

But when she opened her front door, Maggie found herself pleasantly surprised, staring into the eyes of a man who shopped at Nordstrom. Who had sourced his jeans from an Abercrombie or G-Star. Whose dress shoes hadn't been selected in a fluorescently-lit Shoe Barn or the buffet-like stylings of DSW but rather the kind of place where they provided a chair, a clerk to assist you, and if you were looking at the really expensive kicks, a cold glass of sparkling water.

"You're normal," she smiled.

"Debatable," he shot back.

Josh and Maggie stood on the edge of her driveway, outside her apartment building, staring at the blue metallic Fiat that Josh had parked there. Somewhere, a flock of birds flittered by behind them in slo-mo, almost as if a pretentious action film director whose name rhymed with Michael Bay had mandated it so.

"The 2019 Fiat 500," Josh announced dramatically, imagining the song "Oh Yeah" by Yello playing in his head. "Over a million have been made. Comes with a five-speed, semi-auto, Dualogic transmission. Gets twenty-eight miles per gallon in the city, thirty-three on the highway. It has a starting MSRP of sixteen-thousand five-hundred."

Maggie looked at the car, seemingly jealous. "This is your rental?"

"It is." He reached out, running his finger across the front hood and coolly allowing it to glide up into the air. "Usually, they give you a shit box, but I got lucky this time."

"Just out of curiosity," she wondered, "what insurance company do you have?" She seemed especially concerned.

"Universal Car Group."

She threw her hands up into the air. "Me too," she said, realizing the conspiracy that was afoot. "But how could that be?"

"Why, what'd they give you?"

This was technically a first date. Was she really ready to go there? There were rules, of course, about what kinds of personal information you volunteered during such an event. You didn't talk about your family baggage, reveal your current list of medications, or dig deep into your sexual proclivities. You let those seep out over the course of the first six to twelve months while one let the Honeymoon

Period wind down. But answering an innocent question about the rental car you were driving seemed harmless enough, despite what it said about her ability to charm her way into a far better option. *What the fuck*, she thought.

"A Sonata." She made a sick-face. Josh made a sick-face, too.

"Are you going to be okay?" he asked, like she had just told him the cancer had returned.

Gibson's had nothing to do with guitars, or music, or rock bands. It was the surname of Kylie Gibson, the British socialite and trust-fund baby who had decided that the quickest way to become famous in the States was to open a high-end fish and chips restaurant on Sunset near the edge of Silverlake. Yet, in reality, success had nothing to do with your location, she'd found out three months into the endeavor, but rather the buzz you could create. People would go anywhere in Los Angeles if the buzz was there.

Which was why she was hovering over Maggie and Josh, but mostly Maggie, at their prime corner table in the back.

"... and it's a recipe that Nanna Gibson got from her Nan Sophie, which was passed down to me," Kylie rambled on, elbows on the table, leaning in way too close to Maggie's face. "I would just be thrilled for you to try a little of everything, which is why I'm having the kitchen prepare a fantastic tasting menu for you."

Josh was still holding his menu; he hadn't even chosen what to order yet. He looked at Maggie, desperate and famished, like he wanted to say something to doth protest this screeching woman's master plan. Maggie shook her head, in a *don't disturb the bear* kind of way, while she waited for Kylie's gas to run out.

Would it ever?

"Kylie is tireless. Like a machine. Like the *Terminator*," her partner and co-owner in Gibson's had said to the investors ten months prior, during their first funding drive. "She can't be bargained with. She won't feel pity or remorse or fear. And she will absolutely *not* stop, ever. Until she makes you a profit."

"I'm so glad Malin recognized you when you walked in," Kylie continued, resting her hand on Maggie's arm without pity or remorse or fear. Would she absolutely stop, *ever*? "I guess you just show up sometimes unannounced? Is that how it works? Talk to me about your whole process."

"Actually, I made the reservation," Josh piped up. Kylie turned, surprised, like this had been the first time she'd even realized there was someone else sitting at the table. She smiled at him, said nothing, then turned back to Maggie, who was ready to move on.

"You're going to have to leave us now," Maggie said, serious. "We're going to need total and complete silence so we can concentrate on the signals and flavors that our taste buds are preparing to deliver to our brains."

"Oh. *Really?*" Kylie nodded, backing away, gesturing to the two empty tables on either side of Maggie and Josh. "Ok. Then, I'm going to keep these empty," she whispered, smiling and mouthing "Thank you so much" as she disappeared into the kitchen.

Josh put down the menu. "So, you're kind of famous. Is that it?"

Maggie rolled her eyes. "I'm not famous. I'm just a means to their end."

"You must love it. Especially the groveling."

"That is a perk," she said, taking a sip of her drink. "But this gig was never a goal of mine. It's not like I was this little girl dreaming of someday getting to eat for a career. I don't think any girl dreams of that. It just kind of happened in lieu of me having a better plan."

"I hear that," Josh agreed, thinking about his own career path and missed opportunities.

A server sidled up, quietly sliding a small plate of fried olives into the center of the table. "Olives," she whispered, then backed away on her tippy-toes, clearly having been given very specific instructions on how to engage with the VIPs before her. Josh rolled his eyes, sharing a look with Maggie as the server disappeared. There was a long period of silence as the two of them sipped their drinks, took a look around the place, and landed back on each other.

"So, I didn't get a chance to ask you on the phone," Josh began, referencing the elephant in the room. "What made you call me? After, you know, our No Call Thunderdome?"

"That's a great question for Tina Turner," she responded, disappearing into her drink.

"Thanks," Josh said. "But I'd like to hear what you have to say. Is there an answer?"

"Well," she began, lying, "I know how people can get all bunched up over someone else having their confidential paperwork. And since I had yours, and you clearly had *mine*, I figured an exchange of said paperwork was a legitimate, purely platonic, yet completely selfless act on my part." She reached into her pocket, pulling out his auto body receipt, and slid it slowly across the table. "So, here. This is me, being selfless."

Josh picked up the piece of paper gingerly, noticing it looked like it had been opened and closed hundreds of times. He pulled hers out, which looked about the same, sliding it over to her in the tabletop exchange. "Did you sleep with my receipt under your pillow?" he asked. "Be honest."

"Maybe," she said, one-upping him: "Did you photocopy mine so you could have something to remember me by?"

"There's a chance I did," he said. "And did you secretly want to laminate mine and use it as a placemat so every time you ate your Lucky Charms you could look down and remember the make and model of my automobile?"

"Cat's outta the bag."

They laughed. Maggie looked at Josh, dressed like a normal human being, and felt the fleeting comfort she'd felt in the auto body shop rush back into her. There was something about this dude she couldn't put her finger on. Something familiar. Something that put her defensive mechanisms on the back burner. She'd never shied away from telling the truth in the past, so why would she start now? If this ever went anywhere, would she want the first conversation to be based on a silly, trivial lie?

"Truth?" she posed to Josh.

"Truth is good."

"I called you accidentally," she admitted. "I had typed in your number, decided against calling you, then accidentally redialed the number while I was singing in the car. I had no idea I had done it."

"There's no such thing as an accident," Josh said, amused.

"Except the ones that caused us to meet at the auto body shop," she shot back.

"Debatable," Josh replied.

Out of nowhere, two plates of fish and chips appeared on the table. It caused Josh and Maggie to jump out of their skin. The server quickly backed away from the table as the two of them caught him doing so. They looked to each other, laughing at the ridiculousness of it all. Josh liked her smile. It was sweet. And genuine. This didn't feel like work, like the others had.

"Just take it," Josh pleaded with the server by the Square payment terminal, trying to force his credit card on him as he repeatedly backed away, hand outstretched in defense.

"Ms. Gibson says it's on the house," the server said, appearing more nervous by the minute.

"Yes, but this is a first date," Josh explained. "If the meal is free, it's because of Maggie being here, which indirectly would mean that *she* paid for our first date ... which I cannot stand for. It would set a horrible precedent." Josh looked back at Maggie, who was trying to pretend she wasn't watching from back at the table, then spun again to address the server. "First date stories rank up there in significance with marriage proposals and your first-born child. I have to be able to say that I paid for our first date."

"You're already thinking about marriage and babies?" asked the server, cringing. "Maybe you should just focus on tonight?"

Josh glared at the server, then turned back to Maggie, her shoulders rising with a question of what was going on. Frantic, Josh pulled a wad of cash out of his pocket. "Just take this. Take my money. Let her see that you're taking my money." Josh held up the cash so Maggie could see it, then lifted the server's hand, shoving it into his palm. "Close your hand and smile," he whispered under his breath.

The server closed his hand, nodding to Maggie, then gave the kind of big thumbs-up a hostage typically gave to the S.W.A.T. outside through the opaque front bank window. Josh felt a million times better, sauntering back to the table where Maggie was waiting. "So, now what?" she asked, standing up. "Did you have something in mind?"

"I did. I *do*," he said, grabbing his jacket and motioning toward the door.

Maggie made an "ooh" face, clearly impressed as they walked toward the front of Gibson's where Kylie stood. Maggie walked briskly past her, heading for the door. Then she looked back and sarcastically threw out five words she never thought would be taken seriously.

"My advice? Get rid of the fish."

The California Science Center was open daily from 10 a.m. to 5 p.m. When Josh and Maggie rolled up to it, parking behind the loading dock next to the dumpsters, it was most definitely closed.

"So, this is where you work," Maggie said, making note of the lack of visibility in the darkness. "Should I bring my pepper spray or my TigerLady claws? Maybe both?"

"Oh, c'mon," he said, parking the car.

A few knocks and a few minutes later, the double doors to the loading dock opened, revealing a security guard who had clearly been briefed about the evening's activities.

"Mr. Allen, good to see you," said Freddie. "Glad to have you back." He turned to Maggie: "Everybody here's a big fan of Mr. Allen, I just gotta say."

Josh motioned for Maggie to follow him through the doors. "Thanks, Freddie. We'll be about an hour, if that's okay?"

"Whatever you need, Mr. Allen," he replied. "It's all good."

Josh led Maggie down a hall that opened up into the first-floor atrium. "So, you're kind of famous around here, is that it?" she asked him.

"I'm not famous," Josh replied, as they entered the open-air atrium. "I'm just a means to their end."

Maggie looked up and around. The lights had been turned on half-power, but still lit up the facility, creating a sense of wonder. A dinosaur rose high above them from the left corner of the atrium, while a replica of the *Apollo* moon lander was suspended in mid-air on the right. There were self-service kiosks, the admission lines, posters that advertised the latest exhibits, and the Center's *Explorastore*—housing t-shirts, models, puzzles, and more.

"Kind of like an amusement park," Josh said, realizing how right she had been.

Josh watched Maggie, her face lit up by the red and white buttons housed in *Endeavor's* fully operational cockpit control matrix. She sat up tall in one of two control seats, wide-eyed as she ran her fingers across the levers, the buttons, and the graphically enhanced monitors.

"This is amazing," she gushed. "And this is the exact one that—?"

"It flew twenty-five missions, many of which were focused on the construction and outfitting of the International Space Station."

"This was in outer space. And the astronauts sat here," she marveled. She crooked her head to look out of the windshield, the side windows, then behind to look at the instrument clusters around them like a little kid experiencing something for the first time. There was wonder in her eyes, Josh could see it. "God, what an amazing experience to get to go up there. Or to be involved in any way."

"In any way," Josh echoed, his thoughts going back to the JPL NASA debacle. "That was something I always dreamed about doing," he continued, a bit melancholy. "But at least I get to work here, right? It's not a direct connection, but it's close. I mean, the general public isn't allowed to come up here. It's off-limits to anyone who isn't a purple shirt."

Maggie turned. "So, we've finally uncovered the one perk that comes with your regulation uniform."

Josh shook his head, ignoring the barb. Maggie turned the sarcasm knob down to five, turning to him seriously: "So, what? You wanted to be an astronaut?"

"I majored in Math and Engineering at UCLA," he said. "Ever since I was a little kid, I hoped that I'd get a chance to work at NASA or an organization like it. But I guess it just wasn't in the cards."

"Well, did you try?" she asked.

He looked at her. "It just wasn't meant to be."

She looked back up at the buttons and levers. "Am I allowed to—?" Josh nodded, sending her off on a button-pressing tirade of epic proportions.

Josh stared out the window, waxing poetic. He always got that way when he was sitting in such a historic spot. The details alone got him going. "May seventh, Nineteen Ninety-Two. *Endeavor*'s maiden voyage. Commander Daniel Brandenstein was sitting right here. Kevin Chilton, the pilot, right where you are. I can't even imagine the excitement, the tension, the wonder that the crew felt as they lifted off that night from Kennedy Space Center. The blue of the night sky pulling back like a blanket, revealing the sparkling upper atmosphere … the stars coming into view … the sun, the moon."

Maggie looked out the window as he spoke, almost able to visualize it. They looked up in unison, taking it all in. For a moment, it felt like it was just the two of them, out in space, feeling the vast power of the universe.

"Amazing," she marveled. "It must have been beautiful."

Josh nodded, taking her in. "It was … and you are," he said, immediately slapping himself in the subconscious. Those weren't the kind of words that came out of his mouth. Those were the kind of words that a suave, slick shithead might say to get a girl in bed. But that was far from his intention. He wanted to say it because that's what he felt in the moment. In the split second after he did, he hoped she wouldn't read into it the wrong way.

Josh and Maggie were underwater. But they weren't getting wet.

Curved glass panels surrounded them, framing a dreamily lit path under the water, and separating them from the kelp forest and its hundreds of species in the Center's most well-known exhibit. They leaned against one side of the curved glass walls, watching as leopard sharks and moray eels swam above and around them, rising and falling with the water's movement and the wavering lights that reflected against the blue of it all.

Josh watched Maggie watching the sea life. He stared at her for as long as he could without her noticing, then looked away as she turned to look past him in the other direction.

"Do you dance?" she asked, out of the blue. "Like if we were to go somewhere and there was dancing, would you wig out and make up an excuse to *not* dance?"

"I get down. I totally get down."

"That was completely not convincing," she laughed.

"I get down, I do. I'm Mr. Get Down. Gettin' down was like my thing back in the day. There's even periodic gettin' down these days."

Maggie stared at him. "Maybe you should …"

"… stop saying *get down*?" he grinned, embarrassed. She nodded. Vehemently. "Well, it's not like we've got a dance club on the third floor, so we don't have to worry about …"

Maggie turned to Josh, eyebrows raised. "Maybe you don't have one here, but …"

Uh-oh.

Mister Taco was *en fuego.*

The Sunset Boulevard mainstay was popping. Downstairs, hungry patrons powered through a literal ton of tortilla chips, salsa, and gauc, while upstairs they danced to the EDM beats spun by a pair of dueling DJs. In the center, sweating the last five tequila shots out their pores, were Josh and Maggie. From the patterns of sweat on their clothing, they'd been at it for at least thirty minutes.

"You do get down!" Maggie yelled over the pumping beats.

"What'd I tell you!" Josh yelled back, doing some kind of crazy move that swung him behind her, arms moving, then landing back in front of her, face-to-face.

"My bladder is going to explode," she screamed.

"Your *what*?" he screamed back.

"Bathroom?" she screamed, trying a simpler phrase.

"Yes! Bathroom!" he agreed.

The hallway outside the bathrooms was barely lit, the pumping of the upstairs music muted through the ceiling. Josh and Maggie propped themselves up against the wall, opposite the Men's and Women's bathroom doors. On the Men's bathroom door there was a very familiar male frog in a sombrero. On the Women's bathroom door there was a female frog, in a dress, dancing the salsa. Apparently, TLJ Restaurant Designs had grown their business and their wildly popular bathroom door icons significantly over the years.

The two of them leaned against the wall, still out of breath, heads barely touching. Maggie pulled out her cell phone, grabbing Josh and positioning the two of them with their backs to the bathroom doors. "Look sober," she said as she held up the camera and took a blurry, almost unrecognizable selfie. Then she fell back against the wall, propping herself back up.

"I've seen these frogs before," Josh said, running his hand across the male frog's sombrero.

"You're drunk," she said, approaching the female one.

"I am," he grinned, "but I'm serious."

"Well, clearly there's some sad little company out there churning out 'Mimbo Frog' and 'Promiscuous Frog' bathroom door signs for every Mexican restaurant that exists."

"Rockadile's," Josh remembered. "I've seen these little guys in Mexico."

"Rockadile's?" Maggie repeated, remembering. "Did you go there for spring break?"

"April, my junior year at UCLA," he said.

"April, my freshman year at BU," she said back.

The two of them looked at each other, eyes squinted, logic centers blurred. Subconsciously, maybe there was a cloudy memory deep down in each of them like a foggy dream barely discernable in the morning light. But at the moment, it was too far down to grasp. It was also interrupted by both bathroom doors opening at the same time. They awkwardly stepped back, giving passage to those exiting, then shared one last look before disappearing into their respective bathrooms.

Josh and Maggie were going at it.

The front door to his townhouse was still open, keys, wallet, and purse littered on the floor past the Nutid and on the way to the leather Friheten, where they had collapsed, lips locked. His hands cradled her face, fingers stretching up past the base of her neck and through her hair. She leaned in, arms resting on his knees. Her breathing was labored and short, excited but afraid of going too far, too fast. She didn't love feeling so exposed emotionally, a thought that would pop into her head between the physicality of it all. Finally, as her logic centers took control, she pulled back, holding her finger up to pause the moment and take the extra breath she needed. She was still feeling the effects of the alcohol, and so was he.

"I'm no Promiscuous Frog," she said.

"And I'm no … you know," Josh replied, not wanting to say it.

She turned, taking the colorful Funkön from behind her back and cradling it in her lap. Josh took her cues, shifting his position and scooting back to give her some room. She looked around his place, taking it all in. There was a turntable, a modest stack of records, a *Jurassic Park* movie poster, and a bookshelf packed with math and science books, models of dinosaurs, and a Lego model of the *Apollo* spacecraft. Behind the Friheten, sitting on a narrow table, were pictures of him and his parents, a shot of him with Damon and Cody, and an ornate picture frame still rocking the stock photo that came with it. Maggie picked it up, holding the ornate frame out to Josh, eyes questioning.

"That's the Lewis family," he said. Whether he'd come up with their pertinent details on a previous occasion was anyone's guess, but he was fully committing now. "That's Dustin, who works in insurance, his wife Kathy who runs a small letterpress business out of their guest house, and their two kids, Tucker and Skye. They're in Virginia, but that picture was taken in Wilmington, North Carolina. I never quite figured out why they went to Wilmington, but who am I to question their vacation choices."

"Very specific details you've got there," she replied, fascinated.

Josh took it out of her hands, putting it back on the table behind them.

"I don't remember who gave it to me," he said, admitting. "But I loved the frame. Just never had a picture worthy of putting inside it. So, until then, the Lewis family reigns supreme."

There was a long beat. A moment of reflection. Maggie looked up. "I wanted to be a photographer," she said, pushing herself against the arm of the couch, legs crossed, distancing physically as she revealed her emotional core. "I still do."

"So, what's stopping you?"

"Until this week, my boss at the paper. But then he fired our in-house photographer, so I forced him to give me a shot. So, I'm, um, doing that." She seemed unsure.

"That's great! So, you're on your way."

"If he thinks I'm good. But what if I'm not? What if I only think I'm good?" Truth be told, that had always been Maggie's concurrent strength and weakness. Thinking she was good at everything, then worrying that any success was a fluke.

"Someone once said believing in yourself is half the battle."

"What's the other half?"

"Unfortunately, being good," he smiled. "What kind of equipment are you rocking?"

Maggie's face dropped slightly. "I used to have this vintage Nikon SP my father gave me, but someone stole it out from under me during my move here. I was devastated. He would have been, but I never told him." Josh listened, focused. "I have a perfectly fine SLR though. It'll be good. *I'll* be good."

"You will," he nodded. There was something about him saying it that made Maggie believe it. At least for a split second.

"How can you even say that," she said, curiously, "when you hardly even know me?"

Josh paused. "It's weird, but I feel like I'm way past *hardly.*"

"Yeah, huh?" she said, feeling the same.

They both sat quietly. A car sped by with screaming teenagers echoing through the night. Maggie turned back toward Josh. "So, tonight was OK," she said, starting to smile. "If push came to shove, I'd probably give it a seven and a half out of ten."

"Let's go with seven," he joked.

"And I'd really like to stay, but ..."

Josh raised his hands, giving her space. "You can crash here without any baggage. I promise to stay on my side of the bed if you promise to stay on yours. Cool?"

"Cool," she agreed, floored at how easy it had been. Usually, the debate raged on for a significant amount of time, with some men believing that each new hour provided them a new window of opportunity to try again. But not Josh.

Nice, she thought.

Twelve

THE SKY WAS BLUE. And the sun was yellow. *Again.*

Josh lay next to Maggie in his King Slattum, still half-asleep, still wearing their clothes from the night before, peeking out from beneath his oversized Hönsbär. He watched her with fascination as she squinted at the view outside his window, trying to make sense of what she was seeing. She sat up, pushing one of Josh's Jordröks aside in a particularly *jordrökian* way and widening her eyes.

"Is that an IKEA out there?" she asked, crushing Josh's hopes and dreams for a morning debate about illusions, puzzles, and the like.

"Biggest one in the country," he said, dejected. "Sometimes from where I'm sleeping, it looks like the sun and the sky. Like one of those artistic illusions where what you see with your eyes isn't actually what one perceives it to be."

"Kind of like the Penrose stairs?" Maggie asked.

Josh had no words. Lyft would have to live to see another day.

Maggie was famished.

Josh watched her as she mowed her way through the marinated salmon plate, took a bite of her shrimp sandwich, and rotated her attention toward the gorgeous Swedish apple cake that was supposed to be saved for last. She cut a small bite, putting it in her mouth. Her eyes went wide as the "delicately caramelized cinnamon swirl mixed perfectly with the tart, soft apple slices" and she milked the taste for all it was worth. All the while, Josh nibbled at his marinated salmon wrap, while weekend warriors lugged yellow bags with household knickknacks and oversized furniture boxes down the escalator and out the front doors.

Yes, this was the IKEA restaurant, and Maggie had never experienced anything like it.

"I've been reviewing spots for years," she said, excitedly shoveling food into her mouth. "And I have to be honest, this is one of the best. Who would have known?"

"Not me," Josh replied, trying his meal once more to see if he was missing something.

Brian read through the pages, toothpick protruding from his teeth, with a steaming burrito the size of an adult man's arm by his side. Sitting opposite him, periodically shifting her position to avoid the burrito scent wafting in her direction, was Maggie, waiting intently, hoping for a celebration-worthy thumbs-up.

"This is a joke, right?" he asked, throwing the pages across the desk as he took an inhuman bite of his lunch.

"A joke?" Maggie asked.

"This is a review of the café inside IKEA," he said.

"It's a real restaurant," she defended. "They've also got a bistro. Where you can take time out for a *fika*."

"Oh, right," Brian shot back, picking up the pages and tossing each one until he got to the passage he was looking for. "'It's not just a coffee break,'" he read. "'It's a moment to slow down and appreciate the good things in life. Like I did.'" He rolled his eyes, leaning in. "When you said you were going to do both jobs, I didn't quite imagine it would look this half-assed."

"I'm filing it," she said, standing up. "Go eat there. You'll see. It's no joke."

"Where are you going now?" Brian said, standing up after her.

"To do my other job," she said. "The one you'll be paying me for, before too long."

Zack Tolman was smelling grapefruits.

The star of *Sky Spy 3: Free Falling* didn't used to care about grapefruits, or any fruit for that matter. At first, he just cared about smoking pot. Then, he graduated to ecstasy, cocaine, and eventually meth. Before long, the people who cared about him, including his model-actress girlfriend Jasmine Avoneda, who had *Sky Spy 2: Ascendancy* on her very short list of credits, stopped caring altogether. Had it not been for his longtime manager and pitbull Svetlana Rogorov, he would have never got clean, and definitely wouldn't have snagged $5 million for the oft-desired final chapter to the worldwide *Sky Spy* phenomenon.

"I eat nothing but grapefruits from the minute I get up until six-thirty in the evening," he bragged to Maggie, who was checking her light meter and taking test shots on her camera of the craft service table. Which, incidentally, also included pineapples, avocados, apples, and a small tray of cashews.

"What do you do after six-thirty?" Maggie asked, still focused on checking the light in the corner of the lush hotel room.

"Cashews," he said, matter-of-fact, pointing to the aforementioned dish.

"Bet you don't know, out of twenty-nine major stunts in the new film, how many Zack did himself?" Darren posed to Maggie. "*All twenty-nine,*" he answered, without giving her a chance. "Next to Cruise, Zack is the only actor in good enough shape, and with enough faith in his own physicality, to do so."

"I just want the audience to get their money's worth," he said, regurgitating a line that had most likely come from one of twenty-nine major media training sessions, one of which had been attended by his stunt double on a day Zack was busy freefalling out of a plane.

"Ready when you are," Maggie chimed in, slinging her SLR

around her shoulder and adjusting a shade on the left side of the leather chair where Zack would be posing. Zack nodded, following Darren to the space in question, and sitting down. A make-up artist approached, getting rid of some of his facial sheen, and providing powder where it was needed.

Maggie kneeled down, aligning Zack in her crosshairs, preparing to go. Darren leaned down next to her, questioning. "You've got to make him look good."

First of all, Zack was a living Ken doll with stubble. Barring taking a photo of him from the other side of a bed sheet that was partially covering the lens of the camera, he was going to look good. The lighting was set. His face wasn't shiny. The wardrobe was hip. Maggie glared up at Darren to give her space as she snapped away, getting him from all angles. Calling out directions to him, controlling the moment, she was getting every shot she wanted. *I'm a photographer*, she thought giddily as she scuttled across the hotel room floor capturing hundreds of shots. *This is real.* She had stuck to her guns and went after what she wanted. It had delivered in spades. She heard Josh's voice in her head, telling her that she could do this. Telling her that she'd be all good. She'd never had a guy's voice in her head, except for her father's.

Something clearly had changed.

Fred and Eva Gardener *and* Harold and Allie Harrison had requested the presence of over two hundred and fifty people at the wedding of their children, Damon and Lisa. The date had been rescheduled twice, moved venues three times, and eventually landed on a weekend that was now rapidly approaching in two weeks. And much like Damon and Lisa's parents had made a request of the guests, so too had the guests made a simple request of the soon-to-be newlyweds. Namely, that they needed to register for more shit. And stat. Because all that was left on Neiman's was a twenty-four-karat gold taco rack, and the only thing available from Macy's was a set of stainless-steel spatulas. They were guilty of being the worst kind of under-scanners, providing short registry lists with big-ticket items, and now they were going to have to pay the price with another endless afternoon scanning more items at the local Crate and Barrel.

Damon and Josh followed close behind Lisa, a perky, lululemon-wearing, self-anointed "dietetic coach" who had grown her regular client list into the hundreds in just the first year after graduating with her dietetic degree from ASU. She loved puppies, vilified sucralose, and wished that the five percent of incoming queries through her website would stop asking about L. Ron Hubbard and his groundbreaking book *Dianetics*, or learn how to spell it correctly when they typed it into the Google search box.

Damon watched Lisa swing the scanning gun up from her side, logging the code for a strange red ceramic item he was unfamiliar with. He squinted, leaning in to get a better look. "The Le Creuset Cerise Butter Keeper?" he questioned, completely out of his element, and bastardizing its culturally complicated name.

"It's a butter crock, darling," said Lisa, already onto the Decker Galvanized Tray. "Everybody needs a butter crock."

"'Everybody needs a butter crock,'" he repeated into the ether. "What the hell is a butter crock?" Damon asked Josh, picking up what looked like a barbershop's ceramic shaving cream dish.

"You got me," Josh said. "I don't live in this world. I'm just visiting."

"For now," Damon warned him, pointing.

"It keeps butter from spoiling, dummies," Lisa joked, trying to scan Damon's head then crotch with the potentially brain-scrambling, impotence-causing laser beam. He guarded his eyes and loins at the same time, almost knocking over a pyramid of metal cheese graters. "You scramble my DNA or microwave my sperm and it's not just me who's going to be sorry," he joked.

Lisa walked off. Damon watched her go. "Hasn't anyone ever heard of a refrigerator? Those keep butter from spoiling, too." Josh shrugged, as Damon continued to watch Lisa go on a scanning spree across the store. His faux-annoyance gave way to pure delight as he and Josh found a kitchen table on display nearby and sat down like two friends about to dig into a meal. Damon breathed in, letting out an extra-long sigh.

"You're sure, right?" Josh said, gauging his mental state.

Damon got it together, nodding with confidence. "Two weeks to go, my friend, and I'm feeling right as rain. I've crunched the numbers, looked at it every which way but Sunday, and it all comes out in the black." He reached over to Josh, giving his shoulder a squeeze. "She was the one when I first met her, she was the one a year in, and she'll be the one in two weeks when I make her Mrs. Lisa Gardener. She's the one for life. My soulmate. Like I toldja. Like I toldja that night."

And he had. One year ago, to the day.

How it happened had been random and unexpected. After Syracuse, Damon had landed in New Jersey with a math degree and the goal of being an actuary. "Actually an actuary?" Josh had ribbed him, over the phone from California, after hearing the news that he'd be applying to the Trenton-based, well-known actuary hub Investment Partners. Damon had always been cut out for the actuarial sciences. He was always evaluating risk at every turn, providing the odds of potential disaster to Josh and Cody whether it related to asking out a girl, stealing candy from the drug store, or pedaling a bicycle with two other people piled on top over a manmade ramp, traversing a treacherous ravine.

"There's a ninety-five percent chance that one of us is going to break a limb, which will result in a hospital bill that could range between five hundred and two thousand dollars," Damon had said, sitting on the handlebars of Josh's bicycle, looking back at Cody on Josh's shoulders. And one of them *did* … and it cost fifteen hundred bucks.

Working at Investment Partners had allowed Damon to work on both the life and non-life categories, giving him a diverse and lucrative career that put him in the position of evaluating all sorts of scenarios off the "risk menu," as Damon called it. And he was always willing to ensure that those unfamiliar with the gig, or unaware of the profession, were brought into the fold as soon as possible into every new conversation. "I primarily deal with mortality risk, morbidity risk, and investment risk," he once told a pair of women at a local bar, alongside Josh, during the Thanksgiving holiday right after he'd landed the job. "So, that's like life insurance, annuities, pensions, short- and long-term disability insurance, health insurance, health savings accounts, and long-term care insurance," he continued, unaware of the women's complete disinterest, but fully aware of Josh's glee in hearing the speech for the thirtieth time in three weeks. "Also, social insurance programs, politics, budget constraints, changing demographics, medical technology, inflation, and cost of living considerations," he continued.

"We're going to the bathroom," one of the two women interrupted him, never to return.

Years later, he would be a shining example of the rigor and obsessive-compulsiveness that pervaded all great actuaries, landing a spot on a speaking panel at the Western United States Actuarial Conference, just minutes away from Josh's pad. Damon would find himself, one year ago to the day, en route to Josh's couch, by way of the Burbank Airport, unaware that the most significant portion of his trip would have nothing to do with actuarial science whatsoever, but rather meeting and wooing the woman of his dreams. He would bump into her in line at the local Starbucks, where they would find themselves angling for the last of the blueberry scones after Lisa's own roommate, Sasha Kahane, had done her part to devour anything in the cupboard that resembled a breakfast treat.

"You knew after the first date, huh?" Josh asked, trying to remember.

"I knew after the first minute."

"Not possible. Maybe you think you knew that early, but in reality, it had to have been days or weeks later. Months."

Damon shook his head, pulled out his phone, and opened his Notes application. He scrolled down until he'd reached a note from a year ago, titled "Lisa." He slid the phone over to Josh: *Five minutes in. She's totally the one.* Josh eyed it, sliding it back to Damon.

"Possible," Damon confirmed.

Lisa returned, holding up what appeared to be two identical carving knives. "Which one?" she posed, asking Damon. He looked at both. Seriously, there was no difference. "That one," he pointed, clearly the one Lisa had preferred. She smiled, then disappeared back into the sea of scan.

"So?" Damon prompted, raising his eyebrows.

"What?"

"How was last night? Your date with auto body invoice girl. What's her name?"

"Maggie," Josh nodded. "It was good."

"Just *good*?"

"I mean, it was great. She's cool."

Damon looked down his nose at him, skeptical.

"It was a first date. Everyone's on their best behavior during a first date. You don't really get an honest sense of someone on one of those. For all I know she's an undercover Russian spy."

Damon rolled his eyes. "You've spent your entire life waiting for the other shoe to drop. When are you going to stop doing that?"

"When the other shoe stops dropping," Josh said. "You can't come out of a great first date and have unrealistic expectations about where it's going to go."

"But you can hope."

"I hoped before and it didn't pan out. Now I just live and take things as they come."

"Well, I'd like to see you living a little bit more, bud," Damon said, grabbing his shoulder. "When are you seeing her again?"

"Thursday," Maggie said to Robyn, looking through the viewfinder of her camera, and taking pictures of myriad scarves featured in Malibu's own Baylor & Company. "I'm taking him to *Up All Knight*. My friend Cameron is a producer on the show."

"That sounds like it must have gone well. Although don't all first dates go well?"

Maggie had a flash of eleven first dates that didn't go well. Including the time Isaac had misplaced his car after an Insane Clown Posse show at the Forum and their wallets were taken by, well, clowns. There had been the time she met a Tinder date whose picture had not prepared her for the fact that he bore a striking resemblance to her own father (ick). And how could she forget the time that guy named Cole took her to a Mexican joint and mansplained how to eat chips and salsa, how to drink a margarita with salt on the rim, and how to pick up a burrito.

"Try for a full chip, without any cracks, then scoop the salsa from the edge of the dish," he proclaimed, proud of his expertise in the area of cornmeal.

"You really wanna get some salt in every sip," he said, taking an awkward gulp to show her.

"Hold the burrito with both hands and take a generous bite from the top," he had mansplained a third time, which Maggie hadn't totally heard, as she was in the midst of imagining a mariachi guitar crashing down on his skull.

"No, not all first dates go well," she replied.

Robyn followed Maggie as she moved out the front door of the store, situated on the outer edge of the Malibu Country Mart, then framed up the outside shot of the establishment and clicked away. "Well, don't forget," Robyn lectured, "two dates over the course of seven days is the max. And never text after eleven at night."

The *rules*. Maggie didn't prescribe to them. "I'm not playing games. I've never played games. But I'm also not going to jump head first into anything. I'm not going to get sucked into some co-dependent relationship. I'm keeping my emotional distance for now."

"So, you haven't given up the ghost?" she smiled, miming a half-vulgar thrusting motion with her lower torso.

"No. I haven't given up the ghost," she replied. "Although I think you're using the term incorrectly."

Robyn ignored her criticism. "But you like him?"

"As much as I can like a guy I only just met for the first time," she said, heading back into the store. Robyn followed her as they took a few bites of a small lunch platter. Maggie snapped a picture of a beautiful melon, cut open with artistic geometric cuts. "I need to have history with a guy before I can fully go there."

Robyn nodded, taking a bite of some fruit. "My mother always says, 'History isn't necessarily what we read in books, it's the knowledge we acquire by investigation.' So, go investigate, Mags, and see if you like what you find."

Thirteen

TREY KNIGHT WAS ENTERTAINING the studio audience, as usual.

Up All Knight, already in its third season, aired nightly, Monday through Friday, at 1:35 a.m. While its format in its early days had stuck to traditional norms, Trey had decided that his third season needed to shake up the late-night landscape in a significant, groundbreaking new way. As such, he made the executive decision to jettison the traditional monologue and musical guests, and replace them with one of Trey's inspired ideas instead. "A roundtable of guests," he'd tell the production designer, using his hands to illustrate what a circular shape looked like in the real world. "And I want the set to rotate like that sick number in *Hamilton* every time a new guest comes out on stage."

Maggie and Josh watched that afternoon from the stage floor, standing to the side of the studio audience, behind the cameras, and most importantly right next to the craft service table. Maggie sipped an exquisitely made espresso while Josh downed the fourth of five *Treyzies*—sausage and cheese melted into a warm sourdough roll named after Trey and his elementary school cafeteria obsession. Trey, meanwhile, faked a slo-mo walk around the edge of the rotating table as his next guest waited for the carousel to stop so she could get on. The crowd was in stitches … after all, this was the upper-crust comedy they'd come for. They watched it all unfold as the already-present guest, skateboarder Danny Utah (no relationship to Johnny), reached out as he passed her by, dragging her along as the hilarity ensued.

Cameron, holding a clipboard and donning an earpiece and microphone, sidled up to the two of them, pointing to the action. "Fucking batshit crazy, right?" She turned to Josh, extending her hand. "You must be Josh. I'm Cam."

He smiled, mouth full. They shook. And Maggie watched it all unfold with an investigative eye.

It was a three-way dinner. And Cameron was talking a mile a minute.

"And so, I reached over, took a fry out of his lunch, and I chewed it right in front of him without skipping a beat. I didn't know what the hell I was doing, or how he'd react, but it clearly did the trick. Five minutes later I call this bitch up and tell her to pack her bags because she's comin' to L.A." Cameron took a swig of her dry martini, turning to Maggie. "You wouldn't be here right now if I didn't snag this gig." Then she turned to Josh. "Neither would you."

Cameron leaned over to the table next to her, populated by a pair of stuffy, overdressed sixty-somethings. "Just putting it out there now," she said, leaning her head back and motioning to Josh and Maggie, "but these two over here, I either get all the credit, or it's all my fault." The sixty-somethings smiled politely. Maggie pulled at her, dragging her back into their conversation.

"Well, had you not snagged that gig, I'd still be in suburban Chicago trying to turn a liberal arts degree into a depressing little fortune," she said, directing the tale toward Josh. "I didn't have a job. I was living with my parents. I couldn't afford an apartment out here even if I sold my blood *and* eggs. But when Fitzy here got hired on the show, she sent for me. I was kind of like her own little Midwestern mail-order bride. Without having to put out, of course."

Cameron reached over and squeezed her ass. "Oh, she put out!"

Maggie jumped, pushing her hand away, as a pile of menus were handed out to the three of them. The golden font on the front read *Chaat*.

Chaat was the hottest new Indian restaurant on Melrose, and unless you knew about it you couldn't even find it. It wasn't listed, there was no address or phone number available to the general public, and if you pulled up in front of it accidentally, it didn't even look like anything was there. Perhaps that was because it had been camouflaged beneath a worn, ratty sign that read *Coin Operated Laundry: Closed for Repairs*. But inside, it was anything but closed. Waitstaff served a packed house, delivering pungent and colorful dishes, including their signature dish, the Indian Coconut Curry with Red Snapper.

A waiter appeared, standing between Maggie and Josh at the edge of the table. "Are we ready to order, Ms. Mills? I must preface any order tonight with the unfortunate fact that we are completely out of our signature dish due to high demand."

Josh rolled his eyes to Cameron, who cupped her hand to whisper, "Cheap date. You'll never have to pay for food ever again," then flashed him two thumbs-up. Maggie picked up the menu, turning to the waiter, as Josh, for the first time, turned to look as well. He almost jumped out of his chair when he saw him. The waiter was tall, about six feet. Black hair. Sporting a goatee and mutton chops. With the dark bushy eyebrows, his silk yellow shirt, and black velvet vest, he was the spitting image of someone Josh had spent a lot of time with during his formative years. He wanted to reach out and touch him to see if he was real. He wanted to pull out a quarter and stuff it in his pocket. He watched him leave the table, entranced.

"*Zoltar*," Josh blurted out.

"Excuse me?" Maggie asked, mistaking Josh's blurt for a sneeze.

"Our waiter? He's Zoltar. From *Big*?" he said. "The genie who grants Tom Hanks his wish to become … big? In the movie *Big*?"

"Huh, never saw it," Cameron said.

"Yeah, me neither," Maggie replied.

Josh's mouth agape, he couldn't even find the words. Despite seeing the movie at least twelve separate times, at twelve separate ages, he had still scooped up the allegorical bread crumbs of each viewing and found they brought joy and insight into the life he was leading. Thanks to the moral of the story, Josh Allen knew that every adult needed the spirit of a kid inside them. Thanks to the burgeoning romance between young Josh Baskin and "true adult" Susan Lawrence, he learned that women wanted to be with men who respected them; who made them laugh. And thanks to the sci-fi magic that transformed young Josh Baskin into his adult counterpart, Josh Allen steered clear of carnivals, circuses, the creepy contortionists of *Cirque du Soleil*, Internet psychics, covens, cults, the Church of Scientology, and as of this very evening, any waiter who closely resembled the individual famously known as *Zoltar*.

"This is an aberration of epic proportions," he said, looking at Maggie. "You have to see it. It's going to change your life. I promise you."

"Sure. OK. I guess."

"No, not *I guess*. You have to see it. *Tonight*."

"Tonight?" Maggie didn't quite get the urgency.

"I've got it on my phone. We can throw it up on the TV at your place."

"Oh, I see how this guy works," Cameron alluded, winking at Josh.

"No. It's not that," he said, defending himself. "*Big* is a cornerstone of cinematic history. It's a perfect film across the board. It has a timeless message and moral. If you've existed on this planet and not experienced the movie, I simply cannot in good conscience allow you to live another minute more."

"Can we at least eat dinner first?" Maggie asked.

Toto's "Africa" was playing loudly.

The Sonata sped down Ventura Boulevard, clocking in at a mind-numbing twenty-three miles per hour, passing a Hyundai Elantra and a Ford EcoSport. Inside the car, Maggie was driving with

Josh in the passenger seat. They sang together, in unison, throwing caution to the wind. Josh fiddled with his shoulder strap, pulling it for a little more room, and accidentally pulled the entire mechanism out of its socket. He covertly laid it down next to him, holding the strap in place against his chest as to not alert Maggie that the car was more of a lemon than she'd even imagined.

They stopped at a red light as the Elantra and EcoSport caught up. Josh raised his eyebrows.

"Ever see any of the *Fast and Furious* movies?" he asked, as the light turned green.

"I saw the fourth one," she said, surprising him, gently inching her foot onto the gas pedal. The other two eco-friendly cars crept ahead of them down the road.

Josh frowned. "That's the only one that sucked," he said.

"Well, who needs that movie when we've got this car," she said, hitting the pedal with all her might and illustrating her point as the car went from zero to twenty-five in a not-too-fast ten seconds flat.

Big was paused on Maggie's flat-screen TV. On it, Josh Baskin stared into the eyes of his thirty-something-year-old girlfriend, who had just come to the realization that Josh was not an adult on the inside, but in fact a twelve-year-old boy.

On the couch, lit up by only the glow of the paused TV screen, the thirty-five-year-old Josh Allen stared into the thirty-three-year-old eyes of Maggie Mills, who lifted her shirt above her head, revealing her still-affixed bra. At the same time, the twelve-year-old kid in Josh's body looked out from his eyes and saw Maggie in all her glory, forgetting all about the first time he'd seen a naked woman. This wasn't a magazine page in a park. This was real. He felt it in the moment, leaning in to kiss her, but then paused as he was hit with an amusing thought.

"Just like in the movie," he grinned.

Maggie looked unsure, not remembering the reference. "Which part?"

"Uh, when his girlfriend comes over to his penthouse apartment? And she takes off her shirt and turns off the lights? And then Josh turns them back on, because he's stoked to be able to see an adult woman in all her glory?"

Maggie stared at Josh. She leaned in to kiss him, but Josh pulled back.

"Do you not remember?"

Maggie let out a sigh, dropping her arms from around Josh's neck. "I don't know. Maybe I don't." She moved back to kiss Josh but he pulled back again.

"We just watched it."

"Ok. So, I wasn't totally paying attention."

Josh was floored. "You weren't totally paying attention? To one of the most lauded cinematic masterpieces on the face of the earth?"

Maggie looked at Josh, his eyes wild like a lunatic. "I was kinda bored. Look, it's nothing personal. I mean, it's a sweet film, but a modern-day classic? A cinematic masterpiece? Now, say that about *How to Lose a Guy in 10 Days*, and we can talk. But *Big*?"

"You were bored?" he said, pushing back from her.

"Is this a *big* deal?" she asked, smirking, trying to lighten things up.

"Now you're making fun of me?" he shot back.

"Maybe we should try and be adult about this? On the inside and the outside," she posed, still smirking.

"You *are* making fun of me."

"Are we really having a fight about a Tom Hanks movie?" Maggie asked. "Because if we are, I'd rather fight about *Turner and Hooch* and its lack of realism when it comes to police dogs and their functions within established law enforcement."

Josh thought for a moment. Was he really going to make a big deal about this? For someone who had said on multiple occasions that you never show your baggage until at least the six-month period, was he really going to cart out the suitcases and dump out everything he had inside? Right here and now on their second date?

"Yes, we are having a fight about a Tom Hanks movie," he said, doubling down. It was a clearly misguided decision.

Maggie grabbed her shirt, putting it back on, concealing the bra that was once a shining symbol of opportunity. She moved to the doorway of her bedroom. "You can stay or you can go. It's up to you," she said, then disappeared.

Josh sat on the couch, in the glow of the paused TV. He looked up at the image: young Josh Baskin staring into the disappointed eyes of his adult girlfriend, trying to make her understand why he had ultimately decided to become a kid again, leaving all they had developed together behind. He was ending a relationship, but for good reason. He needed to grow up before he could ever take a relationship like that one seriously.

Did Josh need to grow up? The parallels were fascinating, and depressing. He had continually exited relationships over the smallest things, from allergies and bad breath to not considering astronauts courageous to considering a penchant for Grape Nuts to be a personality flaw. The side of Tina that kept him on his toes was clearly at it again. Was that what was happening now? Was he going to sacrifice something he felt had real potential just because she couldn't embrace a feature film in the way Josh did? Was he really turning his world up to DEFCON 1 for that? What would Matthew Broderick think?

"Fuck it," he said, getting up from the couch, flipping off the TV and walking into the darkness of Maggie's bedroom.

She hadn't moved. She was still sitting on the edge of the bed. "Did we just have our first fight?" she asked.

"I think so."

"And it was about a movie?"

"Pretty sure it was."

"And we agree that's exponentially stupid?" she said, taking her shirt back off, and standing up opposite Josh.

He also took off his shirt. "Exponentially," he said, believing it about eighty-five percent. But he was trying. He was trying to not wait for the other shoe to drop. His mind listed off an exhaustive list of other movies from his childhood that he wondered if she'd seen. That he wondered if she'd hate. That he wondered if she'd—

Maggie kissed him, pulling him close. Josh forgot what he was thinking about almost immediately. And then the two of them fell onto the bed, getting back to what they had started before the '80s got in their way.

Maggie's eyes shot open. First confused. Then concerned. *Holy shit.*

What had she done?

She was horrified. She adjusted her body in the bed, turning covertly to see where Josh had ended up. He was there, next to her, facing the other direction. Her mind went over the events of the previous night. The TV show, that hip new restaurant, a famous movie, and an argument no two humans should have ever had. The *sex.* And then …

She removed her hands from underneath her pillow, where they'd been firmly planted all night, and moved them under the covers. When they came back up, she smelled them, horrified. "*Fuck,*" she mouthed to herself as she sat up in bed, looking around the room for anything that could help her out of her current conundrum.

Josh sensed she was awake, turning to look. As he was about to say something, Maggie stopped him, arm outstretched. "You stay right there," she ordered. "Don't come near me."

Josh read into it. "Is this about last night?" he asked. "I mean, I thought it was great. That we were great. Are you having second thoughts—?"

Maggie stopped him. It wasn't about *that.*

He pivoted to the movie. "I was being stupid," he said, admitting it finally. "So, you didn't connect with it. That's cool. I can be down with that."

"It's not about either of those things," she said. She shrugged, her mouth wrinkling as she tried to figure out just how to say it. *Just rip off the Band-Aid,* she said to herself. *Don't beat around the bush. Tell the truth. Own up to it.*

"Then what's wrong?" he said, confused.

She waited a moment. There was no way out. "I wet the bed," she said, mortally embarrassed.

Josh pulled back. "You what?"

Maggie threw back the covers like a magician pulling a cloth off a table covered in crystal goblets. A huge wet stain underneath her torso spread down and across the bed, to just about where Josh's left foot was hovering. He pulled his leg back and sat up, startled. "The bathroom's right here," she said, motioning to the open door adjacent to her bed. "Next to us. Had I gone, you would have heard. I didn't want you to, so I …"

"You held it," Josh replied, sliding his feet a little further away. "*Badly*."

"I think I probably dreamed I was going to the bathroom, because my bladder was so full." She hung her head down. This had never happened to her over the age of three. Josh, sensing the embarrassment, quickly got up from the bed. She watched him, unsure. *Is he going to leave? Is this how it all ends?*

But Josh didn't leave. He ripped the comforter off the bed and threw it to the floor. "You got a washing machine around here?"

Maggie's face dispatched her worry, replacing it with wonder. *Who was this guy?*

It was a small room, hidden underneath the parking garage, affixed with two stacked washer/dryers and a table for folding. Josh and Maggie sat on a wooden bench in front of the washer, watching the sheets tumble head over heels.

"No one's ever washed my sheets for me before," she said, leaning up against him.

"No one's ever urinated in bed next to me," he replied.

"What are you doing for dinner tonight?" she asked, introducing the most memorable segue in the history of segues.

"It's Sunday. Which means I have to go to my parents' house for dinner. It's exponentially anticlimactic."

"I like anticlimactic. Want some company?" she offered, feeling especially connected to him now that he was her Savior of the Damp.

"I'm sure that's exactly what you want for your Sunday night," he lamented. "Joining me and my overbearing, dream-killing, self-important mother and my earnest, in-your-face, Cliff Clavin-esque father as we pretend to enjoy being with each other. I wouldn't wish it on my worst enemy."

"Well, now I really want to go," she laughed as the washer buzzed; the cycle was done. Josh got up, removing the wet sheets and placing them into the dryer. "It sounds far more entertaining than anything I could find to binge tonight."

"It'll be your funeral," Josh said, closing the dryer's door. "Are you sure?"

"No, but that's never stopped me before," she said, raising her eyebrows.

Fourteen

CAMERON HELD HER HEART, eyes swollen with emotion, lip quivering.

"That is the most romantic thing I've ever heard," she gushed. She moved to take a sip of her green juice, then had to stop because she was so verklempt. She got up and grabbed more napkins from the Juice Den-branded self-service station, then returned to sit opposite Maggie.

"You would think it's the most romantic thing ever," Maggie countered. Then thought about it. She nodded, smiling mischievously. "I think I do, too."

"Roses, diamonds, flowers, opening doors, beating the shit outta some guy who called you a skank ..." Cameron continued. "Cliché. Tired. The testosterone-fueled actions of a man just trying to get down to your G-string. But cleaning up your soiled bed sheets? *After* you already had sex with him? Now that's a real man. That's the kind of thing a dude does, maybe if you're lucky, after fifty years together."

Maggie nodded, affected. "It's true. You're right."

"This relationship is on the fast track, that's for sure," Cameron said.

"He invited me to have dinner with him and his parents tonight," Maggie grinned.

"The really fast track," Cameron corrected, eyes wide.

"Is that bad?" Maggie wondered. "I mean, I didn't think it was. How could it be? It's just his parents."

"*Just* his parents," Cameron grinned. "Brace yourself, Mags."

"We had a *Big* fight," Josh said to Damon, as the two of them hiked up the Fryman Canyon loop.

"A big fight about what?" Damon asked, stopping to catch his breath.

"No. A fight about the movie *Big*. She'd never seen it. Then once I forced her to watch it, we fought about the fact that she didn't like it."

"Please tell me you didn't call it a cinematic masterpiece?" Damon pleaded.

Josh looked guilty.

"And what happened *after* you read her the cinematic riot act?"

"We had sex."

Damon stopped, floored. "Let me get this straight. You forced an adult female to watch *Big*, criticized her lack of understanding or interest in the film … and then she *slept* with you?"

"That's right."

"Now that's a woman you don't let go of, my friend," Damon said, impressed. "That's the kind of thing a woman does, maybe if you're lucky, after fifty years together."

Josh nodded, affected. "It's true. You're right."

"This relationship is on the fast track, that's for sure," Damon nodded. "Don't let this one go, buddy. I'm serious."

"I won't," Josh nodded, then remembering, "she's coming to dinner with me at Casa de Allen this evening."

Damon spun, stopping him. "Are you sure that's a good idea? Your mom isn't necessarily the most welcoming individual. I mean she is, but it's all an act."

They kept walking, reaching the top of the trail. Before them, they took in the entire San Fernando Valley, stretching out as far as the eye could see. It was a clear, crisp day. Josh took a breath, sucking in the fresh air.

"What's the worst that could happen?" he posed, then reached down to stretch his hammies.

"Don't ever ask the universe that question," Damon said. "It's bound to give you an answer you don't expect."

When Mel opened the door, he was surprised to see Josh standing with an attractive, enthusiastic young woman.

"Good evening, Mr. Allen," Maggie said, hand outstretched. "I'm Maggie. You have a beautiful home."

"Dad," said Josh. "I hope it's okay that I …"

"Brought someone to dinner without asking permission?" Barbara said, popping up behind Mel like she'd been hiding there all along.

"I rarely ever do," Josh said, defensive. "You should be good hosts and welcome her. And besides, it's my house, too."

"Joshua," Barbara said, scolding. "If you ever checked the shared family account online, you would know that I am presenting my final meal tonight for my class. Tonight, I am serving a meal made up of dishes you'd enjoy at Spago in Beverly Hills."

"That's tonight?" Josh realized, concerned.

"That's tonight," Barbara shot back, eyes raised.

"Oh, just come in," Mel said, ushering them inside. As Maggie walked in ahead of Josh, she could see his face and the sudden realization that tonight's meal had more significance than he originally thought. Spago, Maggie mouthed to Josh, confused. What was going on? What exactly was she walking into?

The *pellucidar*, of course.

There was an Autumn Harvest Pumpkin Soup with a Parmesan Crisp sitting in front of Maggie. Next to her napkin there was a note card that listed out the dinner by each course, with a ranking system that required a score from 1 to 10. There was a pen next to it, fashioned in the shape of a spatula, adding an extra bit of flair to the proceedings. Maggie held up the spatula to Josh, who held up his—a pen in the shape of a knife. He mimed taking the knife and stabbing himself in the neck. Maggie motioned to the scoring card and cringed. Josh pointed down to a bowl of steaming orange liquid, widening his eyes as if to say *just try the damn soup.*

"For the appetizer portion of my final gourmet exam," began Barbara, from the head of the table, "you'll find an Autumn Harvest Pumpkin Soup with a Parmesan Crisp. We'll follow that up tonight with a second course consisting of a Ricotta Gnocchi with Parmigiano Reggiano, a main course of Black Bass in a Sauce Americaine, and finish up the evening with a, drum roll please, Triple Chocolate Soufflé."

"All that, huh?" said Maggie, meaning to say that in her head. "I mean, *wow*," she followed up with quickly. It would have been uncomfortable enough without her food-centric background, but having to gauge Josh's mother's cooking on their first meeting? It had the potential for *Armageddon*-like outcomes.

"Do you have somewhere else to be?" Barbara asked, crunchy.

Josh said nothing, crossing the equator of the *pellucidar* and passing by Maggie. She watched him as he approached his mother, motioning for her to follow him into the kitchen. Barbara watched him disappear through the swinging kitchen door. Mel and Maggie watched her until she finally relented, throwing down her napkin and following Josh inside.

"Just because it wasn't your idea to drag some girl in here off the street for yet another attempt at an arranged marriage doesn't mean you can be rude to Maggie," Josh whisper-yelled at Barbara.

"Don't be ridiculous, Josh," she said, insulted. "Aside from India, China, Pakistan, Israel, Afghanistan, Iran, and Iraq, arranged marriages are a thing of the past."

"Japan, too," he corrected.

"Yes, Japan, too. And sometimes Australia. Point is, there are far more unsupportive locations where you could be having dinner this evening. Be glad you're here. With this family. With me."

So much of their relationship played out like an episode of *Jeopardy*. Perhaps the Alex Trebek in her, the need to control every fact that bubbled to the surface in their lives, had become her way of overcompensating for the lack of authority she enjoyed since they'd moved to Los Angeles. Perhaps her rigidity, and the growing moments of miscommunication and misunderstandings, came from Josh's inability to position his thoughts and opinions in the form of a question. The less time he appeared on the "show," like when he had moved out of the house during the college years, the fewer conflicts there had been. But as always, on those special Sunday-night editions of the program, it seemed as if Barbara had saved up all her energy so she could unload on him. Maybe being in control put her at ease; maybe it made her feel calm. Maybe she just missed being a teacher. All Josh knew was when that Audio Daily Double came up on the board, the last thing he wanted to do was play the game. All it did was push him further away from her.

"I like her," he said, trying to change the mood of the room. "I basically just met her, but I *like* her. You'll like her, too, I guarantee it. When was the last time I brought someone to Sunday dinner?"

"February. Three years ago. The news anchor," Barbara remembered.

"Katie. She wasn't a news anchor."

"Well, she clearly had aspirations to be one with all her play-by-play reporting on absolutely everything we did that entire night," Barbara said, moving to the stove where she plated the gnocchi. "I kept wondering when the weather report was going to come out of her mouth."

Josh sighed and grabbed her by the shoulders. "*Please*," he pleaded. "Be nice."

"And I've always wanted to be a photographer," Maggie continued, sharing the story with Mel from across the table, "so, the opportunity to get out there and prove myself and really show them what I've got, well, it feels a bit like I should have that Carly Simon song 'Let the River Run' playing all the time behind me as my soundtrack.

I mean, it's in my head anyway, so what the hell."

"*Working Girl*, underrated film," Josh volunteered, walking into the room with Barbara on his heels, carrying in the plates of gnocchi. "Harrison Ford."

"Ooh, I like that Harrison Ford," Barbara gushed. "And now he's finally my age," she said, like he wasn't all those years ago.

"And she's an editor, too," Mel spoke up, proudly, like Maggie was his own kid. "We've got an executive in publishing in the *pellicular!*" The two of them had taken the absence of Josh and Barbara as an opportunity to get to know each other, despite Mel asking most of the questions, focusing on her job, her family, and even a few of her proudest moments, including the time she'd been honored by her local Lion's Club for giving back to the community.

"Really, for what section?" Barbara asked as Josh moved around the table and sat back down.

"Nothing in particular," she said, not wanting to throw the figurative food in Barbara's face. It was simpler to leave that small yet significant detail on the back burner for now. Especially since the gnocchi was now in front of her, she had speared a single one for tasting, and it was moving its way up to her cautious, open mouth.

Josh watched her. Mel watched her. Barbara watched her.

Josh was brushing his teeth. Maggie had re-rolled the toilet paper and was now crafting a swan out of what was left. He washed his hands, refolding the hand towel and checking the medicine cabinet to see what prescription drugs his family was on. *Ergo*, they weren't doing anything that two newly dating people with an undeniable physical attraction for each other should be doing in a bathroom this small. But there were clearly larger topics for discussion at hand.

"I can't lie," she said, gingerly placing the toilet paper swan on top of some folded hand towels.

"You have to lie," Josh replied. "It's her final exam."

"Yeah, and why are we grading her? Where's Wolfgang Puck? This is supposed to be his school."

"It's a study-at-home thing."

"And is Wolfgang Puck the *dean* of this school?"

"I don't think so."

"Has she ever seen Wolfgang Puck throughout this entire thing?"

"On a video, I think. Maybe in the brochure."

"Total scam," announced Maggie.

"Well, it's a scam she cares deeply about. It's all she has right now. You have to lie."

"The reason I have the job I have today is because I am totally and completely transparent. In work, in life, in love, in *everything*. The minute I start going against those key tenets, well, who knows what'll happen. I don't want to find out. Do you?"

"You invited yourself tonight. If you hadn't, we wouldn't be in this situation."

She looked at him, seconds away from slapping him upside the face. He noticed. "Can't you give her constructive criticism? And try to be nice about it?"

She thought about it. "I can try, I guess," she said.

"Do or do not," Josh said in a horrible Yoda voice. "There is no try."

Maggie stared at him. *Unamused.*

Maggie had barely taken a bite from each course, but had strategically moved the food around the plate to create the illusion of actively consuming it. While the soup had been taken back into the kitchen, a half-eaten plate of gnocchi, a burned serving of black bass, and a completely deflated chocolate soufflé sat in front of her. She held up her voting card close to her face, the pen perched in her right hand. Barbara watched her intently, as Josh and Mel did their best to finish their own scoring. Mel was first to throw his into the center, which Barbara collected quickly. Then came Josh. Maggie's tongue hung out of her mouth as she put the finishing touches on her ballot.

"Here you go," Maggie cringed, sliding it face down across the table to Barbara. Josh and Maggie watched her like it was a game of Three-Card Monty, sliding Maggie's card into third position behind Mel's and Josh's.

Barbara took her fork, banging it against her wine glass, getting everyone's attention. "Thank you, everybody, for taking the time tonight to grade this wonderful *Spagonian* meal. I'll go ahead and share with you how the scoring netted out." Barbara looked to Mel's card first. "Mel gave the appetizer a nine, *thank you*, the second course an eight point five, *thank you* again. And finished up with two nine point fives for the main course and dessert! That's a …" she put down the card, scratching out the numbers. "Thirty-six point five out of a total forty! Thank you, Mel."

Mel nodded, smiled guiltily to Maggie. He'd seen the soup dribble slowly out of her mouth. But he wasn't an idiot. He shared a bed with Barbara, after all. Sometimes you fought the battles that mattered, and other times you pretended the gnocchi was an eight point five.

Barbara picked up Josh's card, calling out the scores. "We've got a nine for the soup, *thank you*, a ten for the second, main *and* dessert courses!" She was clearly excited. "That's a record-breaking thirty-nine points," she beamed. "Thank you, Joshy."

"Sure, Ma," he said, feeling guilty as he shared a look with Maggie. She gave Josh the stink eye but he couldn't hold the gaze. Instead, he, Mel, and Maggie turned to look at Barbara as she put down Josh's card and picked up the third and final card: Maggie's.

Barbara looked at the card and wrinkled her nose, then cocked her head like she was having trouble understanding. She looked up at Maggie, then an accusatory look at Josh, then back down at the card. She looked up to the ceiling, like she was tallying the numbers, then quietly placed the card face down on the table. Maggie looked everywhere but Barbara's eyes, anticipating what was coming.

"*Eight points,*" Barbara said, disgusted.

"For which?" Mel asked.

"For everything," she spat back.

Maggie straightened herself up, turning to Barbara. "Now, if you'll just give me a second to explain."

"Okay," Barbara said, hurt. "Explain."

Maggie looked to her. Then to Josh. She couldn't feel bad.

That wasn't her. She couldn't walk into this house and pretend to be someone she wasn't. She had to stand strong. Be true to herself. Marshal her strength like Melanie Griffith. The damn Carly Simon song was playing in her head again. And it helped. Her, at least.

"Look, it doesn't bring me any joy to tell you this, but I do think you want real feedback here, not just high scores for the sake of high scores ..." Maggie began.

"The higher the score, the more chances I have at winning the *Sur la Table* sweepstakes," Barbara said, countering her.

Maggie let out a sigh. She had to rip off the Band-Aid once and for all. "Your cooking needs some work," she said, cringing slightly. "Actually, *a lot* of work."

There was a long pause. Silence all around. Maggie looked to Josh, who looked to Barbara, who looked to Mel, who looked to Maggie, who looked at the floor. Everyone was waiting to hear how Barbara would weather the storm. In the end, to no one's surprise, she weathered it *badly*.

"Get out of my house," Barbara said, standing up. "How dare you."

Maggie got up. "You gave me a ballot. To score the meal! I have a legal responsibility to my fellow colleagues and to the industry at large to be completely honest about any and all cuisine that I'm served."

"Which colleagues?" Barbara asked, confused. "*What* industry?"

"I'm a food critic," she said, proudly. "It's what I *do*."

Barbara's eyes went wide. If you looked deep enough you could see the equivalent of the Big Bang explode outwards from her pupils, then cause her entire face to turn beet red. "You brought a food critic into our house? Under my roof?" Barbara spat at Josh. "A *food* critic? You can get out of my house, now."

Josh looked at Barbara, his face growing red. He'd never stood up to her, never felt the passion or reason to do so. But in this moment, something had changed. Had it been Maggie's blatant inability to show fear or shrink back in the face of his mother's wrath?

Had he started to connect with Maggie in such a way that it finally mattered how his mother talked to one of his guests? Had the heartburn, caused by the Autumn Harvest Pumpkin Soup, given him a fire in his belly that he just couldn't contain?

"You cannot talk to her or me that way," he yelled, raising his voice. "If you don't like the way people play your little games, then we won't play them ever again." He took a breath. Mel's eyes were wide, watching it all unfold. "You've spent a lifetime telling everyone else what was wrong with their decisions … with their hopes and dreams. Well, tonight can serve as a reminder of how it feels when someone shits all over those dreams and makes you question exactly the thing *you're* passionate about."

Josh turned to Maggie, grabbing her hand, and pulled her out the door.

Fifteen

MAGGIE WAS DOUBLE-FISTING TACOS.

Both were ingested quickly and without pause, setting off an internal debate in Josh's head about whether any of the previous girls he had dated had ever ingested Mexican food at such a land speed record. Or had gripped the adjacent bottle of water with such force that almost a quarter of the bottle found its way down her throat in no time. Had she even stopped to take a breath throughout the entire endeavor? *I don't think she did*, thought Josh, thinking a backup career in competitive eating might actually be worth exploring. No, Maggie had walked up to the window, guns blazing, stomach growling, determined and focused to experience her first *real* meal of the night in her own time and on her own terms.

Maggie looked up to Josh, clearly aware of his unwavering gaze. "Can't a girl get her taco on without you looking at her like she's defective?" She swallowed the rest of the food, as the employees inside the taco shack behind them began closing up for the night. Josh raised his hands up like he was calling truce. "NFM is in the house," she said. "I'm sorry."

"NFM?" Josh questioned.

"*No food monster*," she replied. "I can thank my dad for that one.

When I was a kid, whenever I was hungry, whenever dinner was a few minutes late, it affected my mood. *No food monster.*" She polished off the last bite of her tacos, washing them down with more water, then sat back as she wiped her mouth. "You ever light it up like that with your mother before?"

Josh thought about it. "No. Not like that."

"So, what was different about tonight?"

"When a parent treats you a certain way over the years," he began, working it out in his head, "it kind of becomes the norm, you know? It's just your *parents.* That's who they are. That's how the family works. I realized tonight, in that moment when she was yelling at you to leave the house, that I've been apologizing my whole life for what has *never* been normal. I've been giving her an out, just because she was my mother. But blood relatives shouldn't get a pass just because they share the same DNA. If they're being assholes, they should be called out as assholes." Josh took a sip of his water. "My mother was being an asshole. To you."

"Her cooking also sucked," Maggie tested, cautiously. Josh looked up. "That's where you laugh, I realize it's okay to laugh because you know I'm kidding, then I join in on the laughing *with* you," she said.

Josh laughed. And Maggie joined in.

"Just be glad you didn't meet me during her marzipan phase," Josh warned, recalling how the obsession had become so all-encompassing that he and his father had denoted the months prior to Barbara's almond-paste obsession as "B.M." (before marzipan). Unfortunately, all their clever attempts to speak in judgmental code while around her often made things worse.

"I think about B.M. a lot these days and how hard it is for me," Mel had said one morning at the breakfast table to high-school-aged Josh, lamenting about Barbara's unstoppable desire to create sixteen unique marzipan statues of Mel in all sorts of athletic poses he could never recreate in real life. Barbara, it seemed, had overheard and misconstrued the conversation like a perfectly crafted episode of *Three's Company*; at least that was the only explanation for the prune-centric meals that curiously found their way into heavy rotation in the family's meal plan.

For Josh it was just one of her many obsessions. "I think that was before her calligraphy and taxidermy phases, but after her fidget spinner phase."

"Doesn't sound any worse than my mother's obsession with scrapbooking," Maggie added. "Every minute of my life is represented somewhere, on a page, with cute shadowboxed letters, colorful patterned backgrounds, and an inspirational quote about either God, family, love, or courage. Every time she visits, she drops another *War & Peace*-sized book on me."

"Do you get along with your parents?" Josh asked.

"I did. I *do*," she thought out loud. "I'm closest with my father. He gets me. He always has. And I've got mad respect for the man. He was always there for me, always had the best advice, always was looking out for me. He's the only man in my life who I've felt that way about. His word is solid, and his words are truth."

"Tough shoes," Josh said. "Maybe someday I'll get a chance to meet him."

At the age of twenty-four, high-on-life Spencer McCurdy led a group of college-aged students in through the double doors of the California Science Center.

They wore pre-printed guest passes that had been provided to them by the internship office at Pasadena's JPL NASA, and the laminated name tag "Mr. McCurdy" wore plainly designated him as an "Associate Engineering Technician" for JPL's Office of Planetary Sciences. He pointed to the *Apollo* model hanging from the ceiling as a few green-shirts approached him, clearly remembering him from his own Science Center internship days.

"It's been an amazing experience," he told the green-shirts, looking happy and enthusiastic and fulfilled and accomplished and living his best life and reaching for the stars and achieving his dreams and about a hundred other inspirational categorizations that Josh, watching him from afar, imagined he had used in conversations, at high school reunions, and in flowery fonts set upon colorful backgrounds on his Instagram page (@McCosmonaut).

Spencer corralled the group, moving them through the center of the first-floor lobby, heading toward Josh as he stood by the Help Desk.

Josh remembered that summer morning in 2016 when he had been guilted into giving Spencer a ride to the Center, and spent the latter portion of the ride hearing him passionately speak about how he had, at the age of five, planned out his entire life.

"When I was just five years old, I had planned out my entire life," he said, just like that.

He had explained to Josh how all his adolescent experiences, including the almost blind support of his parents, was directly responsible for his snagging the internship at the Center, and how everything he had yet to do would place him in the formidable position to secure a position at JPL NASA. Josh remembered wishing he could unlock the door to the car as he sped around a particularly dangerous curve, cradling the edge of a steep, water-filled ravine, and push Spencer out. Had he done so, perhaps the moment that was about to occur would have never occurred at all.

"Mr. Allen?" Spencer said, stopping as he recognized him.

Mister? How dare he call me Mister, Josh thought, faking a smile as he turned toward Spencer and his group of lemmings. "Wow. Hi, Spencer," Josh faked his surprise, eyeing Spencer's JPL NASA name tag, replete with the cool NASA logo.

Spencer turned to the group of interns. "Everyone? This is Mr. Allen."

Gah, Mister. Please stop calling me that.

"He was in charge of planning the exhibits here at the Center when I was an intern a long time ago." The interns nodded, mildly impressed. "And can you tell them what you're doing now?" he posed.

Josh thought about the question and the complications the question presented. It was both a simple question and an extremely complicated one. "Well, I'm planning the exhibits," he said, anticlimactically.

Oof.

"So, *still,*" Spencer said, unbelieving, since in his world, if you were *still* doing anything you had done before, you weren't evolving at all. The interns nodded, a little less impressed. "Like, exactly the same day to day?" he confirmed, not helping the already tense situation in Josh's head.

Josh smiled, ignoring the follow-up. "And I see you're at JPL?" Josh asked, already knowing the answer.

Spencer held out his nametag. Even the lamination looked better than the lamination of Josh's name tag. The edges were rounded, while Josh's were square and frayed. The picture of Spencer looked like a professional had taken it, while Josh's picture looked like it had been taken by a three-year-old who had taken his uncle's cell phone, drooled on the screen, then accidentally snapped a partially askew picture. And there was the NASA logo. The damn NASA logo. It was screaming at Josh. Poking at him. Getting under his skin. How could he compete with the NASA logo?

How had Spencer done it when Josh had failed?

"Yes, I'm at NASA," Spencer replied, driving a dagger right through Josh's left ventricle.

Maggie entered her apartment, hands full with her morning coffee, pastry, and green juice.

"Tomorrow night at six," she said, into her cell phone, juggling everything in her arms as she kicked the door closed with her foot. "Yes, *Mother,*" she continued, "I'll pick you both up at the hotel and take you to a place with normal food." She listened. A male voice was speaking slowly, with focus. "Yes, Dad. They'll probably give it to us for free so you don't have to worry about me depleting my checking account to pay for an insanely priced, hyped-up meal." She nodded a few more times, taking a sip of her coffee and then preparing to hang up. "Yes," she finished up. "Okay. I'll see you then."

Click.

Her *parents*. They were *visiting*. Again. When she had first moved to Los Angeles, it had been mind-numbingly bi-weekly. There had been lunches, dinners, rides to work. Her mother had cleaned out her closets fourteen times, packing them with organizers and wooden blocks that smelled like hamsters and their offspring. Her father had threatened the cable company, which was the Internet company, which was *also* the telephone company, which was the *exact* company who canceled all of her services after he had kept them on the line for what had clocked in at seven hours and sixteen minutes. They had slept on her couch, blasted their Sharper Image noise machine loudly, and woke her up each morning at 5 a.m. when her father made his spirulina protein shake. These days, years since Maggie had faked a note to her parents on a page of the Homeowner Association's letterhead, informing them that their visits had to be less frequent (or result in a significant fine for their daughter), it was generally once or twice a year. Which was doable.

Still, she hated having to face them alone.

Maggie sat at her kitchen counter, where she had a perfect view of her bulletin board, affixed with the latest pictures of her life. She eyed a new one, pinned to the bottom right corner. She got up, moving to take a closer look.

It was the selfie she had taken of her and Josh at Mister Taco. Blurry, but cute. She plucked it off the board, looking at it more closely, then smiled. Maybe she'd tell him after all. Sometimes *maybe* meant *yes*.

She picked up her phone and dialed his number.

This time, on purpose.

Josh was eating Cheetos.

He had been for some time, polishing off his fifth bag as an entire second grade class of children wandered past, then stopped to stare at him wide-eyed. Like monkeys throwing feces behind a glass partition, this was a sight to see, except Josh was far more fascinating and far less vomit inducing. The caked-on orange powder gave him a Joker-esque grin and his inability to care what people thought about him, how he looked, or where he was going professionally lent to the overall "accident on the side of the road" fascination of it all.

He looked up at the children, contemplating sharing some potentially horrible life advice, when his cell phone rang. He answered it, without even looking to see who it was.

"So," Maggie began, excitedly, "My parents are in town and I'm getting dinner with them tomorrow night. I wanted to see if you wanted to return the favor and cause chaos with my family."

He stuffed another handful of Cheetos into his mouth. "Sure, I guess," he said, mouth full, dejected.

Maggie could sense it. "So that's a no, then?"

He swallowed. "Sure! I guess!" he tried again, with feeling.

Maggie could still sense it. "Maybe I shouldn't have asked."

"I'd be happy to go," he said, not wanting to upset the apple cart, but had the apple cart been a metaphor for his life, it would already have been upset, turned over, and crushed.

"In a not-so-happy kind of way?" she asked, concerned.

"I'll be good," he straightened up, wiping the cheese dust off his chin. "I'd love to go."

"Great!" she replied, returning to her original excitement.

Yeah, just great, he thought, wallowing in self-pity.

Frank and Jean Mills were enjoying their cold shots of ceviche, compliments of the chef.

They had come to play, so to speak, dressing up like Midwestern parents who thought dinner in Beverly Hills meant khakis, a V-neck sweater, and a matronly sundress. Their eyes were rarely on Maggie and Josh, instead scanning the main dining room of Cain's to see if anyone famous, whose name they'd never remember correctly, was there on this particular night.

"Is that Fred Selleck?" her mother asked.

"Don't you mean *Tom* Selleck?" Maggie replied, embarrassed.

"That's right," her father confirmed. "From *Magnet P.I.*"

Maggie rolled her eyes. "No. That's not Fred Selleck from *Magnet P.I.*"

Josh sat across from Maggie's father, a thick scrapbook perched in his lap. Jean periodically leaned over to see where in the timeline Josh was currently at, pointing and smiling to a variety of shots as he made his way through. The scrapbook, denoted "13" on the cover, represented Maggie's thirteenth year in life. Josh pretended to be interested, despite his head being somewhere else completely. Somewhere where his confidence in himself had been destroyed; where his faith in his future had been demolished.

"So, Josh," Frank said, buttering a small pretzel bread roll. "You should feel extremely honored to be here with us tonight." Josh looked up from the scrapbook, not sure exactly what he meant. "I can't remember the last time Maggie introduced us to anyone she was …" Frank wasn't sure how to categorize it.

"Seeing?" Maggie provided the term for the table.

"Right, that," Frank replied. "And remind me again where the two of you met?"

"The auto body shop," Josh replied.

"Riiiiiight," Frank replied, his reaction dripping with judgment. "What were you driving? Was it a BMW seven series?"

"A *three* series," Josh grumbled back.

"Oh," Maggie's father replied, less than impressed.

Maggie shared a polite smile with her father and mother, who lifted the scrapbook from in front of Josh and placed it back in front of herself. The pages were open to a particular memory, couched under a two-page headline that read "Niagara Falls." The photos covered the endless car trip, pictures of the family at rest stops and restaurants, and a few photos at a familiar location stuck in time.

The Apple Blossom Festival in Newfane, New York.

There was one particular photo, that had Josh actually seen, or Maggie actually remembered, would have transformed the moment and the relationship into something much more fantastical. It would have confirmed for the two of them just why they had felt a connection so strong from the outset. It was a color photo that pictured Maggie, at age thirteen, sitting on a bench next to Josh, wearing a Civil War-era costume, looking perturbed as Maggie mugged for her mother. Yes, their paths had crossed multiple times before, but the two of them had never remembered. Perhaps they weren't ready. Perhaps it hadn't been time.

"All ready for your salad course?" said the waiter, placing the salads in front of everyone. Jean closed the scrapbook, making room.

"So, darling? How's the job?" Jean asked Maggie, taking a bite of her Caesar.

Maggie motioned to the food around the table. "Clearly, it's great. And lucrative."

"Are they letting you take any pictures?" Frank asked.

"That's what I was going to tell you guys," she said, perking up. "Brian, the publisher, he's got me out doing some assignments after we lost our full-time photographer. It's still early stages, but I'm feeling really confident that I'll get to start doubling down on that area at the paper."

Frank perked up. "The Nikon coming in handy for that?"

Agh, the Nikon, Maggie thought. Upon hearing the name of the antique camera her father had given her at the age of eight, Josh looked up as well. He knew the story. It was just that Maggie's father didn't.

"Obviously things move fast these days and the kind of technology required for these kinds of shoots is …" Maggie began, lining up her faux-defense, "and it's a *film* camera … but I get to use it every so often for more artistic or retro looks."

"Well, take care of that baby," Frank said. "It's a classic." Frank took a bite of his salad, then turned his attention to Josh. "And what about you?"

"Could you be a little more specific?" Josh asked, eyeing Maggie.

"Your work. Your job. Like us old folks like to ask, what are your plans for the future?"

"He's going to work at NASA," Maggie was quick to reply, which immediately rubbed Josh the wrong way. This wasn't the day to go there.

It reminded him of his run-in with Spencer, the fight with his mother, the baggage over all the years. His hopes, his dreams, *especially* his failures ... they all came rushing back.

"I'm not going to work at NASA," he said, feeling bad for himself. "I wanted to, once, but I basically grew up in a family where your hopes and dreams were discouraged if they seemed unrealistic. So, after trying once, I basically decided to give up."

Well, that was *one* way to inspire the family of the girl you were dating.

"But you have a good job now?" Jean said, trying to help. "It sounds like you love that job?"

Josh thought about the question. "You know, my boss asked me that the other day. Did I *love* the job? I told her I did." Maggie and Jean looked relieved. "But I was lying. Probably because I was worried she was going to fire me. Or that there were staff cuts coming. But I realized in that one moment that I wasn't so sure anymore. I mean, I've been there *ten* years. And what has it gotten me? Sure, it's nice to know other young kids are feeding their hopes and dreams, and I think that's important. But, deep down, every time I see one of them dreaming big, I can't help but ask, what about *me*? Why not *me*? What did *I* do to deserve this?" He banged his fists on the table, rattling the stemware as he repeated, "WHAT. DID. I. DO??"

It was deathly quiet. Everyone in the entire restaurant stared at him, mouths agape. It was really embarrassing.

"Aren't I worthy?" he meekly whispered, then took a mindless bite out of a small buttered pretzel roll. Which just happened to be Jean's. Maggie's mother turned to Josh, seemingly affected by his blatant bread borrowing. She held out her hand and Josh lethargically let it fall out of his mouth, half-chewed, into her palm.

As usual, Frank was the first to speak up. "So, basically you hate your job and you've given up your dreams?"

"Not *basically*," he said, correcting. "*Exactly.*"

The look on Frank Mills's face spoke volumes.

Frank and Jean stood by the valet as Maggie pulled Josh aside.

Around them, music from the '80s played over the valet station's speakers, drowning out the noise of the city street.

"Do you mind taking a Lyft?" she asked, awkwardly. "I'm just going to take them back to the hotel and then go back to my place."

"Should we meet up later?" Josh asked, curious.

Maggie let out a sigh. Not tonight," she said. "But ... I'll call you."

Josh knew what that meant. You didn't need to be in MENSA to figure it out. He clearly knew what was up. "I had a bad day today," he said, trying to explain. "I didn't mean for it to hang over dinner like a cloud of ..."

"Of *shit*?" she volunteered.

"Well, I wouldn't say *shit*."

"I would," Maggie replied.

"Well, people have bad days," he said, defending himself.

"Yes, they do," she confirmed. Maggie turned to look over at her parents who were waving her to join them; the Sonata had arrived and it was time to go.

"So, let me tell you about *mine*," he said, pleading.

"Can we talk about this tomorrow?" Maggie asked. "Or later this week?"

"Are we actually going to?" Josh asked.

Maggie looked back at her parents, then to Josh. "Maybe this is moving too fast," she said. "Maybe *we're* moving too fast."

"Says your father," Josh lamented. "But what do you think?"

She thought about it. Then thought about it some more. She turned to look over her shoulder where her parents were waiting just as Chicago's "You're the Inspiration" began to play on the speakers. Josh almost had an aneurism. The dichotomy wasn't lost on him. There was no beach. No top of a Ferris Wheel. No romantic couple chasing each other through a park, on the top of a red rock cliff, somewhere in Sedona, Arizona.

No. There was just *shit*.

"Maybe tomorrow I'll know," Maggie finally said, giving Josh a platonic nudge on his left forearm.

"Can we talk tomorrow, then?" Josh asked, eyeing her father.

"I have to go," Maggie said, turning and walking back to her parents. Josh watched her go. Waved to her parents. They waved back barely, getting into the car. He looked to Maggie, trying to get her attention.

But he couldn't.

Thirty-One Years Later

JOSH WOKE UP.

These days, anytime it happened, it was a wonderfully surprising feeling, ranking right up there with regular (and successful) trips to the bathroom, navigating the particularly narrow set of cobblestone stairs that led up to the Chalet de l'Oasis, and completing that weekly sudoku puzzle in *Le Monde*. "After all," as Josh had once said to his next-door neighbor, Guillaume Cantet, "at the age of sixty-five, any daily accomplishment or small step forward represented real, concrete, substantive progress in life."

On this particular day, as was the case on most, Josh enjoyed the luxury of continuing to lay still in the oversized bed, watching his chest rise and fall as the breeze from the open window turned curtains into living, dancing beings. He stared out at the sky, a crisp blue hue, providing a home for the bright yellow of the rising sun. He squinted at the beauty, remembering a time when such things were only illusions. Then he sat up, eyeing the side of the bed he hadn't actively used, and swung his legs over onto the floor. They were older and grayer but not weak or frail. As for his face, he had forgone the beard that most of the friends his age now embraced, leaving bare a visage that had lived a life that didn't always necessarily land how he'd expected, but had given him moments of joy he wouldn't forget.

Josh made his way through the morning's usual activities. A shower and a shave, a breakfast of coffee and toast, a trip outside to water the plants in front of the quaint, two-story French provincial home. It had a steep roof and a classic brick exterior, and was set back significantly from the main road, hidden by tall trees and a manicured hedge. Josh turned off the water, moving along the side of the house and around back where a six-thousand-square-foot grass area was fenced in and protected. At the far side of it, large pallets of stones sat untouched, alongside piles of lumber, unopened boxes of metal parts, and an already set circular concrete foundation. Josh lorded over it, making mental checks as he eyed the supplies, the rebar that formed a tall, round skeleton, and the position of the sun in the sky.

Yes, he thought. *Today is finally going to be the day.*

Sèvres, France, wasn't far from Paris.

Located in the department of Hauts-de-Seine, just six miles from the center of the city, it was situated far enough away that the bustle and noise never impeded the suburb's ability to feel more like its own special protected land. Josh had spent nineteen years in Paris before leaving for Sèvres, deciding that a more rural existence that gave him room to stretch was exactly what he desired. God knows, after all those years packed into a flat like a sardine, and the years prior living in the shadow of the blue and yellow monolith, he needed nature. And fresh air. And freedom. Fortunately, it was also far enough away from the center of Paris that when the sun went down and the night sky emerged, he could look up and see stars and constellations free of the light pollution so prevalent just a mere six miles away.

It also didn't hurt that the Avenue de l'Observatoire was only a twenty-nine-minute drive, home to the Paris Observatory since Louis XIV had supported its construction and completion in 1671, and Josh's second home ever since he had developed relationships with the caretakers of the center in the early twenties. When he visited, he was like a kid in a candy shop, no matter his age.

At thirty, at forty, at fifty, and even now at sixty-five, he still felt an excitement bubbling up inside him each time he closed in on the Boulevard de Port Royal. As the self-driving car rounded the turn toward the final stretch, approaching the grassy knoll that surrounded the observatory, he would feel his pulse quicken despite having been there hundreds of times before. He would take a breath to calm his excitement as he passed dozens of French astronomers who were housed there, down the hallways and past the tours and students, and on his way to meet Dr. Emile Laurent in the Central Hall.

Dr. Emile Laurent had come to the Paris Observatory straight out of the Paris-Sorbonne where he had secured his PhD in Astronomy. When he started, he was nothing more than a glorified research assistant, but it was his vast intellect, genuine nature, and ability to focus on logic over emotion that quickly helped him rise through the ranks. Within a decade he was overseeing hundreds of researchers and strategizing their overarching projects while prioritizing how and when internal and external stakeholders were using the telescope to search the heavens for the next groundbreaking discovery. Every once in a while, when trying to schedule time, newly appointed researchers would innocently ask Dr. Laurent about that infamous ninety-minute block that was always blacked out on the scheduling system. What was it for? What secret organization was leveraging the telescope during those prime nighttime minutes? But there were no answers and the staff quickly learned not to search for them, because that's just how Dr. Laurent wanted it to be.

"How's EGS-ur4-3 doing today?" Josh asked Dr. Laurent, leaning down to get a daytime look through the telescope. Dr. Laurent, moving slower these days as he approached seventy-five, picked up a cup of tea and made his way to the chair nearby. As he sat, he positioned the cup with purpose, away from his research papers but still within reach. He pushed his hand through his wispy white hair, matting it down in the back.

"Still there," he said sardonically with a thick French accent. He took a sip of his tea, then put his glasses on so he could read the top sheet on a stack of paperwork. "Still sending us short radio bursts every few months … from fourteen million light-years away."

"That's amazing." Josh stood to sit opposite Dr. Laurent. "All those potential discoveries out there? Think of how they could change the face of our existence."

"It still won't change the fact that I have to walk Ulysses every morning and clean up after him." Dr. Laurent laughed.

Josh joined in, reflecting. "I guess you still have to live your life, no matter what the universe has in store."

Dr. Laurent took off his glasses, sliding closer to Josh. "Speaking of which. Is everything in place?"

"Would I be here if it weren't?"

Dr. Laurent nodded. "Silly me." He moved toward the edge of the room where he unlocked a metal closet, swinging the door open to reveal a sizeable storage room. Josh watched him intently as he disappeared into the room, then re-emerged pushing a cart loaded with a large brown box. Dr. Laurent tapped the top. "Go ahead. Take a look."

Josh's eyes lit up as he grabbed a nearby knife, cutting through the top. These weren't the eyes of a sixty-five-year-old, no. It was the same look of a four-year-old staring up at the night sky through a toy telescope, pointing and telling his parents that he "wanted to go there." Had he looked in a mirror at that moment, the sixty-five-year-old face would have thrown off the concentration of the child still inside.

"It's a Zeiss," Dr. Laurent said, as Josh opened the box and carefully lifted out a telescope lens. "Objective diameter of nine and a half inches. Two hundred forty-two millimeters. A focal ratio of fourteen point eight." It was gibberish to most, but to Josh it was exactly what he needed. It was exactly what they had discussed when the initial plans had been drawn up.

"It's beautiful," Josh said, noticeably moved. "Thank you."

"Thank *you*," Dr. Laurent said, giving Josh a pat on the back and scuffling back to the chair where he put his glasses back on and took another sip of his tea.

While Emile wasn't his father, and could never replace Mel, he had been a true mentor to Josh over the years, especially during times of loneliness and isolation. Especially when he had first come to Paris, a stranger in a strange land. But now, he felt at home. He felt like he had a place. Which is why the time had come to finally pull the trigger on a dream he'd never had the courage to chase after.

"Will you stop standing there spinning," Dr. Laurent said, without turning to look at Josh. "I've got research to do … and you've got an observatory to finish."

Sixty-one years, two months, twelve days, fourteen minutes, and thirty-three seconds. It's how long it had taken for Josh's four-year-old dream of "going there" to become a reality.

The prep work over the previous weeks, the cement slab, the masonry work, the electrical, it had all made today's construction go without a hitch. The construction crew, made up of local contractors and combined with Josh's own circle of expert professionals, got the structure up in hours, then secured the technology and equipment in the base of the structure in half that time. The small crane, which had been sitting out on the street for days in preparation of the event, was finally able to do its job, lifting a polished stainless-steel dome from the shipping container it had come in, and allowing for the crew to secure it firmly in place.

Charlie Legune, who had helped find the perfect place and positioning for the backyard observatory, stood next to him, surveying the cylindrical structure as the crane retreated back out to the street. "Spectacular," he whispered, with a French accent. "*Je suis envieux.*"

"Well, you can come and use it anytime you want," Josh said.

Charlie disappeared, only to return with the refractor in his white-gloved hands. "Will you do the honors?"

Inside, Josh climbed the circular metallic steps surrounding the telescope's mechanism, leading up to the very top. There, two additional men waited, with the guts of the telescope open and ready to receive what Dr. Laurent had so generously provided.

Josh handed over the lens and the men put it inside, closing the casing.

It was nighttime. Everyone was gone.

Josh sat in a rickety old chair, the observatory structure lit up from within, a shaft of light protruding from the top of the dome and into the night sky. Josh took a sip of wine, then approached the open door to the structure.

He looked up at it, took a breath, and let it out. There were people he wished could be here. But sometimes, not everything worked out the way you wanted. Sometimes the universe had other plans. Ironically, tonight, Josh had his own plans for the universe.

He stepped inside, closing the door, and climbed the stairs.

Sixteen

MAGGIE MINDLESSLY TOOK PHOTO after photo of her half-eaten chocolate croissant.

Alyssa watched her, hands on her hips, standing off to the side near the green screen setup, draped around the latest book she'd reviewed for the upcoming issue of *The 818*. The book, *Mr. Jangles Has a Problem*, was a "cautionary tale of one man's quest to bring music back into the lives of the citizens of a small rural town" after a seventy-five-year-old clause in the county's bylaws banned musical theater for good. Dean Agers's debut novel had been receiving amazing reviews since the advance copies had gone out, and Alyssa had been immediately taken by what she called its "retro '50s new-age message" and its final, rollicking chapter where Billy Ray Thomas and his fellow Shriners put on the entire *Gold Diggers of 1933* musical in drag.

"Good to go over here," Alyssa said to Maggie, picking up her dog Chumley in the process. She approached Maggie, blocking her eyeline through the camera. "Did you hear what I said?"

Maggie sat up, swinging the camera away from her morning snack, and turned to Alyssa. "I think I made a mistake," she said.

"Probably should have stuck to restaurant reviews, yeah?" Alyssa asked.

It snapped Maggie out of her fog. "No, I'm not talking about this," she said, pointing to the book perched on a stand, ready for its closeup. "I'm talking about this guy." She held up her phone and that grainy, half-drunk selfie from Mister Taco.

Alyssa lit up. "I'm here for you," she said, moving close to Maggie. "I give a lot of my girlfriends relationship advice, so I'm kind of an expert."

"I usually don't ask girls for relationship advice," Maggie said, cringing.

"Why not?"

"Because they're not guys. Girls tell you to do the things they hope might work, while guys tell you to do the things they know will."

"But if you're asking for advice," Alyssa said, "then you must care."

"I guess."

"So, what mistake do you think you made?" she asked, reaching over and taking a bite of the croissant. "You know, it can sometimes feel like we did something wrong, when in actuality we were acting on our own instincts. And sometimes, acting on your instincts may not be a bad thing. Sometimes it's good."

"I ghosted this guy because my father didn't like him."

"Okay," Alyssa contemplated, "… *bad* thing. Never let your father make decisions about who to date. A father's advice to his daughter is always focused on keeping her away from men."

"But my father," Maggie began, drawing a glare from Alyssa, "he's always been there for me. He's my guy."

"I thought *this* guy," Alyssa said, pointing to the cell phone picture, "was your guy."

Maggie let out a breath, her whole body shrinking down a few feet.

"You know what your problem is, Mags?"

"No, Alyssa. But I'm sure you're going to tell me."

"You care too much about what your father thinks and you're letting it block the happy."

Alyssa pulled out her phone, taking a picture of Maggie's face, then quickly showed her the snap. She looked dejected, tired, and generally miserable. "Do you like what you see? Is this the Maggie you want to be? Isn't it time to let the happy in?"

Technology Through the Ages was shaping up.

Josh walked through the third-floor exhibit-in-progress with co-worker David by his side, cross-referencing the layout plans on David's clipboard with walls and panels that Center staff were erecting. They passed by the diorama of '60s album covers, antique turntables already secured in a row of plexiglass boxes, and found their way into the section earmarked for the '30s. There, workers hung a huge silkscreened image of *The Television Ghost*, one of the first TV programs to ever grace black and white televisions. In front of the image, others were unboxing three antique TVs from large wooden crates.

"The Geloso came in this morning," David said, referring to one of the antiques, "but we had the Bush and Baird since last week. They're amazing specimens, if you ask me. The Geloso is on loan from the Museum of TV and Radio, while the other two were donated by the Kecks."

"Mmhmm," Josh said, scrolling through his phone to see if he had any missed calls.

"And over here," David pointed, urging Josh to follow, "we've got the riser all ready for the Volkswagen Bug. That's being delivered tomorrow AM."

"Mmhmm," Josh said again, really not paying attention.

David stopped. Waited. Eventually Josh looked up, realizing the updates had stopped. "Is that it?"

"Isn't that the question I should be asking you?" he volleyed back.

Josh shook himself back to the present, taking the clipboard out of David's hands and giving his surroundings a once-over. He nodded. "This looks good," he said. "Keep me posted on the Anderson donations. I can't wait to see that Trash-Eighty when it comes in."

"So, we're done?" David asked.

"Yup. I'll see you back downstairs after I do my rounds."

Josh wandered the halls, passing by the Air and Space pavilion, through the World of Life and past the entrance to where *Endeavor* was housed. He peered in, eyeing the students who gathered to get a glimpse at the hulking space shuttle, then passed into the Ecosystems exhibit where throngs of children crowded the marine "touch tanks." They reached out, eyes wide, feeling starfish, eels, and stingrays. They cackled with glee, living in the present, with no worries or stresses or angst over life.

"Enjoy it while you can," he muttered under his breath to a little boy and girl holding hands as they passed. "Because it's all going to come crashing down when she tells the class you're her boyfriend." The little boy looked up, pulling his hand away as he ran off. The little girl looked up to Josh, her lip quivering. Josh stood proud, hands on his hips like a modern-day superhero whose superpower was quashing the happiness derived from love. He felt *proud*. He felt *accomplished*. He felt *sickened*. What the hell was he doing?

He looked at his cell phone again. No missed calls.

He'd been trying to get her for three days and she hadn't returned the call. It left him to replay the evening in question back in his mind hundreds of times, eventually realizing that his downer of an attitude might have had an impact on her and her parents' impressions of him. But it had been a bad day. His blue sky had faded to gray. His passion had gone away.

He'd also been playing "Bad Day" by Daniel Powter in his car, on repeat, and it had to stop because it was permeating every single one of his thoughts, every time he had one.

"'Well, you need a blue-sky holiday,'" he'd told David, who he'd found struggling with the logistics around acquiring a few of the late additions to the technology exhibit.

"'Sometimes the system goes on the blink, and the whole thing turns out wrong,'" he'd said to T, who was dealing with a particularly annoying glitch in the mailing list she'd mail-merged for the official invitations.

"'You kick up the leaves and the magic is lost,'" he'd said to one of the Science Center gardeners, who was using a leaf blower to clear off the concrete area in front of the facility.

Josh looked back to the touch tanks, noticing a crowd of children surrounding a purple-shirted team member who had not been there before. He watched as the person lifted a starfish out of the water, extending it so dozens of children could touch its arms. He angled his view, trying to get a glimpse of their face but they were blocked by the crowd. He moved closer, curious. Had it been a green-shirt he wouldn't have been so thrown off. But a *purple* shirt? A nearby teacher called out to her students, pulling the lot of them away from the touch tank and parting the way for Josh to approach. As the purple-shirt came into focus, he saw that it was none other than Maggie.

He stopped his approach, surprised. She made up the difference, moving to him. The two stood opposite each other in the center of children-caused chaos.

"Like it?" she asked, pointing to the purple shirt. It wasn't regulation by any means. She had clearly purchased it from somewhere like The Gap.

"I could have you arrested for impersonating an employee," he said, motioning behind her to a security guard at the periphery.

"But you won't," she said, confident. "Because you're glad to see me."

"I've been the one calling you," he said. "And you ..."

"I'm sorry," she said, genuinely. "You freaked out, then I freaked out, and then ..."

"Your *father*."

"Yeah, he basically freaked out too. But put yourself in his position. Your daughter introduces you to a dude she's hanging with and he tells the entire table he has no goals, hates his job, and has given up on his dreams. What was that? Was that real?"

Josh let out a breath. Of course it was real, he'd tell Maggie. He was coming off a milestone argument with his mother that had drudged up his past regrets, then an ego-crushing run-in with his intern-nemesis that reminded him his present wasn't so great either. On top of it all, he'd walked into a Chicago-style interrogation with twelve bags of Cheeto powder still coursing through his veins, then found himself under pressure to answer the kind of question all TV dads asked their daughter's suitors: What are you going to do with your life? All Josh could think about was what he hadn't done with his life. Specifically, JPL NASA.

"You applied to JPL?" Maggie asked, surprised.

"And I got rejected. I never reapplied. My mom discouraged me against it and the idiot that I was, I listened. Eventually, when I finally got around to thinking about trying again, it was too late."

"It's never too late," she interjected. "If you can wear that shirt in public, you can do anything."

He laughed.

She grabbed his arm. It wasn't the "there's a speeding truck coming your way" kind of arm grab; nor was it the "oh my God, what is that hovering in the sky" kind of arm grab. It was an "I like you" kind of arm grab, firm and interested. He looked down at her hand, then up to her eyes.

"I like you, too," he said, knowing exactly what she was thinking.

"So, can we pick this back up where we left off?" Maggie asked, then cringed. "Before the dinner, though it'd be great if we could pretend that the bed wetting thing never happened."

"I've been trying."

"I'll do anything if you can really, totally forget."

"Anything?" he said, with something very specific in mind.

"I mean, I guess," she cocked her head, worried. "What is it?"

Josh smiled, then cringed.

Lisa had the mic.

The candles, lit up from all four corners of the Redwood Room, gave the rustic, wooden ballroom a quaint, personal setting. Guests packed the tables, fully invested in the speeches that were now going full force. Josh and Maggie sat next to each other at a twelve-top, alongside a crew of well-dressed friends who were all in various stages of alcohol poisoning now that their jobs in the wedding party were done. They listened as Lisa directed her attention to Sasha Kahane, her old roommate, a platinum blonde hanging on tightly to her unimpressed Armenian boyfriend, Davit.

The wedding ceremony had been *Da-mazing*, which in the Damon to English Dictionary that Josh, Cody, and Damon had created back in sixth grade, was defined as *having amazing properties by incorporating the inclusion of at least one (1) Damon*. And as this wedding did, indeed, include one Damon, plus a Lisa, and approximately two hundred and fifty smiling, gift-carrying supporters, no one would argue with the adolescent logic at play. In addition, no one, including Fred and Eva Gardener *and* Harold and Allie Harrison, would argue over the flower arrangements, the inordinate amount of hors d'oeuvres, the per-plate price of the wagyu beef, the bags of blueberry scones as party favors, or the song that Damon and Lisa would dance to when they first came into the room: "She Blinded Me With Science" by Thomas Dolby. Yes, Lisa saw fit to see that through, to ensure there were no wedding coups, or else there would be …

"… *hell* to pay!" Lisa's booming voice came over the speakers, as she pointed to Sasha over at the wedding party table, the crowd laughing along with her as she laid out her and Damon's origin story. "I told her, I said, if you eat that last blueberry scone you are going to be sorry in a major way. And she still did. To this day she denies eating it, but crumbs on your chin and in your bedsheets *do … not … lie*, girlfriend!" The crowd laughed riotously, turning to Sasha as she waved off the accusation. "But I would have been sorry, it turns out, if she *hadn't*," Lisa continued, walking back to the head table, and pointing directly at her handsome groom. "I wouldn't have met this troublemaker," she joked. "Because had she not eaten that scone, I never would have had to hoof it down to the Starbucks. Had I not hoofed it down to the Starbucks, I would have never stood in line directly behind this goof-head. And had there not only been one blueberry scone left, the two of us wouldn't have argued over just who was justified in purchasing it."

Damon grabbed the mic, leaning in. "To be clear, she warned me off with horror stories of how the last scone always has the most bacteria." The crowd laughed and Damon finished his thought. "Then she bought it for herself! She blinded me with her beauty … *and science.*"

"But I eventually shared it with him, and the rest was history. So, thank you, Sasha, for being a selfish food-stealing ingrate … *said with love.* Because if you hadn't been true to your own questionable instincts, none of us would be here today!"

The crowd cheered. Sasha cocked her head, unsure if she was being complimented. Maggie leaned into Josh. "Is that true?"

"Wild, right?" he said, leaning in. "I wonder if they would have met if Sasha hadn't caused her to go down to Starbucks. He was staying with me for three days, crashing on my couch while he was attending a conference for work. He didn't live out here. He rarely visited. What are the chances they would have ever crossed paths again?"

"What does Damon say?"

"He says they're soulmates. He says no matter what, they would have met. That if they hadn't that day at Starbucks, the universe would have found another way to make it happen."

"And do you believe that? About soulmates? About destiny and fate?" she asked.

"I'd like to think so," he said, smiling. "My dad does, for sure. You should've heard the speech he gave my mom when he asked her to marry him. He practically told her the universe had willed it to happen. What about you?"

She thought for a beat and shrugged. She didn't have an answer.

The wedding party inhabitants were floored.

In Los Angeles, when you went to a wedding, most of the people you met worked in quote-unquote Hollywood, where they were talent, they worked for talent, or they served talent. The people at the outer edges of that world—the criminal lawyers and the doctors and the sanitation engineers and the bail bondsmen, and the so on and so forth, insert blue-collar, state-sponsored, non-profit *this*, and unprofitable *that*—they never crossed paths with the quote-unquote masses. Yes, even the vice president of exhibits at places like the California Science Center.

"You don't work in the entertainment industry?" a TV publicist asked Josh.

"Like, the job you do, has nothing to do with movies?" a screenwriter wondered, trying to wrap his head around this thing.

"But at your job, I'm sure you've done some big deals with the studios or other content companies to create entertainment-*related* exhibits tied to movie releases, right?" asked a casting director. The questions came fast and furious. They came from actresses, directors, costume designers, entertainment lawyers, and personal assistants. They didn't want to hear about the day-to-day of the industry professionals at the table. Heck, that was boring as *shit*. They were endlessly fascinated at Josh's seemingly blue-collar, science-focused, downtown-centric job. Did he have to go to college for a job like that? Did he ever use the IMAX screen to watch football games? Was the salary good? Did he get health benefits? Did he have a key so he could get in after hours and show people a good time?

"Definitely not," Josh warned them, sharing a mischievous look with Maggie. "That would be against the rules."

It was Josh's fifteen minutes of fame. "You're famous," Maggie whispered.

"It's a publicly managed educational organization," he explained. "We have a Board of Trustees, donors, affiliations with groups like the Smithsonian," he continued. "We have over four hundred species of plants and animals featured in the facility, too."

"Real animals?" a producer asked. "Not a CGI IMAX movie of what looks like real animals?"

"Yes. Real flesh-and-blood animals."

The table *ooh'd* and *aah'd*.

Josh and Maggie rocked back and forth, her head on his shoulder, his arm around her waist as INXS' "Never Tear Us Apart" swirled around them and the other couples on the dance floor. Maggie lifted her head and pulled back into the traditional junior high slow dance position. "How long were they together before they got married?"

"Just a year. It happened quick," he said.

"So, they both clearly knew."

"If you ask them, that's what they'll tell you."

"But how do you really know, though?" she wondered. "How do you know it's the right person?"

"I guess you hope there are signs. You know?" Josh said, moving her into the center of the dance floor.

"Signs?" she asked. "What kind of signs?"

"Signs that you're supposed to be together. Good signs. Moments, coincidences, opportunities, mutual appreciation for the same movies," he joked, then getting serious. "Feelings. Feelings like you've known the other person longer than you actually have. Deep-down, soul-level stuff."

Maggie nudged him. "I wish there was some organization like the DMV that would just send you a piece of paper that showed who, exactly, you were supposed to be with. Take all the guesswork and emotional trauma out of the equation. It might have helped me save some time over the years."

"But then you wouldn't be who you are today."

He was right, when she really thought about it. Every single significant or cringe-inducing moment she could still visualize from her past had some impact on who she had become. Being mugged by insane clowns had made her more skeptical of people who wore masks, both figurative and literal. Failing to become valedictorian during her senior year because of a C plus in English had driven her to improve her writing skills. Food poisoning from churros made her swear off sugar and get healthier, while losing her summer job as a legal clerk in Joliet, Illinois, had been such a demoralizing experience that she vowed she would never take any job for granted; nor would she leave one without having another. And speaking of demoralizing? Paris. Paris alone and the aftermath had kept her single long enough to meet someone who actually made her want to grab his arm, look up at him, and use her doe-eyed skills (the result of appearing in a high school production of *Into the Woods*) to communicate just how she felt. Yet, even as she cycled through all the examples, there was a niggling feeling that she still needed—

"—proof. Proof that the other person is the person you're supposed to be with."

"The only proof you get is after. At the end. Only then do you know if you picked wisely."

"Or at the divorce proceedings. You'd know then, too."

"Yes, the divorce would probably give it away."

They laughed as Damon and Lisa twirled over to their part of the dance floor. Hugs and high-fives all around as "Relax!" by Frankie Goes to Hollywood started playing.

"Thank you, guys, so much for coming!" Lisa beamed.

"It was a beautiful ceremony," Maggie chimed in.

"And a great party," Josh added.

"Don't forget your complimentary scones," Damon said. "If you don't take your bags with you, we'll be forced to eat five hundred pounds of the things." Lisa poked him, playfully.

Damon pulled Josh aside. "Bring it in, buddy," he said, hugging him. It was a meaningful moment, the result of thirty or more years of friendship. It was a moment that could have never happened had it not been for Mel deciding to move the family to California. Or Josh deciding to buy a townhouse in Burbank. Or Sasha deciding to eat the last scone. Or … Or … Or … The moments were numerous, but the outcomes were singular in their significance.

"Have a great honeymoon in Hawaii," Josh said, pulling back. "Where are you staying?"

"Four Seasons Maui," he said. "Lowest percentage of food poisoning or beach accidents. I did the risk assessment before we put down our deposit."

"It sounds so romantic," Maggie said.

"Romance isn't about the place. Or the situation. Or how much money you spend. Romance can happen anywhere. Because no matter where you go, there you are. It's about the people." Damon leaned over to kiss his bride. After he'd done so, he turned back to Josh and Maggie. "When you realize it was meant to be, nothing can stand in your way. Not even scones," he said, pulling a half-eaten one from his pocket and taking a bite.

Josh and Maggie took it all in, smiling.

Was it really that easy?

Seventeen

IT WAS A FAMILIAL staring contest of epic proportions.

There had been other staring contests in the past where the stakes had been far less serious. When Josh was seventeen, there had been the staring contest for the keys to the family Volvo, resulting in Mel bursting a collection of blood vessels in his "driving eye" after trying to keep up with Josh's superhuman ability to stay wide-eyed in a moisture-free environment. There had been the Staring Wars of 1999, when Josh had been fourteen, deciding which poor soul would be responsible for retrieving the supplemental movie snacks for *Star Wars I: The Phantom Menace* despite the trailers already playing. And no mere mortal could forget the Care Stare of 2009, when Barbara and Josh went head-to-head in an attempt to force the other to take care of Mel, bedridden from a nasty case of strep throat that no one wanted to catch.

As for the epic proportions at hand, tonight's Dare Stare concerned one thing and one thing only: an apology. Would Barbara give one? Would Josh? Would either of them, more stubborn than the other, find it in their heart to take one for the team and apologize for the events of the previous Sunday night, let alone the previous thirty or so years?

Josh sat on one side of the table, a Diet Coke sitting in a tall, ice-filled glass in front of him. He watched the bubbles as they rose to the top, then lifted up into the air. On the other side sat Barbara, hands wrapped around a hot cup of tea, dripping honey into the center hypnotically, entranced. And then there was Mel, sitting between the two on the third edge of the table, watching both of them like a judge at a mute version of the U.S. Open.

"Although I opened up the floor fifteen minutes ago for introductory statements," Mel spoke up, voice cracking, "I'll re-open the floor again in the event anyone would like to chime in." Barbara looked at Josh, like if anyone was going to chime in it had better be him.

"Why should I start?" Josh asked.

"Because you clearly have an opinion about me that you'd like to share."

They both returned their focus to the drinks in front of them. Mel rolled his eyes like the worst mediator on the face of the earth. "I saw that," Barbara commented.

"Which I'm fine with," he said, "because this is ridiculous. You're two adults, yes, it's true. You're now at the point in your lives where you should be able to communicate like two mature, well-adjusted people."

"Well, I'm not going first," Barbara said. Mel turned to Josh, putting his hand on his son's arm. Josh relented, letting out a sigh. He reached out, took a big gulp of his drink, then wiped his mouth.

While he hadn't realized it until the night of his mother's cooking finale, he'd been waiting to have this conversation for years. It's just that he'd been so deathly afraid of her skull opening up and releasing her own motherly version of the Kraken. Yes, he'd not had the courage to do it. Not until now. Yet in the seconds it took for him to take a big gulp of his drink and wipe his mouth, the thoughts raced at a blistering pace. Was he about to really do this? Where would he begin? Would he blow up their entire relationship? She had been such a towering figure of authority, thanks to her ingrained teacher mentality, that he was second-guessing himself. She had conditioned him to her controlling ways. He had internalized them, regulated them, normalized them. But lately, he had started to see the cracks in the foundation of her logic. He had to tell her how he really felt.

"When I was four …" he began. Barbara threw up her hands. *Is this the starry sky incident all over again?*, her expression shot back. She opened her mouth, about to throw down, but Mel stopped her mid-breath. With one fatherly look, he handed the floor back to Josh.

"I'm sorry, but it all goes back to that," he said, continuing. "You shut me down. You squashed my dreams, telling me they weren't realistic. That conditioned me to take the easier, less complicated routes in life, for fear of failing at the riskier opportunities. I went through life thinking I didn't deserve those kinds of opportunities. I settled for things I *knew* I could do instead. And in the process, I limited myself from the things I wanted to do. Every time I was faced with something that scared me, all I could hear was your voice reminding me about unrealistic expectations. Now, I'm not here to tell you it's all your fault, but I'm here to ask you to at least take some responsibility in that. To recognize that I don't want to be that person any longer, and to support me in making that change. The other night it all came to a head and came vomiting out of me. I'm sorry for that, but there was no other way."

Barbara sat back, arms crossed. But her skull didn't open and the Kraken didn't emerge. She took another sip of her drink, then leaned across the table. "Don't manufacture false memories," she said, defensive. "I've been there for you from the moment you were born. Looking out for you. Making sure you had the tools to become a contributing member of society! Part of being a parent is making sure your kids are aware of the challenges. Life's tough, Josh. Life doesn't always give you what you want. Sometimes what you expected turns out to never materialize. Do you think my life is exactly how I wanted it to be? Well, it's not."

"Barbara, come on now …" Mel tried to slow her roll.

"*Mature adults*, right, Mel?" she shot back. "If we're all mature adults, then why should I censor how I feel?" She turned back to Josh.

"Life is like rolling a die, darling. You might want it to come up six but it may only come up three. You don't see me complaining, do you? Because in the end, it's no one's fault but mine. In the end, I should have fought harder against your father taking that job at ValleyCon. Then, maybe, I could have retained my tenure and become a full professor at Stony Brook. But I didn't. But you don't see me blaming him for it, do you? No. All the blame rests firmly on my head."

"Well, you did kind of blame me," Mel spoke up, sheepishly.

Barbara spun to him. "What did I say?"

"It was more of a look. A repetitive, daily, agitated *look*. Kind of like you wanted to punch me in the face." She looked at him with an agitated look like she wanted to punch him in the face. "Just like that," he pointed.

Barbara let out a huge breath, her shoulders dropping to her side. "But you know what I did, Josh?" she continued. "I worked with the hand I was dealt. I found other things to keep me busy. I tried to forget about the things I had wanted for myself, and focused on the things I *had* instead." She stood firm and tall.

"And are you happy?" Josh asked, taking her hand.

She looked down at his hand holding hers. "I don't know," she replied as her eyes started to mist up.

"Well, I want to be. I want you to *let* me be."

The tears started to flow freely. She picked up a napkin, dabbing her eyes. There was a guilt in her eyes as she gave Josh the once-over, then turned to Mel for that familiar embrace. He got up, pulling her close, embracing her like a weighted blanket stuffed with the memories of all the good times. "We love you," Mel said.

She turned to Josh, eyes red, looking for confirmation.

"Yes, of course, me too," he confirmed. "But that doesn't change the fact that I don't want to forget about the things I want for myself either. Yes, I want your support. Yes, I want your counsel. But if you can't do that, I just want you to close your mouth and keep your opinion to yourself."

Barbara wiggled out of the weighted embrace and turned to Josh. And nodded. With her mouth closed.

While Josh and Maggie would never come out and say it directly, the truth was, they were looking for proof.

Proof that they belonged together. Proof that they were a perfect match. Proof that their presence in each other's lives was important, and that they'd never try to keep the other person away from those significant parts of their lives. Proof that they had grown out of their old baggage. Proof that they were listening. Proof that they were excited by each other, both physically and mentally. Proof that they had a sense of humor, that they *cared*, and that if something were to ever go sideways in their lives, the first person they'd think of, the first person they'd call, would be the other one.

There was the time Maggie dragged Josh to an evening of karaoke with *The 818* team, bastardizing the lyrics to The Rolling Stones' "(I Can't Get No) Satisfaction," being too slow with the lyrics to R.E.M.'s "It's the End of the World as We Know It" and being too drunk to read the lyrics to "Islands in the Stream," despite doing her best Dolly Parton to Josh's Kenny Rogers. He'd meet everyone, be welcomed into their group selfies (hashtag *818ers*), and even spend twenty minutes listening to Robyn's sob story about how her overbearing mother and conservative upbringing caused her to become the fashion-forward female she was today. When they'd return to Maggie's house later that night, she'd hook up her phone to her portable digital printer and affix the group selfie to a part of her bulletin board that was quickly becoming Josh-inated. And Josh would take the same picture, centered on him, Maggie, and *half* of Robyn, and do something daring. He'd make it his phone's wallpaper image, throwing caution to the wind.

Josh would drag Maggie to the Technology Through the Ages exhibit preparation on a Saturday afternoon, including her in the unboxing, taping, tacking, and hanging that he and the rest of the team always did a week before an exhibit's launch. Despite not being nearly as fun as bastardizing song lyrics, Maggie would get to meet Diana in the flesh, who would already be there supervising the team from her perch, as she took a voracious bite out of a monstrous kale BLT.

"I'm pleased to share if …" Diana began, but quickly looked away to prevent any significant eye contact, for fear of someone actually taking her up on the offer.

"Thank God for you," Maggie proclaimed, quickly lunging for the half of the sandwich Diana wasn't eating and opening her mouth to an ungodly diameter to take a bite. "I was about to unleash the NFM and nobody, and I mean nobody, wants to see that."

"It's true," Josh agreed. "You definitely don't want to experience the NFM."

Diana sat stunned as the other half of her beloved BLT was now in the hands of Maggie. The rest of the team eyed her with mad respect, floored by her fearless food fetching, then flashed Josh the kind of overwhelmingly approving glance that he rarely got from anyone. Diana's disappointment segued into a smile.

"The one who would slay the giant," Annabelle whispered to Josh.

Ah, Maggie. She could fit in with his co-workers, pillage his boss's lunch, and still solicit a polite smile from her when it was all said and done.

Proof.

There was the night Josh took Maggie to meet John Williams at The Hollywood Bowl, if by "meet" one meant sitting nowhere near the stage and with no personal connections to engineer such proximity in the first place. He would secure their dinner and drinks, purchase two black t-shirts with the maestro's face emblazoned across them, and wait for the perfect moment to hold up his bin of popcorn and casually extend it toward Maggie's fidgeting hands. He would wait for the music to swell during the perfect moment in "The Flying Sequence" from *Superman: The Movie*, then fight back against all the historical baggage he'd been carrying for years.

"You can have some if you want," he'd say, cringing inside while he held the bucket out in front of her. And she would smile, appreciate the generosity, and without any idea of the significance of the moment, stuff her mouth.

Yes, my friends. More proof.

She'd buy him the Lego exclusive VIP Tyrannosaurus Rex set, remembering that he'd had his eye on it for months, calling it "the most anatomically-correct Lego version of a prehistoric lifeform ever." *Proof.* They'd spend hours in bed together, kissing and laughing, then play Trivial Pursuit: '90s Edition under the covers by the light of their phones. Significant *proof.* He'd put himself out there for the comedy of it all, purposefully wetting the bed on *his* side, so she'd finally feel like she wasn't the only one whose life had been affected by bladder baggage.

Proof. But awkward, over-the-top kind of proof.

Sometimes, they sat quietly together, saying nothing for hours. Sitting on her couch, or on his Friheten, scrolling through their phones, listening to music, periodically glancing over at the other person just to know they were there. It was comfortable. It was calming. And it felt right.

Until one Sunday morning, it *didn't.*

It started with a sock.

It was light-blue, bordering on turquoise, with a jagged white stripe. There was a subtle mesh that extended down and around the ankle, for what the relentlessly targeted Facebook ads claimed could both prevent the festering "plantar fasciitis" as well as the infamous, yet never-before-heard-of *gardener's thoe*. It was currently fully encasing Maggie's right foot, which Josh eyed from his side of the couch, as it wiggled back and forth from underneath the Vinkelfly she'd grabbed to keep warm. There was something about the foot inside of the sock. It was *cute*. Or maybe Josh was just sweet on Maggie, so any affection he felt for her was easily assigned to her exposed appendages. He didn't know quite why he was, in that moment, so drawn to it, but he was.

So, he squeezed it. A small, insignificant, affectionate squeeze.

Maggie looked down at her foot, then regarded the Friheten she and Josh were sharing. She eyed him. His place on the couch. Looked back down at her own foot. Then she shivered. Not a cold shiver, but the kind that was often followed by a masked man and a butcher knife coming through your sliding glass door. She got up quickly, pushing the Vinkelfly aside, and moved into the kitchen where she uncharacteristically rifled through the fridge for a drink. Once there, she found a beer, cracking it open, then sat down at the table staring at the open bottle.

It was Sunday morning. Eggs, sure. Coffee, OK. Smoothies, maybe. But beer?

Josh turned around from the Friheten. "It's always five o'clock somewhere?" he joked, referring to the Corona Light she lifted up, taking a swig. "Are you okay?"

She sat, catatonic. Staring.

Without a response, Josh moved into the kitchen, sitting opposite her. He reached out and touched her arm, which she quickly pulled back. She couldn't look him in the eyes. "Maggie," he said. "What the hell is it?"

She peered into Josh's clueless yet concerned eyes. "Not *what*," she said to Josh, taking another sip of her early morning breakfast beer, which seemed to momentarily pull her out of her head. "More like who."

"Who?" he said, turning rigid. "What do you mean, *who*?"

She took a breath. "Gabriel Marchand," she said, cringing.

Fuck, Josh thought. *Gabriel Marchand*. His imagination started to spin, and spin *hard*.

Gabriel Marchand, heir to a fortune that had been tallied at almost four billion the last time *Fortune* magazine had made one of those lists. *Gabriel* Marchand, the Ferrari-sponsored French race car driver who had won *Le Mans* over sixteen times, beating his longtime rival Francois Belleguile by rounding the corner and winning the race on, get this, *four* flat tires! Gabriel *Marchand*, the son of the creative business mind behind Perrier sparkling water, croissants stuffed with chocolate, and the motorized scooters you could find littering the streets of every major metropolis in North America. Gabriel Marchand ... that *asshole*, Josh thought, actually knowing nothing about him but feeling perfectly able to make up the stories about his fictitious lives as they raced through his head. *Who was he? Had Maggie found someone new?* Maybe Josh should have never shared that popcorn in the first place; what if the sharing of the popcorn had been the catalyst for Maggie finding someone new? He visualized Maggie standing over him as he set his new lock screen on his phone. Had he moved too fast? Had he missed the signs? *Fuck.* You never put someone on your phone as the lock screen until you were really, truly, exponentially serious.

"That beer is liquid courage, is that it?" Josh asked, nervous.

"Liquid courage … for what?" Maggie asked.

"So, you can tell me that …" he began, not wanting to say it, "… you're seeing someone else."

She laughed. A pretty sizeable one. "No," she said, insulted. "I'm not seeing someone else. Gabriel was someone I dated when I was working abroad in Paris. Right after college."

"And he's turned his Olympic Gold medals into a commentator job at one of the networks out here in Hollywood, is that it?" he said, trying to crunch the numbers. "And you ran into him and all those feelings came rushing back?" Josh's manic spin cycle gave Maggie a moment to take a deep breath, her shoulders coming down as her body relaxed.

"He was my first love," Maggie said.

She laid it out. How she'd fallen for him hard. How she'd opened her heart, sharing every intimate part of herself with the amateur pub owner slash wine connoisseur slash lifeguard. How he'd said the words; the ones that reciprocated the ones she'd said. That things, for a long clip, had been wonderful, almost magical. The magic lasted for exactly a year, until the three hundred and sixty-sixth day jumped up and bit her in the ass.

"One day I came home to my flat to find him packing up all his things," she said, remembering the painful moment. "When he saw me, there was no emotion. No apologetic look on his face. He was completely unemotional. Matter-of-fact. He told me he was leaving, and that was that."

"Because?"

"*Just because*," Maggie explained. There had been no other woman, no terminal disease, no visa issues. None of it. "He'd literally just woken up that morning and decided it was time to move on. I don't think I got out of bed for a month. Paris took on this negative aura everywhere I looked. A place I'd once dreamed of was now a nightmare. Around that time I vowed never to return to that godforsaken place ever again."

Josh did the math in his head. It still wasn't adding up. Why was Maggie bringing him up now, especially if she wasn't seeing him, missing him, or longing for him? Why was Gabriel Marchand, the lifeguard who saved an entire family of homeless Londoners from drowning in the English Channel, coming up now?

"You touched my foot," Maggie volunteered, then looked away.

I touched your foot, he let roll around in his head. They were having a serious conversation about loves lost and found because he ...

"You're scared of getting hurt again," Josh said, finally understanding as he got up and pulled a second Corona Light from the fridge. "Is that what's going on here?"

"Maybe," she said, looking embarrassed.

"Well," he began, "maybe Tina Moretti was *my* Gabriel Marchand."

"Tina Moretti?"

He sat back, taking a sip of the beer. "We were close friends," he began, reminiscing. His eyes looked up to the ceiling. "I liked her, I did. I think subconsciously maybe I did feel some kind of a connection with her. But that wasn't what I was shooting for when I asked her out that night. It wasn't supposed to be a big deal. But then, there we were, out together at the movies, and I ... I ... *Fuck*, I'll never forget that night."

Maggie listened, looking horrified. "What did you *do*?" she asked.

"I shared my popcorn with her."

Maggie cocked her head. "I'm sorry?" she said, not getting it.

"She took that generosity as a sign of me wanting to be serious with her. She even went to school the next day and told everyone we were boyfriend and girlfriend. It was horribly embarrassing. People laughed. It took me weeks to convince all the kids that she had interpreted this insignificant thing as a desire for something bigger. But the bottom line was that I'd crossed a line and things went sideways. That relationship, the friendship, it imploded all because of a small, insignificant gesture that I should have never made in the first place."

"How old were you when this happened?" she asked, still unpacking it all.

"I was five. It was kindergarten. Still, what I'm trying to say is ..."

"*Five*?" she almost blew a gasket, then cackled. "How can you compare my heartbreaking, depression-causing PTSD relationship trauma to that?"

"Love does not care if you are five, fifteen, or fifty," he said, insulted.

"No, love *does* care," she said, matter-of-fact.

"My point?" he threw out, waiting for her to nod for him to continue. "Back then, I accidentally shared some popcorn with a girl and she thought I had fallen for her. But when I touched your foot," he said, seeing her start to come around, "I did it on purpose because I wanted you to know that I already have."

"Well, shit," she said, taking one deep swig of the beer. "You're just as crazy as me."

Eighteen

AT THE AGE OF fifteen, Brian Epstein divorced his parents.

The night he told them of his plans was a sticky, humid Floridian night. The sound of crickets buzzed through the open back door, lending a soundtrack to the moment, as Brian sat down in the overstuffed corduroy couch and explained to his parents in the most respectful, eloquent way just why it was going to have to be this way.

"You're horrible, unmotivated, intellectually immature parents and I could do better on my own," he said, clearly missing the emotional intelligence chip that allowed for normal people to let others down with respect and care. But all he could think of, in the moment, was that the couch was covered in allergy-inducing dog hair, his father would never have a job of any true significance, and that his five years of paper delivery savings ($12,560) was more than enough to get him out to the West Coast where he could start his new chapter free of these down-home, back-woods chains.

They would mutter something about doing the best they could, and his mother would attempt to pull him in for an embrace, but there was already a duffel by the front door, a behemoth-sized sandwich wrapped in a brown paper bag by his side, and a taxi in the alleyway honking out back.

At the age of twenty-three, Brian Epstein would break up with his hair stylist Phoebe, after eight stylish years together.

They had been through a lot. The relationship had lasted the test of time and the ever-changing landscape of barbicide. With her as his guide, his hairs had experienced the crew cut and the pompadour and the undercut and the quaff and the side part and the fringe and the man bun and even the bowl cut. He spent most of his time in the chair talking about his work and the women he was dating and contemplating if that new copy editor job at *The 818* would be the right thing to do. He talked about his hopes and his dreams for a long career in the world of locally sourced, nationally relevant, Gen-Y journalism. Every once in a while, the topics turned to more serious subjects like split ends, hair loss, and scalpish skin tags. Once in a blue moon, she'd do what most of her clients wished she would do but which wasn't a part of the job: she'd trim his eyebrows out of the goodness of her heart.

But when it came time to break up with her, he was still clearly missing that chip.

"The bottom line is you never have anything interesting or insightful to say," he had said, as she was cleaning up the back of his neck with an electric hair trimmer. "You're also just mediocre at your craft. Every time I walk past the Paul Mitchell hair college at the mall and see the work those fake hair stylists are doing on those fake mannequin heads, I wonder why their fake is better than your real."

She would mutter something about doing the best she could, and attempt to pull him in for an embrace after she'd applied the requisite fiber paste, but he had already covertly paid for the bill, snagged a handful of Oreos off the complimentary food table, and had an Uber sitting outside waiting for him to bolt.

And so, it was no surprise, at the age of forty-eight, Brian Epstein would sling a similarly honest yet completely inappropriate set of words at Maggie, as she stood over his desk, staring at a pile of the photos she'd taken at her last three shoots. The last three shoots that represented a dream in the works, a moment in time she had desperately hoped to experience. His feedback would mean the difference between a career she had fallen into and a career she wanted in on.

"You suck, kid," he said, looking like he'd worn to work whatever he'd worn to bed. "I could hire a monkey to take pictures and they'd look better than these."

Somewhere in the background, "the monkey" cleared his throat. Maggie turned to see someone she'd never met before sitting on his couch, camera gear at his feet, listening awkwardly from where he sat. "Stringer," Brian threw out, lending some 411 to the awkward scenario at hand. The stringer waved sheepishly.

"You're certifiable," Maggie said, fighting back emotion with pure force. She picked up a few of the photos and put them directly in front of him. "You can't tell me these aren't solid shots. The depth, the composition, the lighting?" Brian was already over this whole thing, half looking at a page of text, half eating something questionable out of an old Chinese food container. "Brian!" she said firmly, trying to get his attention.

"I'm gonna go use the bathroom," said the monkey, getting up and leaving the room.

Brian looked down his nose, through his glasses, at Maggie, then picked up one of the pictures she'd shoved under his nose. He stared at it. Shook his head. Stared at it some more. Then turned it around and placed it gingerly at the other edge of the table, on Maggie's side. "Nope," he said. "We're not some artistic, hoity-toity rag looking for award-winning photography. I don't care about depth or composition. I'm looking for serviceable photos that complement but don't overshadow the writing! C'mon, Mags. You had your chance. We had an agreement. You said you'd leave this alone if I wasn't feeling it."

"Give me another chance," she pleaded, grabbing onto Brian's arm in the most unaffectionate way possible. He pulled it back, bothered, smoothing out his sleeve. "I'll be more pedestrian! Boring! Is that it? Is that what you want?"

"You've missed the point completely," he said, spinning around to find an old coffee cup that still had some liquid left. He tried it, made a face, then poured it out into the garbage.

Maggie was spinning. "This was my dream," she said, quietly, then reiterated. "This has always been my dream. Being a photographer. Can't you just—?"

"Sometimes dreams don't pay the bills, Mills," he said, appearing pleased with the rhyme. "But what does pay your bills is writing restaurant reviews. Ones for restaurants that don't occupy the same space as furniture dollies. So. Do you think you can find some of that dream juice to keep writing those pieces? I guarantee you, those will pay your bills."

Maggie was tearing up. She didn't want to tear up. *Fuck no*, she thought in her head, *don't give this asshole the pleasure. Suck it up*, she said to herself, breathing deeply and letting out a long, audible *swoosh*. Meanwhile, the monkey returned, saw Maggie's face, then turned right back around and left the room.

"I could've handled it," she said, gathering her photos into a clean stack.

Brian looked up, nodding. Placating.

Maggie picked up her stack of photos and exited the office. She walked quickly to her desk, grabbing her purse, and headed toward the elevator where she rapidly pushed the down arrow button. You know, *that* down arrow button.

She waited. And waited. And waited some more.

She wanted to cry. But she didn't want to cry here. She wanted to call someone. But who could she call? Should she call her parents? *No, they'd just worry and suggest moving back home to Chicago*, she thought. What about Cameron? *No, she'd always warned her against pursuing photography as a career.* She needed to talk to someone who would listen, hear where she was coming from, who understood her and could help her figure out what she was going to do next. She was surprised when his face popped up in her head, then (pleasantly) not surprised at all.

She pulled out her phone, scrolled to the J's, and dialed Josh's number.

Josh was standing at the real podium, doing a faux speech.

Around him, Technology Through the Ages stretched from wall to wall, stunning visuals wrapping around the antique technologies that had been secured for the exhibit. There were televisions, record players, automobiles, video games, computers, cameras, military technology, and more. Josh looked down to where the audience would be, facing Diana. She watched him, squinting as he practiced his speech, taking it all in as his cell phone buzzed from his pocket. He reached for it, declining the call without looking.

"'People will forget what you said, people will forget what you did, but people will never forget how you made them feel,'" Diana proclaimed, her voice echoing throughout the hall. "Maya Angelou," she finished up, adding a dramatic period to the quote.

"And what exactly would you like me to make them feel?" Josh asked.

Diana stepped toward him, reaching the edge of the stage and whispering up to him at the podium. "I would like you to make them feel generous," she smiled. "This facility runs on generosity and the dollars that come with such emotions."

Josh stepped down to her level, making a mental note. Calling out the board members and the trustees and the donations they had already made to the exhibit would help. A particularly heartwarming story and a potential ugly cry could do wonders as well.

"Is everything absolutely buttoned up for Friday?" Diana asked.

"We're good," Josh replied, feeling his phone vibrate again, this time taking it out to look and spotting Maggie's name on the screen. "Everything's buttoned up."

"Do you need to get that?" Diana asked, referencing the phone.

Josh rolled his eyes. He did. He held up his finger, then picked up the phone. "Hi, I'm in the middle of …" he said, then her voice cut through it all. She was upset, crying uncontrollably, trying to get the words out but barely making sense. Josh had never heard her this way before. The words "I need you" were just about all he could hear, and all he needed to hear. "Okay," he said quickly. "I'm on my way."

He hung up the phone, turning to Diana. "Maggie?" she asked.

"Maggie," he confirmed. "I need to …"

Diana didn't need to know. She waved him off. "Go," she directed him. "But when you come back there's some unfinished business I need to talk to you about."

Josh had turned to bolt, then stopped dead in his tracks. He looked to her, concerned.

"It's good," she said, smiling. "Really good."

It was really bad.

Maggie's face was swollen, with tissue remnants hanging from various orifices. She had changed her work top into a stained Boston U sweatshirt, but was still wearing her work bottoms. One shoe was off, with the sock only, the other still on. The minute she opened the door, she turned, hobbling toward the center of her living room like the Hunchback of Notre Dame, as the tears began streaming yet again. She collapsed on the floor in the center of what some might have confused for a sacrifice ritual, with candles and pictures everywhere. Even her latest scrapbook ("13"), as delivered by her mother the previous week, sat open by her feet, like she'd been taking a depressing look back at when things had been more innocent and fulfilling.

Josh closed the door, standing over her as she wept from the center of it all. "What's wrong?" he said, kneeling down next to her, her left eye twitching like it was sending a message via Morse Code. He picked up a stack of tissues that had been ripped out of the pink cardboard box and handed them to her. "Maggie, what is it?"

She waved her arms, pointing aimlessly at the stacks of pictures all around her, then started crying again uncontrollably. She caught her reflection in the flat-screen TV, only to remember flashbacks to some of her other greatest ugly cries. There was the first time she'd dropped a perfectly good ice cream cone on the ground at the age of four. The time she found herself all alone at home during the night of her junior prom. There was Gabriel Marchand. And a moment that felt awfully similar because the locations were the same: the time her camera had been stolen on moving day and Maggie sat here in the once-unfurnished apartment trying to figure out how she'd ever break the news.

"Brian said my work ..." she pointed to the pictures, "... sucked," she huffed. "He's not going to give me the job."

Josh sat down opposite her. She looked at him, pleading. "Aw, shit. I'm so sorry," he said. "I know how much this meant to you, and trust me when I tell you that I know how much it sucks when the dream doesn't land the way you imagined it would."

"It sucks big time," she said, sniffling. "It was my one chance." She looked up to him, eyes swollen, then wiped her nose with her sleeve.

Josh looked down around his feet, where all the photos Maggie had taken were spread out. He picked up a handful, flipping through them one by one. Josh's face transitioned from "between a rock and a hard place" to "suddenly surprised."

"What?" Maggie said. "You hate them, don't you?"

Josh looked around at the other pictures on the floor.

"You're a great writer," he said, the words acting as a shiny object to focus on.

"Answer the question," she said, pleading.

"What do you want me to tell you?"

"The truth."

"Your pictures," he began, clearly choosing his words carefully, "leave something to be desired."

Maggie's ugly cry became five times more ludicrous than her worst historical ugly cry. She collapsed back onto the floor, her arms and legs moving back and forth like she was making a snow angel in the pile of pictures. As she did so, some of the cringe-worthy photos gave way to stacks of others Josh hadn't seen before. They were Maggie's test shots. The ones that had mostly been of the food, the craft service tables, her morning croissant. Josh's eyes widened as he reached around her and plucked them from the floor. He held up a shot of grapefruits, one of a chocolate croissant.

"What are those?" she said, sitting up, the waterworks slowing.

"You tell me," Josh replied.

She grabbed them. "Just some test shots," she said, disregarding them.

"These are good, Maggie," Josh complimented, picking up the ones she'd discarded and finding a few more buried in the pile at his feet. "These are really good. These, I like." He threw them at her, smiling. She picked them up, her eyes widening to get a better look. She wasn't sure.

"Who says you have to take pictures of people? You could take pictures of food."

"A food photographer?" Maggie said, as the light bulb went off in her head.

The memories flooded back. The moment when her father had given her the Nikon SP, the weeks and months that followed as she tromped around the house taking pictures of everything. When she had graduated from pictures of people and animals, she recalled sitting in the kitchen taking pictures of the fruit bowl, the meals her mother would make, boxes of cereal and bowls of ice cream. "You should take the pictures for the boxes in the supermarket," her mother had said, making Maggie feel proud. "For the magazines, too." It was strange how memories came and went, only to resurface when they were poked and prodded. Only to rush back, along with the accompanying emotion, at a future moment in time. The floodgates opened for Maggie. She remembered then and it made everything clear for her now.

"A food photographer," she said, with no question in her mind. "How could I have not seen it?" She pulled herself closer to Josh, looking him deep in the eyes. "How did you?"

"It was right there in front of you the whole time," he smiled.

Maggie looked down as a thought hit her, then looked back up with an even bigger smile. "What?" Josh asked. Maggie adjusted her posture, swinging her right foot to the front and positioning it on Josh's lap.

"Go ahead," she said. "Do it."

Josh reached out, touched her foot, and leaned in to kiss Maggie. She wrapped her hands around him tightly as the two kissed, arms reaching, breath heaving. But in the midst of it all, as things started to heat up even more, Josh's eyes shifted. Maggie sensed something was up, pulling back. "What is it?" she asked, concerned.

Josh reached past her, sliding the scrapbook toward them. It was opened to the two pages with the header "Niagara Falls." There, in the center of the second page, was a picture. It was a picture of Maggie, at age thirteen, sarcastically smiling at the camera. And next to her? A teenager dressed up in Civil War garb, clearly embarrassed that he had been forced to dress up in an outfit that was now being memorialized forever in some other family's photo album. Ironically, that exact photo album was now right in front of them.

"That's me," Josh said, stunned. "And that's you."

It was strange how memories came and went, only to resurface when they were poked and prodded. Only to rush back, along with the accompanying emotion, at a future moment in time.

Maggie stared at Josh, looked down at the picture, looked back up. "Stop screwing around," she said, unbelieving.

"I'm not screwing around," he said, pulling out his phone and opening the photo application. He scrolled back to the albums that held some of the ancient childhood pictures he had scanned and imported back in his *Throwback Thursday* phase. He turned the phone to Maggie to show her. It was a picture of Josh, dressed up in the Civil War outfit, posing with his parents during the same Niagara Falls trip. It was *him*. He was *there*. They had met before.

"Your mother made you wear that outfit," Maggie remembered.

"You were sarcastic and acerbic that day," Josh recalled.

"You knew a lot about apple butter," Maggie added, slowly remembering.

"You pretended to know a lot about *a lot*," Josh grinned.

There was a long silence. The two taking each other in, passing the picture back and forth so they could further examine the evidence. It was spiritual, universal evidence. It was confirmation that the feelings they were having, the connection they had felt, the thing they couldn't put their finger on, was, in actuality, something that had been growing since they had been kids. Since they had met for the first time. It was absolutely mind-blowing. And also?

It was *proof*.

"That *was* you," Maggie said, eyes wide.

"This explains a lot," Josh agreed. Maggie put aside the scrapbook. He put down his phone. And they embraced.

Because when you realize it was meant to be, nothing could stand in your way.

Nineteen

WHEN BERTRAM SÖHM WAS twenty years old, he would say goodbye to the Hochschule für Technik und Wirtschaft and transfer to UCLA in order to continue his college education in the States.

It's not that the HTW in Berlin was a bad school. In fact, it was one of the largest public universities in Eastern Germany, with engineering and computer science programs that rivaled the best around. But Bertram had dreams of working in aerospace, and the civil engineering major, plus the proximity to JPL NASA in Pasadena, was a plus. And trading in the "perfectly mediocre weather" of Berlin for the barely wavering seventy-two degrees of California was one of the perks he was willing to accept, nay embrace.

The fact that UCLA held an annual Oktoberfest celebration was another.

Diana Rowland had been nursing the same beer for hours, due to the fact that it was housed in a glass stein about the size of her five-foot-six torso. There was music and dancing and the usual requisite chaos that was necessary for an Oktoberfest to be considered successful, and she sat completely content to watch it all unfold from the safety of her seat at the edge of the beer garden. Bertram had been watching her from the other side of the long wooden table for at least thirty minutes, wondering if she had transferred to UCLA just like him. Usually, it was the foreign transfer students who found their way to Oktoberfest during those first few weeks, longing for some flavor of European tradition and hoping to meet others who were doing the same. So, it wasn't strange or awkward, in Bertram's mind, to slide down and make his move. In German.

"*Kommst du oft hierher*?" he asked, wondering if she'd come here before.

Diana looked up, surprised. Her eyes glowed, her hair long and lustrous. Ironically, despite all the years that would eventually go by, the chasm between college-aged Diana and Science Center Diana would not be that huge. Her spirit and her demeanor, and her proclivity and passion for language, science, history, art, and literature, would never not be a part of her.

She smiled a bright, engaging smile. "*Es ist erst mein zweites Mal*," she replied in perfect German, responding that it was only her second time.

"*Du kommst aus Deutschland, wie ich*?" he nodded, asking if she was from Germany, just like him.

"I'm American," she said, flashing a flirty smile, then taking an impressive swig of her beer. "But I've always wanted to go."

"Perhaps that is something we could accomplish together," he said in English, sliding marginally closer to her at the edge of the bench.

"That's awfully presumptuous of you," Diana shot back.

He looked at the huge stein of beer she had made nary a dent in, tapping it with his hand. "As was *this*, of you," he said, referring to her lack of progress.

"I had to buy one or they wouldn't let me sit in the beer garden and people watch," she replied, sheepishly. "I could never drink it all."

"And are you enjoying the watching of the people?" he asked, smiling. Ah, that smile. It was the smile that always secured Bertram his morning coffee for free, and it would be the smile that would ensnare Diana's interest now and forever more. Bertram took a swig of his beer, tapped the glass, and said, "'You can do what you have to do, and sometimes you can do it even better than you think you can.'"

"Did you just make that up?" she asked, impressed.

"No," he replied, winding up with the answer. "Jimmy Carter did."

Diana smiled.

She was smitten.

Diana sat behind her desk, hands folded atop a stack of papers. She was bouncing in her seat with enthusiasm, staring at Josh who sat opposite her. *Whenever she looked this happy,* Josh thought, *there was another powder blue Manolo Blahnik somewhere, getting ready to drop.* He cleared his throat, feeling generally uneasy as she looked him up and down.

"Well, Winnfield," she said, lightening up the mood, "it's all come down to this."

"It's all come down to … what?" Josh normally would have thrown out a Vega retort, but his head was somewhere else entirely. He wanted to know what was going on. He waited for Diana, always the consummate professional when it came to dramatic pauses and ellipses, only to have the moment disrupted by his vibrating phone, perched on the edge of her desk. The screen lit up, showcasing Josh's recent wallpaper change, with him, Maggie, and a partial view of Robyn. Diana glanced over to the phone as Josh pocketed it and refocused his attention.

"You sat in that chair almost ten years ago," she continued. "You did what any intelligent, driven student of science would do in the face of failure and rejection. You looked outside of yourself, identified new pathways and opportunities for success, and barreled down that road without ever looking back. But like many scientists, you let your surroundings lull you into a false sense of security. You became complacent, Josh. And you know how I abhor that word."

"This is a wonderfully inspiring pep talk, so far," Josh said, sarcastic. "May I say that your management style leaves something to be desired?"

Diana removed her folded hands from the papers on her desk, picking up the stapled stack and handing it over to Josh. "The anthropologist Margaret Mead once said, 'The notion that we are products of our environment is our greatest sin; we are products of our choices.' With that in mind, I made a choice for you ... because I knew you would never make it on your own."

Josh looked down at the stack of papers. At the top, in a gold-embossed circular logo, was the lowercase letter *e*. And next to it, the letters ESA, spelled out to read European Space Agency. It was an application. It had already been filled out. Josh flipped through the pages, handwritten with perfect penmanship, with a flowery recommendation page written by Diana, work experience, and examples of what he'd been doing at the Science Center. "What is this for?" he asked, half stunned.

"For a Lead Project Engineering role at the European Space Agency," she said, eyes wide with anticipation. "Working on the team responsible for their unmanned exploration missions; working alongside team members from all twenty-two partner countries at their headquarters in Paris."

Paris, France?

"I ... I ..." Josh didn't know what to say. "I don't know what to say. Did I mention that I don't know what to say?" He was spinning.

"Say *thank you*," she replied, "and then mark down on your calendar Wednesday at three o'clock, because that's when the in-person interview with Bertram Söhm will be."

"Bertram Söhm?"

"Director General of the Agency," she clarified.

Josh could feel Diana's gaze burning a hole through his head like a superhero gone rogue, as he mindlessly opened and closed the paperwork. "It's not JPL, I know," Diana said. "But if you ask me, it's better."

"It's in Paris." Paris was not Pasadena. Paris was nowhere near Maggie. His mind raced. He thought about the night before. The picture that had revealed they had known each other far longer than they had ever imagined. The way he felt about her. He didn't want to abandon the kind of progress they had made with each other just for the prospects of a new job. *But it's not just a new job, he'd think to himself.* It was a new opportunity. A new chapter. A way to accomplish the goals he had always dreamed of. But it was in Paris. *Fuck,* he thought. *What am I going to do?*

"*Paree,*" she said, pronouncing it with the correct Frenchness, "is significantly better than Pasadena, wouldn't you say? Don't misunderstand me, Old Pasadena is perfectly charming, but it can't hold a candle to the Louvre. Or Notre Dame. Or the Arc." She sat back in her chair, taking a sip of her tea. But Josh looked unsure. Because he *was.* In a big way. Maybe he'd gotten too comfortable, too used to his environment like Diana had pointed out. Maybe all these years of settling had finally extinguished the passion he had for his dreams. Maybe the recent developments with Maggie had made all of that seem OK, because he finally had something in his life that made him feel accomplished. Was he making excuses for himself? Was he trying to justify making no changes in his life? Was he afraid?

"Isn't this still your dream?" Diana asked, interrupting his stream of consciousness.

He thought for a moment. Deep down, the child was still inside. Still wide-eyed and passionate about all things dinosaurs and outer space and the infinite universe. That child still got excited each and every day he rolled up to the Science Center. Each time he got to sit in the cockpit of *Endeavor.* Each time he looked up at the night sky. It was still his dream. He just never thought he'd ever have the chance at realizing it.

He'd given up.

"It is," he said, feeling guilty as hell the second after the words came out of his mouth.

"Then stop moping in my office and go," she pressured. "It's just a meeting. You're not committing to anything." Josh seemed a little more comfortable. "Just relax and be yourself. That's all Bertram needs to see."

I'm not committing to anything, he said to himself. *It's just a meeting,* he justified. It seemed reasonable. There was nothing wrong with having a conversation, right? Seeing what he had to say? People always said that you took meetings no matter what, because you never knew what could come from them. No one could fault him for that.

Josh got up, tucking the papers into his back pocket and pushing the guest chair back in place. "And when you see him, do me one favor?" Diana said. Josh turned back, waiting.

"Tell him I said *'Ich vermisse dich'*—he'll know what that means."

Josh nodded, writing it down, then exited into the hall, taking a deep breath.

Just a meeting. Not a big deal.

Maggie wouldn't even have to know.

Josh was wearing a suit.

Even after all these years, it still fit him like a glove. It may not have been as fashion-forward as it had been the day he'd interviewed with Diana for the Science Center position, but anything that fit a man ten years prior was always an instance worth celebrating. He moved casually from the valet roundabout, in through the shaded front lounge, and out toward the doors that opened up to the outside dining balcony, which overlooked the Pacific Ocean. Bertram had asked to meet there.

Josh looked out the doors of the Loews Hotel, scanning the outside dining area. For three in the afternoon it was empty, hovering between the late lunchtime crowd and the early afternoon alcoholics. And there, sitting alone, looking like a modern-day hybrid of Freud meets Steve Jobs, was Bertram. He'd clearly been rejoicing in the Southern California weather, wearing a flowing white linen shirt, a pair of khaki shorts, sunglasses, and a hip pair of Nike flip-flops.

And Josh was wearing a suit. *Overdressed*, he said to himself, judgmental.

Bertram looked up as Josh exited the doors to the outside dining area, getting up himself as Josh approached. He was a genial, friendly man with kind eyes who reached out to shake Josh's hand, motioning for Josh to join him at the table where a huge basket of warm bread had already landed. "Look at this wonderful bread," Bertram proclaimed.

Josh sat down. "Diana Rowland says *ich germisse dich*," he said, feeling proud, unknowingly replacing the "v" in *vermisse* with a "g" instead. "They were only two letters apart," he'd defend later when he'd recounted the horribly funny, psycho-themed message he had actually delivered instead.

"You are stalking me?" Bertram asked, confused, yet accurately translating the mistake.

It's only a meeting, Josh said to himself, trying to lessen the embarrassing blow.

They laughed. They talked. They spoke, *in the same language*, about science and space travel, about engineering and astrophysics, about their matched passions for the unknown. Bertram laid out the position, an exciting opportunity to be a part of something groundbreaking. To be a part of something that was, literally, out of this world. When all was said and done, it felt as if they had talked for hours. In reality, it had only been forty-five minutes.

It could have been five minutes. It didn't much matter. Because when it was time for Josh to leave, as he got back into his car, he felt guilty as hell.

Paris.

It was a long shot anyway. Why worry?

Maggie's morning ritual was *en fuego*.

She was moving a mile a minute, like Belle on speed, consistently five steps ahead of Josh as he struggled to keep up. But she was excited and she couldn't contain it. Life had possibilities now that it hadn't presented before. She had been so jazzed that she had sent twenty-eight e-mails, made thirty-nine calls, and had fourteen conversations about her potential new career direction, and that had all been in the last two and a half hours.

"*Bonjour!*" she'd announce to the barista at Le Pain Quotidien, who handed her an espresso noisette over the counter. Josh would cringe, not only at the word, but at his entire surroundings … the epitome of a Parisian café, replete with barrels filled with fresh French bread, adorably beautiful fruit tarts, and servers periodically prattling on to each other in terse French phrases. It made him ill. What in the hell was the universe trying to tell him?

"And there's nothing preventing me from leveraging my relationships with the people in the food industry who I'm close with," Maggie excitedly relayed to Josh as they entered the neighborhood deli, where she high-fived the clerk and pulled down a chocolate croissant in a brown paper bag. Maggie held it up in Josh's face, taunting him. "Would you like some of my croissant?" she said, enunciating the French accent.

What are you trying to say? Josh would lash out at the infinite universe, who was toying with his finite patience.

"So I keep working at *The 818* and see if I can build up the photography business, and at some point when I can't do both, that's when I pull the trigger and go full-agro pro," Maggie explained to Josh, showing off the list of to-do's she had generated in her phone's Notes app the night before, then snagging her green drink from the owner at the Juice Den. "There are so many restaurants in Los Angeles," she continued, as they walked back onto the street, "that there's a real opportunity for growth. Henry Louton, the general manager of Treat, already called me to say he thinks he might have a gig for me. Bottom line? I am in the perfect place for the next chapter in my life."

Yes. Los Angeles. The perfect place … for her next chapter … in *her* life.

Josh swallowed.

It was the universe's fault that Josh felt kind of sick.

Josh and Maggie sat on the curb, out in front of Good News.

She flipped through multiple magazines. There were the food magazines with the glossy, professional photos. There were the photography magazines, with the glossy, professional tutorials on photographing food. There was an *US Weekly*, oft considered the junk food of the publication world, reminding Josh on a weekly basis that the celebrities he often saw were *just ... like ... him*. Josh sat, trying to stay focused and present, but his thoughts kept rising back up.

"Celebrities are *just like you*," Maggie said, holding up an *US Weekly* double-page spread on actors who had found their soulmates on the movie sets of Hollywood. Josh regarded the pages, flashed a polite smile, then looked back to the road ahead where cars passed by in droves. Maggie eyed him, seemingly sensing something off, then reached into her purse and pulled out the picture. Yes, that picture. The picture of the two of them at Niagara Falls.

She held it out in front of them. "What do you think this means?" she asked.

Josh eyed the photo. There was no denying the fact that it was wild. Stunning, in fact. That they had met so long ago only to have reconnected so many years later. Did it mean they belonged together? Did it mean they were soulmates? Did it mean the universe had willed it? But had it been the universe at play, then why had it seen fit to put him in a suit, down by the beach, talking about a job that he would have jumped at had it materialized just months ago?

"If *my* dad were here right now, he'd say that we were clearly supposed to meet again. He might even say that we were soulmates, fated to be together since the dawn of time. Or thirteen and fifteen, respectively," he qualified.

"If my dad were here right now," Maggie said, eyeing the picture more closely, "he would have called it a strange coincidence and nothing more. He'd tell me to stop overthinking and focus on making the best decisions for me."

While Josh couldn't admit it, there was something about her father's logic that made sense, too.

Maggie looked to Josh, smiling. "We disagree with both of our fathers, don't we?"

"Maybe we should just agree on what we think," Josh said, taking the picture and giving it an extra close look. It was undeniable. Maybe he agreed more with his own father. "Maybe the past doesn't matter, truly," he continued. "Maybe all that matters is that we met now."

"I think we met now," she said, winding up for a joke, "because you didn't take my advice then about your fashion sense or your inability to stand up to your mother."

"We may never know," he said.

"Oh, we know," she smiled. "I know."

Josh smiled, then thought more deeply. "We don't seem to change much over the course of our lives, despite thinking we do," he realized. "You and I? We're still dealing with the same issues we had back then."

"With one exception," she pointed out, garnering his glance in her direction. "I'm here. And you're there. And maybe that'll make all the difference."

"Do you think?" Josh wondered.

"I vowed to never reference *Dirty Dancing*," she said, "but I've never felt like this before."

Josh sat back, hands on the sidewalk behind him. "Do you swear it's the truth, and you owe it all to me?"

"Ask Bill Medley," she laughed. "They're his words." She snapped the picture back from Josh's hands, then grabbed the magazines under her arm. "Just promise me one thing, okay, buddy?"

"What's that?" he said, pulling his keys out of his pocket.

"Don't ever become a Gabriel Marchand," she said, turning the French name into an expletive. "Because if you do, I'll kill ya."

Josh gulped. "Noted."

Twenty

THE BELLEVUE FIRE DEPARTMENT was on the scene.

Jane Anderson stood on the front grass of her suburban two-story house, rain pouring down on her, which would normally have been a really great thing had she called about a fire. But this wasn't a fire. This was something far more unexplainable. No one was wounded, as far as she could tell, and no one was having a heart attack or needed any jaws of any life at all. It was just that her twelve-year-old son, Bruce, was kind of, generally, awkwardly indisposed.

"He's, uh, trapped in his room," Jane would say to the 911 dispatcher when she called.

"And the door to this bedroom is locked, ma'am?" the dispatcher would ask, confirming.

"No, the door is unlocked."

"And you can't get in? Is he holding it shut? Is he a teenager?" the dispatcher would ask, clearly not a stranger to the adolescent annoyances that often came across the line.

"Yes, he's a teenager. And no, he's not holding it shut."

"Ma'am, I'm unclear of what the issue is then, exactly."

The issue, of course, was that Bruce had grown up with a penchant for collecting things. For gathering items of questionable historical significance or value. For riding his bike aimlessly in the suburban neighborhoods behind Bellevue and Issaquah and Redmond, and coming home with a backpack filled with things that used to have value, and were now simply junk. The problem with junk, of course, was that when you piled it high, it would all eventually come crashing down. And if you were as unlucky as Bruce, it would block your bedroom door and trap you under a broken '70s-era air hockey game, a folded ping pong table from South Korea, and twelve Ziploc bags filled with over a thousand Matchbox cars.

Yes, it had been just like the James Franco film *127 Hours*, yet for Bruce, it had only been twenty-seven minutes when the axe came crashing through his door.

"I'm not a hoarder," he would tell his mother and father later that day, after he'd been rescued from within his own personal Jenga-fied hell. "I'm a collector. And collectors get rich."

"If you're lucky," his father would say, having just walked through the door at the end of the day and at his wits' end with the crap piling up in the garage, "you'll make between sixteen and twenty-six dollars per hour … as a collector of garbage."

The Bellevue Fire Department would need that axe to get through, as simply taking the door off the hinges wouldn't do the trick. And as they chopped away to try and make their way through, Bruce would scream from the inside for them to hack anywhere they wanted except for the upper right corner of the doorjamb. Because that's where, lodged at a strange angle, and still mint, new-in-box, was the famous '70s-era TRS-80, the most well-known computer of its time.

Someday, of course, just like Bruce, it would have its own fifteen minutes of fame.

Bruce was always fascinated with how money and success could change a bad word into a good word.

He knew alcoholics who were down on their luck, in dead-end jobs and with familial problems. He also knew alcoholics who ran major corporations, were raking in the cash, had multiple homes, and spoke to large crowds about their success. But they weren't called alcoholics; they were called luminaries. He knew deadbeats, without a dollar to their name, often wandering from one city to the next, without ever putting down roots or signing up for life's responsibilities. He also knew deadbeats who were financially independent, took ten-day-long mindfulness retreats, and flew on airplanes to cities they'd never been to on a whim. But they weren't called deadbeats; they were miraculously called journeymen. If he could just find the success in hoarding, matching it with a financial windfall, he could easily start referring to himself as something far more impressive.

So, it was nary a surprise that when Bruce had made hundreds of thousands of dollars by retrieving, repairing, advertising, and selling the things other people saw as garbage, he became defined not as a hoarder, but as a legitimate, bona fide collector.

By the time he was twenty-nine, Bruce had turned hundreds of thousands into millions by smartly investing in the early Microsofts and Apples and Facebooks. He had turned those profits into buzz, starting his investment portfolio company Andoco off the backs of his super rich friends. They would tell two friends, and their friends would tell two friends, and so on and so forth like a modern-day retelling of the Selsun Blue commercials. It would allow him to get involved in philanthropies and charities and speak to large rooms about his five-step program to identifying opportunities in the market. His overarching theme, which was often reprinted on banners, business cards, and on the website of Andoco, was simple and impactful: *If You Love It, Invest In It.*

And since Bruce loved himself, he invested in such.

Eventually, when the money was enough and he had been finally referred to as one of Seattle's most fascinating luminaries in a *Wall Street Journal* article highlighting his rise to financial freedom, he packed up his house, moved to Southern California, and started a new chapter.

Some who knew him started referring to him as a journeyman.

Jane Singh had never stolen a thing in her life.

Except for a pack of gum when she was ten from the local drug store, a Cabbage Patch doll from the bargain bin outside a Toys "R" Us, and a copy of *Duran Duran's* Greatest on compact disc, she was practically a poster child for honesty and integrity.

These were the opportunistic moments in her past, when taking something that wasn't hers didn't require an *Oceans 11*-esque master plan or a group of her closest friends to manage every aspect of the operation. No, these were the moments when someone had left something sitting out, clearly not concerned about losing it, and so it seemed perfectly reasonable to walk right by, pick it up, and be on her way. How different was it from finding a twenty-dollar bill on the ground?

It wasn't, she'd tell herself, quieting the voices of reason and responsibility.

And it wasn't like Jane was hard up for cash, or living on the street, or even struggling to pay her bills. She was a woman in modern-day civilized society, who periodically gave in to the prehistoric instincts of hunting and gathering, which in present-day Los Angeles, had rapidly evolved into the act of stealing and profiting—from finding that rare book in her parents' closet and selling it on eBay, to picking up that chair someone had left in front of their house and getting rid of it on Craigslist, to regifting that Marvel-licensed Tony Stark Crock Pot instead of having to spend her hard-earned money on another birthday gift from the god-awful Hot Topic.

She was a collector, she'd tell her children, who were often complaining from the backseat of the SUV, as she lugged yet another item off the street and onto their laps.

So it seemed normal, on that summer afternoon in Studio City, as she walked back from lunch to her office on Ventura, to pick up the camera and walk off with it. It was just sitting there, on the street, on a patch of grass in front of an apartment complex, next to boxes labeled *bedroom* and *bathroom*, and clearly had been set out for the next garbage pickup. It was the same old story, Jane told herself as she scooped it up and continued walking—sometimes people grew tired of the things in their lives, and were happy to see they had found a new home.

"Like Jessie in *Toy Story 2*," her seven-year-old daughter Millicent would agree.

The camera was in mint condition. A Nikon SP, Jane would proclaim as she opened up the smart leather case and looked inside to find a touching message ironed-on at the back. It read, *To Maggie, a student of life. Love, Dad.*

"There's a really touching story here," she'd tell the clerk at the Beauty and Essex pawn shop as she handed it over, taking $450 in cash for the trade as she pointed out the sweet note inside. "Whoever ends up with this beauty," she continued, wanting to impress the clerk, "well, it will have clearly been the result of fate."

"It's clearly fate," the Beauty and Essex clerk said to Bruce, as he took the Nikon SP out from under the glass cabinet, its $3500 price tag swinging from the strap. "This baby was manufactured in the fifties," he continued. "A rare example of a timeless classic."

"I know exactly when it was manufactured," Bruce said, his face lighting up, trying to keep his excitement at bay. He knew that in the coming months the Center would be mounting an exhibit centered around the technologies of the past decades, and as chair emeritus he was always looking for ways to contribute. He had earmarked the TRS-80, still mint-in-box, but hoo-boy, the '57 Nikon would be extremely well-received. Diana and her team would be over the moon, and at this point in Bruce's life, it was the small gestures of generosity that gave him the most mileage.

He slapped down his credit card, which was linked to his bank account, which was still flush with cash thanks to the years of ludicrously inflated valuations of tech companies, and paid for the item in full. He'd call the Science Center team later that week, letting them know just what he had up for grabs.

"Garbage indeed," he scoffed to himself, still carrying the emotional baggage that stemmed from his father's lack of faith in his business endeavors, as he exited the pawn shop and headed back out to Hollywood Boulevard. *One person's garbage is another person's treasure*, he thought.

It was truer than he could ever imagine.

Bruce couldn't take his eyes off of himself.

It was a color photo, surrounded by the kind of text he recommended should be surrounding his image: all compliments, flattering rumors, inflated statements about his impact on the financial landscape, and the story behind how he'd landed yet another antique of immeasurable value. He eyed the plexiglass box, the Nikon SP seemingly hovering above the leather case, its familiar message to Maggie now front and center.

"You've done a great job as usual," Bruce said, turning to David and Annabelle. When you were someone like Bruce Anderson, with the history he had with the Center, you were given a very special preview of how the items you donated would be presented to the general public. Bruce was pleased. His face was all over the place, tied to the computers, cameras, and even the Morse Code machine he'd collected and donated.

"People will ask you to tell the story," Annabelle chimed in, always focusing on the public-facing narrative. "Are you prepared to tell it?"

"It's very simple," he replied. "I found it in Hollywood at—"

"No," Annabelle interrupted. "I mean the story about—" she leaned in to get a closer look at the message in the camera case, "*Maggie*. And her father."

"Well, they were most definitely close," Bruce spun, having no clue. "It's an old camera, so the original owners are probably dead and gone by now."

"But do you actually know?" David chimed in.

While Bruce always wanted to have the answer, he was at a loss in this current situation. "All I know is what you know," he said, tapping on the plexiglass box. He kneeled down to get a closer look. "And we may never know more than that."

David and Annabelle kneeled down to get on Bruce's level; all three gazed into the box, wondering just what the story behind the camera might have been. But as was typically the case with old artifacts, the stories behind them were faded and lost.

Until they weren't.

Twenty-One

STARSHIP WAS PLAYING.

She was sitting in a plastic molded chair in the Western Auto Body "luxury box," watching as *he* rifled through the janky drawers under the broken flat-screen TV, looking for something to keep them from dying of malnourishment while they waited for their paperwork. *She* texted the play-by-play to a girlfriend in between his periodic head-twist and smile, as he displaced a thousand or so coffee stirrers while digging for gold. He wasn't suave by any means, but she'd spent her entire life in horrible relationships stewarded by the suave of society, and maybe now was the time to zig when she'd normally have zagged.

She'd been driving too close to the bike lane, swerving at the last minute to miss the crowd of pedestrians she'd raced toward after swerving to miss the bike. Her Volvo, the safest of safe, handed down from her parents after they'd gone electric, careened over an embankment and into a retaining wall; she landed here twenty-four hours later. *He*, on the other hand, had recently seen *Fast & Furious* (the fourth one, his favorite) and thanks to the myriad how-to videos on YouTube concerning the installation of nitrous oxide, he had done just that. All it had done was cause his engine to explode and the entire front of his Mustang to splinter into a hundred colorful pieces.

Starship's "We Built this City" ended. Starship's "We Built This City" began.

The sound of car repair from the garage echoed throughout the establishment as he sat back down next to her, leaving a seat between. The two of them looked toward the front desk where the clerk repeated her usual disinterested disclaimer: that until the paperwork was ready, they weren't going nowhere. Then, she turned back to the customers who had already been waiting, holding out their invoices so they could finally say goodbye to this godforsaken place.

It was Josh. And it was Maggie.

They stared at *him*, sitting two seats away from *her* in an attempt to not show his interest. They stared at *her*, marveling at her ability to focus on her cell phone with one eye, while the other casually kept tabs on his movements. They were totally into each other, that was obvious. They were smitten. Interested. Under each other's spell. Had it been this obvious with them? Had they appeared to fight the attraction with such transparency that it had all but forced the two of them together? It was like watching the moment they'd met from another perspective, with two actors playing the roles of Guy in Purple with Heart and Food Girl with Attitude.

"What is it with this place?" Maggie said, eyeing the couple.

"Well, it ain't the magazine selection," Josh joked.

"Betcha he doesn't ask for her number," Maggie surmised.

"Betcha *she* won't either."

"That's why I do this," the clerk said, holding up their two invoices, then illustrating her devious plan as she switched each person's paperwork with the other person's keys. Josh and Maggie looked at her, stunned. "You two? Total accident. But then I did it again for shits and giggles. Sometimes you gotta give folks a nudge."

Maggie got back into her Tesla.

She closed the door, sinking into the driver's seat like it was a

Tempur-Pedic mattress, sighing with joy as her phone's Bluetooth connected to the in-car stereo and started playing The Boss. She adjusted the mirrors, pulled her seatbelt across her body, and inched out from the garage toward the major crossroad in front of her.

She checked her mirrors, then looked in the rear view. Josh smiled back from behind the wheel of his BMW. He inched up behind her, as she inched forward, giving her a big thumbs-up.

The coast was clear. She lunged forward to merge into the main thoroughfare; Josh saw her moving at a clip and hit the gas at the same time, expecting her to fly out into the road. But at the last minute, a car came out of nowhere, causing Maggie to hit the brakes just as Josh's car was lunging forward.

The front of *his* car and the back of *hers* met each other in a loud crash. Both cars' airbags deployed, inflating into their faces in a burst of air.

Minutes later, Josh and Maggie stood before the clerk.

She handed over both invoices and associated keys, then joked like she was going to switch them.

"We're good," Josh said, dejected.

"Yeah, we're good," Maggie agreed, more dejected than him.

Twenty-Two

"DROP-DEAD GORGEOUS," CAMERON GUSHED, as Maggie exited her bedroom wearing an elegant, long black dress, then spinning like a Disney princess lacking true poise and basic human reflexes. As the dervish whirled, her left leg clipped the edge of her bedroom side table, knocking into a lamp and sending it crashing onto the floor.

"My two cents?" Cameron cautiously offered up. "Don't spin. Anywhere."

"Fine," she grumbled, "but how's the dress?" She wanted to look good for Josh. She'd be meeting his co-workers and his boss for the first time. This exhibit represented months of work. He was proud of it. She wanted him to be proud of her. He was even giving the keynote speech. Maybe he'd mention her and how all of her support over this short period of time had been the key reason for the success of the project. She imagined him doing so, her spinning in her dress, and knocking over a table Brady Bunch-style, sending a three-tiered cake and a huge punch bowl crashing to the floor.

"When I said drop-dead gorgeous, that was about the dress," Cameron said.

"Can you say it again? About both of us?"

"When did you get so needy?" Cameron threw her arms up, then collapsed onto Maggie's bed. "It's amazing you've found any man willing to spend an extended amount of time with you, with all of your self-absorbed idiosyncrasies."

It was a statement so full of truth, so true to Maggie, that it gave her pause. She moved over to the chair next to her bed. Cameron flipped onto her stomach, head in her hands. "What is it now?" she asked.

"It's just … You're right. It is amazing," Maggie said, smiling.

"Oh boy," Cameron said, looking more closely at Maggie. "You went and done it, didn't you? I can see it in your face." Maggie looked to Cam—*did what*? "You went and opened up your heart to the guy and now you are gonna get Paris'd all over again."

"What does that even mean?" Maggie spat back. "I'm gonna get Paris'd?"

"Screwed. And not in the good way," she said. "There's a waiting period, you know? It's like a year or something. You can't get too attached before then because no one's being themselves anyway. And if you do … You *did* in Paris. And what happened?"

"I'm being myself. And he's being himself. There's no deception here. There's no lying or games. This was meant to be," she said, enjoying the freedom of saying it out loud. *Meant to be*, she repeated in her head. "You know, Cam, I didn't know for sure when I met him, but certain things recently have made me sure. So, I opened myself up to him. *To this*. I opened up my heart so I could show him that all that baggage wouldn't stand in our way."

Cameron sat up. "Wearing your big girl panties now, aren't ya?" It was a crude metaphor, but appropriate nonetheless.

"He's the one," Maggie said, confident. "There's nothing he could do to change that."

It was like every single award show ever produced.

"This is basically like the Oscars," Annabelle said to Maggie as she hovered next to her near the red carpet, the step-and-repeat, and the lone camera crew from the local PBS affiliate. Well-dressed guests, VIPs, board members, and trustees gathered in droves, taking pictures on the red carpet before slowly making their way down to the first-floor atrium's elevators, which were already taking people to the third-floor exhibit.

"So, like, you televise it or something?" Maggie asked, noticing the lone camera crew. "And there are awards, too?" Annabelle suddenly got red, like she'd been caught in a lie. As head of communications for the Center, and always self-conscious that she wasn't working to Diana's high standards, she often made things seem bigger than they were, then backtracked when she got caught.

Annabelle pulled out her trusty notebook and furiously jotted down a few thoughts. "Awards," she said as she scribbled, thinking through how she could really ramp this exhibit up for the next time. "And we televise it?"

Maggie smiled politely, watching Annabelle steal all her pedestrian, seen-it-done-it ideas like they were newly discovered gems on an archeological dig.

No, it wasn't like any award show ever produced.

Maggie moved through the pockets of well-dressed VIPs, following the pathway that took her past, well, technology through the ages.

The team had done an amazing job. The production design was flawless. Visually, the floor-to-ceiling graphics told the story, surrounding each decade and its rare booty of then-groundbreaking technologies in engrossing detail. Maggie perused it all, periodically doing an under-the-radar spin, going against every piece of advice Cameron had given her. But *fuck it*. She felt good. She looked good. She was happy. It didn't matter that she knew absolutely no one here; she didn't care. People around her took notice—who was this attractive, light, happy person doing Ginger Rogers moves every ten steps or so? And where was her Fred Astaire? Thankfully, had the reference been made, at least sixty-five percent of the AARP members in the house would have smiled knowingly.

Maggie moved past the '60s, turning toward the '50s, peering curiously into the Volkswagen Bug that sat atop a raised platform. It was a bright yellow, beaming the reflections from the overhead lights in multiple directions and momentarily blinding her as she pivoted her head in an attempt to regain her sight. She turned toward the tall plexiglass box that housed the 1957 Nikon SP. *The camera her father had given her.* It was there. It had been lost, it had been found, and it had been subsequently donated.

But Maggie's eyesight, blurred from the lights, was slowly coming back into focus. Just as she was about to see what was in front of her, someone, from somewhere else, called out her name. She would have no idea the Nikon SP was there.

"Maggie?"

Maggie spun, but not on purpose. Standing behind her, clearly having been dressed by a semi-famous, semi-local fashion designer, was Robyn. *Robyn from work.* Here. At the California Science Center's premiere opening. "Robyn?" she said, surprised, as she embraced her tightly.

"What are you doing here?" Robyn asked, confused.

"What are *you* doing here?" Maggie asked back.

"She's here because her *mother* works here," another voice chimed in. They turned. There was Diana, who might as well have been Princess Diana: the combination of her elegant dress, sparkling jewelry, and perfectly prim expression communicated nothing less than top-shelf royalty. Even if it was faux royalty with a side of cultured 'tude, Maggie immediately felt less than, eyeing her own dress and feeling overshadowed by this brand-new addition to the conversation. Robyn, clearly having had to face this larger-than-life personality throughout her life, shrunk back as Diana gobbled up all the oxygen in their pocket of the room.

"Mom's the head of all exhibits here at the Center," Robyn explained.

"And very generous with her artisan BLTs whenever there are hungry guests like me sitting next to her at the table," Maggie joked, giving Diana's arm a familiar squeeze as Robyn realized there was already a connection between her mother and Maggie.

"Wait. You both ... ? What a small world," Robyn marveled.

"How come you never told me your mother ... this mother, worked *here*?" Maggie asked. "I wouldn't have guessed in a million years."

"Well, fashion and science rarely go together," Robyn joked, then reduced her smile as her mother gave her an unflattering glance.

"Without science," Diana spoke, "there would be no fashion. And without technology, there would be no dresses," she punctuated, eyeing both of their outfits.

"Without dresses, this would be a much more casual affair, which I had originally pitched but was overruled," came *another* voice, chiming in from behind. The three women turned to find Josh, dressed in a sharp suit, standing behind them. He had finally splurged for something of this decade, of this moment. He looked *good*.

Maggie and Josh shared a look of mutual attraction, which wasn't lost on Diana or Robyn. Robyn nodded a hello to Josh, who seemed to realize there was something more significant going on here in the Circle of Three, as it would be known from that point forward, than he had previously thought.

Maggie pointed to Robyn. "Robyn, who you've met ..." Then she pointed to Diana. "Is Diana's *daughter*." Maggie pointed to Josh, then back to herself. "Which means, screw Kevin Bacon. We've been one degree apart for *five years*."

"*Footloose*," Josh said to Diana, trying to give her some context to the Bacon reference.

"Mom wouldn't know that movie," Robyn clarified, "because my childhood was basically ... *Footloose*," she laughed. "Music, movies, television, all banned."

This was clearly way too much *Footloose* for Diana, who had other things to contend with. "Can we speak for a second?" she directed at Josh, who gave Maggie a finger in midair, as if to say he'd be just a minute. The two of them walked off, past the stanchions, beyond the stage and podium, and behind the curtain.

"C'mon, let's go get a drink," Robyn urged, pulling Maggie toward the bar. "I don't know about you, but I suspect I'm going to need it."

Diana adjusted Josh's black tie, cinching the knot and pulling it tight.

He crooked his neck, making room for the added pressure, as the two of them stood on the other side of the dark red curtains. Diana took a step back, giving him a once-over. She nodded, clearly impressed. "You look good, Josh," she said, patting his chest with kid gloves. "You ready?"

Was he ready? He was never ready. Despite the fact that he had done these speeches before, he always felt uneasy right before going up. It was the uncertainty of it all. The not knowing. Would it turn out OK? Would it go off without a hitch? Were there other metaphoric phrases he could use to give himself more agita in his head? Plus, this was no Oceans Alive exhibit or Black Holes Are Among Us experience. This was the one where Maggie was standing out in the audience, watching. This was the first time she'd see him in his element, in front of the board and the trustees. This had weight to it in a way the others hadn't. And on top of it all, he could hardly breathe, now that Diana had, for all intents and purposes, strangled him with his tie.

"Totally ready," he said in a raspy neck-cinched voice.

Diana smiled. "Good," she said, looking like she wanted to say something else, but refraining. Everyone knew, including Josh, that when she had some intel of any significance, it was hard to get her to keep her mouth shut.

"What?" Josh asked, sensing it. Wondering if it was about tonight.

Diana shook her head in an aw-shucks kind of way. She couldn't keep it in.

"I talked to Bertram. They're going to offer you the job," she said. "It's all happening, Josh," she continued. "It may have taken longer than you originally had hoped, but life isn't a sprint, it's a marathon. And you, my friend, are rounding the turn and barreling down the final stretch. I've worked it out with Bertram. You'll work here until the end of the summer, then start fresh in Paris in the fall. Six months, Josh. *Six months.*"

Josh's mind raced. It had only been a meeting. And now they were going to offer him the job? He felt the weight of the situation pressing down upon him; he hadn't told Maggie because he never thought it would come to this. But now that it had? This isn't how it was supposed to play out. *But it's the chance of a lifetime*, the other voice in his head suggested. A way to get his life back on track. But what about Maggie? Things were going well. The signs were there. If that was true, then why would something so destructive, like an official offer for a dream job, suddenly materialize out of nowhere?

"Aren't you excited?" Diana said, snapping Josh out of his head.

"Yes, of course," he shot back, providing enough volume to convince Diana in spades.

"Good," Diana nodded. "I just wanted to make sure you were viewing it the same way I was," she said, satisfied. "As the great opportunity it is."

Josh was at the podium.

"I'd like to welcome all of our esteemed guests, board members, and trustees of the Center here tonight," he said, his voice booming through the third floor's audio system. He gripped the podium tightly, holding on for dear life, although no one else could sense the tension that had suddenly risen up inside of him.

"Without your support, financial contributions, and enthusiasm," he continued, "tonight's opening of Technology Through the Ages would have never come to fruition."

Maggie stood in the middle of the crowd, drink in hand, eyes wide with interest at Josh's speech. Beside her stood Robyn on one side, Diana on the other. The Circle of Three watched, entranced, as Josh began to walk the crowd through the work that had been accomplished in a relatively short time. Diana had a thought, then turned to look at Maggie, smiling. Maggie noticed it out of the corner of her eye, then turned when she couldn't ignore it any further.

Diana raised her eyebrows.

"Did you … want to say something?" Maggie asked.

Diana pursed her lips, but it was clear that her mind was stronger than her mouth. "Josh has some absolutely stellar news he's going to share with you later."

Stellar news? Maggie turned to look at Josh up on the podium, whose mouth was still moving but the words weren't registering. She had other, more serious things to focus on. Like, for example, a packet of *absolutely stellar news* that his boss knew about, but which Josh hadn't mentioned. There was *good* news and there was *great* news, but *stellar* news? You could save the good and great for later; stellar had to be now.

Diana's brain apparently wasn't satisfied with the vague phrases that had come out of her mouth. She needed her mouth to be more specific. So, her brain made it so, without giving any thought to what it might mean. "He interviewed for an amazing position at the European Space Agency," she blurted out. "The kind of dream job he's been desperate to find for as long as I've known him." She pursed her lips again.

"And he got it. He got the job," she said, shaking Maggie's arm and forcing a feeling of vertigo to rise up inside of her. "In Paris!"

Excusemewhat … Paris?

Diana smiled. Up at the podium, Josh was smiling. All the people around her, including Robyn, were smiling. All Maggie could think to do was down the rest of her drink.

She looked up at Josh. His mouth was moving, but the words seemed muted, the expressions moving at a snail's pace. *He'd applied for a job?* She looked away. *In Paris?* The vertigo was joined by nausea, which was joined by a tightness in her stomach.

Diana turned back to the podium, like she hadn't just thrown a huge monkey wrench into Maggie's world. Maggie stood there, unable to concentrate. Unable to process it all. She had opened her heart to him and this is what he had done in return? She caught Josh's eye up on stage, narrowed her glance, then spun on her heels in a very non-Ginger Rogers way and pushed through the crowd, past the atrium, toward the stairs, and out the hall. Josh watched it happen. Then looked to Diana, who gave him an oblivious thumbs-up.

Gabriel Marchand already had his bags packed.

He had emptied the bathroom's medicine cabinet of his personal effects, removed the clothing he'd stored in the top two drawers of the armoire in the corner of the bedroom, and had taken the practically new container of protein powder from above the refrigerator and placed it by the front door so he wouldn't forget it on his way out. There was no way he was leaving behind a container that had cost him forty-one Euros. That being said, he really wasn't a fan of direct confrontation, which is why he had timed his exit strategy for when Maggie was planning to be at Versailles taking pictures of the gardens.

So, it had been surprising when she had walked through the door just as he was getting ready to leave.

"My darling," he said to her in a silky-smooth, almond milk latte kind of way. They would be the last two words Gabriel would utter to Maggie that would not elicit a horrible feeling in the pit of her stomach. From that point forward she would feel nothing but that horrible feeling for hours and days and weeks and months. His lack of explanation and reasoning would just make her feel more stupid than she already did.

How could I have not seen this coming? She would ask herself that question when she walked in the door, while she listened quietly to his wafer-thin explanation, as he carried his items out the door, and as he disappeared from her life forever.

Perhaps the memory had never fully left her at all.

How could I have not seen this coming? Maggie bolted down the atrium stairs, past the last-minute stragglers taking pictures on the red carpet, and past Annabelle at the front door.

"You're leaving already?" she asked, to which Maggie said nothing as she speed-walked out the double doors to the concrete waiting area outside.

Maggie struggled to walk faster despite the snug-fitting dress trying to slow her roll. She exited the sitting areas in front of the Center, then entered the rose garden on her way to the parking lot. In the background, Josh sprinted after her. "Maggie!" he yelled.

Maggie wiped her eyes, taking a deep breath to keep her emotions in check, and turned as Josh reached her. He was out of breath, his bowtie unraveled, his shirt coming undone. He leaned down, putting weight on his knees as he tried to regain some level of composure. Maggie stood there, angry, betrayed. Waiting to see what silky-smooth, almond milk latte phrases might find their way out of his mouth. She had been here before. Her walls were coming back up at a breakneck speed.

"Why did you run out?" he said, still recovering from the 100-yard dash. "What happened?"

She stared at him, saying nothing. *How could I not have seen this coming?*

"What did Diana say to you?" he tried a second time, arching his back and putting his hands behind his neck to stretch it out.

"Did you apply for a job at the European Space Agency?"

His face dropped. He moved over to a stone bench just behind her, sitting down. He motioned for her to sit opposite him. "Sit down," he said. "*Please*, sit down."

She reluctantly moved to the bench, arms crossed, walls up. "Did you apply for a job at the European Space Agency?" she asked again, this time sounding more hurt than before.

Josh took a breath. Exhaled. "Technically, no. I didn't."

"Technically?"

"Diana filled out the application for me."

"And they offered it to you?"

"They're going to," he said.

She let it sink in. The duplicitous nature of it all. The lack of trust. The cowardice. She turned back toward Josh, staring him right in the eyes. "You're Gabriel Marchand," she said.

"I am *not* Gabriel Marchand," he shot back. "Look," he began, starting to wind up the explanation machine.

But Maggie didn't want to hear it. "I let you touch my foot," she said, completely serious. "I opened up to you, and you did this to me? Clearly, you never felt the way I do." She turned, starting to walk away.

Josh got up, stepping after her. "But I *do*," he shouted.

She turned. "It's fine, Josh. Go chase your dream. I just thought, stupidly, that those dreams included me. But they don't if you're living on another continent altogether." She spun, leaving Josh standing there in the cold.

Josh might as well have been a background extra for *The Walking Dead* with all the slow walking, feet-shuffling, and moaning he was doing as he returned into the belly of the beast. He was firmly planted in his own head, unfocused on the VIP guests that swirled around him in slo-mo as he passed through the first-floor atrium. He replayed the events with Maggie. Why had he let her go? *Idiot.* Why didn't he make some kind of sweeping emotional proclamation about how he felt? *Dolt.* Why didn't he just come out and tell her what he had decided about the job and not beat around the bush? He wandered into the elevator, pressing the button for the third floor, and watched as the doors slowly started to close.

"Hold the door!" a voice shouted, a tuxedo-laden arm jamming in through the narrow space. It was none other than Bruce Anderson, Chair Emeritus, a smiling, genial, energetic man in his sixties who was a cross between a Teflon Congressman and an infomercial host. Josh looked up, snapping himself out of the raging internal battle.

"Mr. Anderson, hello."

"You did a fantastic job with the event tonight," he said, grinning wide, as the doors to the elevator closed tight. "The entire exhibit? Top notch." His expression changed to that of a disapproving mentor. "But out there in the rose garden? With that young lady?

Left something to be desired, if I may be so bold."

"Life troubles," Josh said, dejected, as the doors to the elevator opened and the third-floor festivities came roaring back into view. Bruce took a step out, motioning for Josh to follow.

"Walk with me," he suggested, although coming from Bruce Anderson, it was more of a demand. Josh walked alongside him as they made their way into the '80s era and strolled down the path. On all sides, guests marveled at the rare items on display, periodically nodding to Bruce and Josh.

"I've been collecting things ever since I was a snot-nosed kid," Bruce began, turning to Josh as they walked. "It started as a hobby, then a way to prove someone wrong, then it turned into a very lucrative business. One day I woke up and I had amassed so many things that I realized I couldn't hold on to absolutely everything. And despite having had moments of pure joy with each of the items I'd found … having a unique story and set of memories tied to each? I had to let some of them go."

They entered the '70s era, where Bruce stopped alongside the display case housing the TRS-80. He pointed to it. "Picked that baby up when I was twelve. But I decided it was time to give it up and let others find the joy in it." They crossed over the walkway and into the backside of the '50s era.

"Well, we appreciate it immensely," Josh said, still in his head. "*I* appreciate it. The guests of the Center are going to appreciate it as well."

Bruce stopped him, this time next to the Nikon SP display. "It's the same with the people in your life," he said. "Sometimes, after all the good memories and experiences, it's time to let them go, too." Josh snapped back, realizing this whole speech was his way of giving him advice. "Maybe you and the young lady have seen your best days? Maybe it's time to let her go."

Josh moved to the other side of the camera display. He looked up at the well-regarded, well-off, well-worn philanthropist journeyman and cocked his head. "With all due respect, sir, while I appreciate your perspective, you're way off-base. You don't know me or her."

It was at that moment that Josh caught a view of the Nikon SP. When he looked down, he could, for the first time, see the message ironed-on inside. *To Maggie, a student of life. Love, Dad.*

The world stopped in its tracks as the realization washed over him. He looked back up at Bruce like a man who had figured out the code to the universe.

"There are signs," Josh said as he kneeled down to get a better look. It was still pristine, as was the case, representative of one particular caretaker and the meaning the camera had held for her.

"Is that so?" Bruce replied, kneeling down to see what Josh was glancing at. "And what are the signs telling you?"

Josh looked Bruce directly in the eyes.

"To not let her go."

Twenty-Three

THREE MAILBOXES SAT IN the center of the office.

They were all different sizes and colors, some made of faux metal while others were made of foam. They all had been made by the production designer of *Up All Knight* and three production assistants were jammed into each of them like sardines. Cameron eyed them from behind her desk.

"Which do you think?" Cameron asked Maggie, who was curled up on her oversized couch at the far side of the room. "Make the flaps move again," she barked to the staff members hidden inside. Comically, each of the slotted doors where the mail was supposed to go in started flapping back and forth. Two looked janky, making the decision pretty straightforward.

"Remember," Maggie said, face swollen from the last hour of emotion. "You're not curing cancer here. You're …" Maggie forgot what this was even for. "What are you doing again?"

Cameron sighed. She'd explained the cutting-edge comedy bit three times already. "Trey's going to hide in the mailbox and we're going to set him up outside the Hollywood Post Office. Then when people come to put their mail inside? Comedy ensues."

"Does it ensue?" Maggie poked fun.

"Oh, it ensues," Cameron shot back, waving off the mailboxes. "Let's go with that one," she said, pointing to the clear winner. Heads suddenly appearing out the top of the mailboxes, they wandered out, crashing into the wall as they attempted to leave. The two women watched them go, then Cameron shut the door.

"You know you can't sit here all day," Cameron said, moving back to her desk. "I've got work to do, and you need to snap out of it."

Maggie let out a sarcastic *HA!* as her phone vibrated—it was Josh again. Seventeen missed calls. Seventeen calls she had chosen *not* to answer. She held up her phone to Cameron.

"Seriously, Mags. I know you liked him, but he clearly had other plans. So, you move on. You shake it off. You block him and you find someone new."

"I opened myself up to him."

"And that's okay! That's what they call a healthy relationship. One where you actually let your damn walls down for a minute. I mean, think about that." Cameron moved over to the couch, opposite Maggie, taking her hands. "You had a *healthy* relationship. Then it crashed and burned and now you're really depressed and sad, and life feels like it's completely over, but … *healthy relationship!*"

Maggie looked up at Cameron. "Do I *look* healthy?" Her face was a swollen mess. Cameron's mouth opened in an attempt to triage the situation with a compliment, but thank god, she didn't have to.

The door to the office burst open and Trey slid in like he was on an airport people mover, coming to rest in the middle of the room, his hands and face painted sky blue.

I remember the Blue Man Group, Maggie thought to herself, fondly recalling when her parents had taken her to see them at the age of ten. Her brother had eaten five churros and thrown up in the middle of it, but the memories of that overcast Chicago day still held firm.

"Is this really necessary?" Trey complained. He noticed Maggie sitting next to Cameron, and gave her a nod.

"You're a mailbox," Cameron said. "Of course it's necessary."

"There's something extremely un-*woke* about painting me blue, Cam. We're playing with fire here. I can feel it."

"Yes," Cameron said, fed up, "the Smurfs are really going to have a field day with your insensitive comedy bits. We'll ready the statement for when they have their Spokesmurfs attack you on Twitter with a Smurftacular meme."

Trey turned to Maggie, changing the subject entirely.

"Now what is going on *here*," he said, sitting down next to her. "You been crying about somethin', Mags? Tell Treyvon what's up."

Over the years, Maggie had spent a good amount of time around the *Up All Knight* set, in Cameron's office, at the afterparties. Trey knew her, but not well enough, because he wasn't that type of guy. He was a drive-by socializer, quick with the quip, hyper with the hello, and A.D.D. with the advice. One never went to Trey for advice on purpose, but when he wanted to give it to you, you had to sit there and listen.

"It's about a boy." Cameron widened her eyes.

"A cheating boy?" Trey wondered, the whites of his eyes popping out from the blue of his face. Maggie shook her head. "A boy who broke up with you?" Maggie shook her head again. "Then what the heck are we talkin' about?"

Cameron looked to Maggie for her OK, then laid it out: "The dude applied for a job out of the country, and didn't tell her. They were gelling, connecting, the whole nine. So, to find out that he might just go M.I.A. and leave her behind? Kind of bullshit. Kind of backstabby."

"But the dude never said that. Amiright?"

"Well, no," Maggie replied. "But—"

"Did this brother take the job?" Trey interrupted, spinning up even more.

"I think so," Maggie said. "I don't know," Maggie amended.

"Girl, you are writing a check right now for a bill that may never come."

Maggie stared blankly at Trey. Then turned to Cameron. Her breaking of eye contact with Trey only caused him to shift his body back into her line of sight. "Are you Bran Stark?" he asked, exasperated.

Maggie shrugged, completely oblivious to the reference.

He leaned in closer. The blue face paint made it even more uncomfortable. "I ask the Lady of Studio City again," he said, voice growing louder. "Are … you … Bran Stark?"

"Who?" Maggie asked, confused.

Cameron leaned into Maggie. "*Game of Thrones* dude," she said, rolling her eyes.

"Second son and fourth child of Lord Eddard and Lady Catelyn Stark of Winterfell. He got these creepy white eyeballs rollin' back in his head, but it was all good because he could see into the future with 'em. But you? You can't see into the future, girl. So maybe stop worrying about shit that hasn't happened yet and shake off the shade."

Maggie stared blankly and shrugged.

Trey threw his hands up, having reached his breaking point. "S'all the wisdom I got, girl." He turned back to Cameron, holding up his blue-hued hands. "We sure?" he asked, to which Cameron gave him a frustrated glance. "We're *sure*, okay. We're golden." The door shut, and he was gone.

Cameron turned to Maggie, refocusing. "He's a child," she said.

"Yes," she agreed. "Yes, he is."

"But in his own childlike way, he's got a point."

"About the blue face paint or shaking off the shade?" Maggie said, raising her eyebrows.

Cameron took a swig of her cold coffee. "Maybe if you can't see into the future, you shouldn't react like you're already there."

Barbara and Mel listened while Josh laid it all down.

The European Space Agency, the Lead Project Engineering job, the way Diana had let it slip to Maggie, and the dramatic aftermath. It's not every day you find out that your only child has an amazing new job opportunity that could result in him moving five thousand miles away. They took it pretty well, all things considered.

"I think I'm going to throw up," Barbara said, getting up and pouring herself a cold glass of ice water.

But *could result* was not *actually result*, and Josh still had no idea what he was going to do. "It's not something I was chasing," he said, pushing back his hair with his hands. "Diana applied for me, then convinced me to take the meeting. I never thought it could be a possibility, because …" He trailed off.

"Because it seemed unrealistic?" Mel posed, as Josh nodded in agreement.

Barbara sat back down. "So, now what?" she asked. "What do you need from us?"

Josh had never heard it presented in such a non-confrontational way. He looked to Mel, who eyed him as if to say "don't question it, just go with it." "Advice? Thoughts? Opinions?" he said, realizing that when he *asked* for it, he was okay to receive it. "It's a great opportunity, but …"

"It's Maggie," Barbara said, trying to stay neutral.

"I know you don't like her," Josh replied, "but yeah, it's Maggie."

"I never said I didn't like her."

"You threw her out of the house," Josh shot back.

"Do I like negative feedback?" she said. "Does anyone? No. Did I overreact? Maybe. But do I respect someone standing up for what they believe in? Yes." Josh's face loosened at the sound of her words.

"Look, we can't tell you what to do, Joshy," Mel continued, putting his arm around him. "You're not a kid anymore. You've got to make these decisions on your own." Mel turned to Barbara. "Tell the kid you agree."

Josh turned to Barbara. Mel turned to Barbara. Barbara bit her lip because you can't change a woman in her sixties, let alone a woman like Barbara, period. "I think you've been chasing this dream for most of your life," she continued, "and I think it's about time you caught it."

"She's right," Josh said, turning to Mel.

"But I also think you've been chasing *another* dream," she said, drawing Josh's attention back to her. "And dare I say, Maggie might actually represent the potential of *that*."

"So, you're saying I go after both?" Josh asked.

"If she's truly the one," Mel chimed in, "and you choose her? Maybe then everything else will fall in line."

If you believed in the all-knowing, all-powerful, all-infinite universe, then it made sense. In the moment, it even appeared to make sense to Barbara. "Go get her," Barbara said. "Maybe if it's meant to be, it'll all work out in the end."

Mel followed Josh out the front doors and down the stairs, a folded piece of paper in his hands as he watched his son get into another, less exciting rental car. Josh pulled the shoulder belt across his chest and lowered the window. "What is it, Dad?"

Mel swallowed, looked to the sky, then back at Josh. "That night Maggie was here, while you were in the kitchen talking to your mother, we had a very telling conversation, just the two of us."

"That's nice, Dad," Josh said, starting up the car. "Can we talk later? I feel like I should get going."

"She told me about her family, her friends, about growing up in Chicago," Mel went on, ignoring Josh's desire to leave. "And I asked her a question that I like to ask everyone. Namely, what were those special childhood milestones, those moments she would never forget."

Now Josh was growing impatient. These stories always went on far longer than they needed to.

"And do you know what she said?"

"No, but I'm sure you're going to tell me."

"Astute child of mine, you are correct," he said, grinning. "She told me about the time she was one of two hundred and fifty students from across this great land of ours. Honored for her philanthropic contributions to her local community. It was sponsored by The Lion's Club, and she flew, all expenses paid, to Dallas, Texas, for a weekend celebration."

"Dallas?" Josh asked, remembering. "The Lion's Club?"

Mel lifted up the piece of paper, handing it to Josh through the open car window. When he opened it, he could see that it was a list of Lion's Club Community Honorees, dated May 2002. Josh's name was circled in an alphabetical list of two hundred and forty-nine others. "I kept the program from that day," Mel said, eyes wide. "You were there."

"I remember," Josh replied, stunned.

Mel tapped at the piece of paper. "And so was she." Mel's voice raised as he slapped the top of the car with excitement. Josh stared at the piece of paper and the distance between his name up there in the A's, and her name, way down in the M's. They had been there together, at the same time.

Josh dug into his back pocket, pulling out his cell phone and scrolling to the most recent photos on the device. He selected the picture from Maggie's scrapbook—the Niagara Falls shot. He turned the phone to his father, showing him what he'd found. His father immediately knew what he was looking at.

"I know over the years I haven't completely bought into your whole fate of the universe thing," Josh said, winding up for an apology. "But I'm kinda feeling it right about now."

Mel stared at the picture. "Amazing," he said. "Undeniable."

Josh nodded, staring at the picture, his father … *the list*.

"So, what in the hell are you waiting for, Joshy?" Mel said, hitting the top of the car with unbridled emotion, throwing the phone back into his lap. "Go! *Go go go!*"

Twenty-Four

MAGGIE SLUMPED IN THE oversized red leather chair at the head of the table.

Around her, *The 818* staff jockeyed for the last of the salt bagels, slathering cream cheese and airlifting smelly lox onto their plates, all while giving the stringer monkey in the corner major props for being the first person to ever bring legitimate snacks to a weekly meeting. Maggie watched them, almost as if they were moving in slow motion around her, running through the speech she had practiced all night long, sick to her stomach. Not only was she out in a metaphorical boat without a metaphorical oar, but she was not-so-metaphorically alone. It was something she'd never let bother her before, something she wore like a badge of honor … but now that she'd tasted what it was like to have someone in your life who cared, well … it kind of bit ass.

Metaphorically, of course.

Brian sloppily shoved the last bite of his bagel into his hole, leaving a mess of cream cheese to collect in the corners of his mouth. "Let's get into it, people," he grumbled. "Talk me through what you're working on for the next issue." Carly, ever the enthusiastic world-changer, sat up straight like she was determined to share a new idea she'd already previewed with Brian. "You mention climate change or weather control, and I ban you from this meeting forever," he said, shutting her down.

Darren sat up, pad at the ready. "I've got time scheduled to go visit Kaylee Simpson," he said, reading from his chicken scratches. "We're going to talk about her new movie *Sriracha*, her new make-up line Oh Kay Cosmetics, and she's agreed to show off her Hollywood Hills home, which is completely self-sustainable and off the grid. She's very pro-environment, so we can cover that angle as well."

"Now that, I like," Brian said. Darren perked up. Carly threw her hands in the air, dejected.

Maggie was still in her head, not paying attention. "Are you okay?" Robyn whispered. "I heard what happened the other night at the Center, and …" Maggie reached out to touch Robyn's arm, silencing her, then glared at the stringer monkey in the corner and Brian at the head of the class. "I'm going to be just fine," she whispered back, saying it almost as much for herself as anyone else, then clearing her throat.

"I'll go next," Maggie announced, cutting off the last of Darren's updates. Everyone turned to her, including Brian.

Maggie reached into her folio and pulled out a typewritten, stapled print-out. "My restaurant review for Chaat. Three out of four forks." The room commented: how great they had heard Chaat was, how they wanted to go, how they couldn't wait to hear what Maggie had to say. "It's also going to be the last restaurant review I file for *The 818*," she said. Brian, who had been dangling a piece of lox over his mouth, stopped dead in his tracks.

"Your last?" he said, almost choking.

"I've done everything I can do here," Maggie replied. "I'm extremely thankful for the opportunity you provided me, but it's time for me to set out on a new chapter. Something that makes me happy. Something I'm good at. Something that doesn't require me to eat all the time. It's tiring, honestly, and I'm on Prevacid now for acid reflux, and it's just … I'm very thankful, did I say that?"

"This is about me not letting you take photos, is that it?" Brian asked.

"This is exactly about that," Maggie said, nodding with confidence. "But that was the best thing you could have ever done for me, Bri. Because if you hadn't, I never would have realized what I really wanted to do with my life." Carly watched the tennis match of words go back and forth with morbid fascination.

"Which is what?" Brian spat, annoyed.

Maggie opened her mouth, clearly on the verge of sharing a well-thought-out response to one of life's ultimate questions. But instead, the double doors to Brian's office burst open, and everyone turned to see who was crashing their meeting.

It was Josh Allen.

He was being chased by a nervous receptionist who was trying to keep him from walking into the staff meeting, but having very little luck in doing so. "I tried to get him to …" she exclaimed frantically as she attempted to chase Josh down, but it was too late.

Everyone turned; it was like watching an accident on the freeway about to happen. Maggie sat up in her chair and shared a look with Robyn. "Just give me a second," Josh said, walking into the room like he owned the place and scanning the shelves behind Brian's desk. He located a Bluetooth speaker, which he set on the desk behind everyone. Then he pulled out his cell phone, switched on the Bluetooth signal, and held down the button at the top of the speaker. "Sometimes this takes a minute or so to sync up," he said as the bleep/blurb/bloop of Bluetooth technology did, well … its thing.

He waited. They waited. This was worse than the elevator. Brian didn't understand what was going on. "Who the hell are you and why the hell are you in this office?" Brian said.

Robyn was watching Maggie, staring unemotional at Josh. "We know this crazy, misguided person," Robyn clarified. "And so does my mother."

Brian sat back down, dumbfounded. He looked to Robyn, who mouthed "her boyfriend," right around the time the Bluetooth connection engaged and the music started playing.

It was Chicago's "You're the Inspiration." The romantic, harmonized, Peter Cetera of it all. The ultimate love ballad, soulmate anthem that young Josh had dreamed of someday playing as not-so-young anymore, Josh. And so, he just stood there, arms crossed, staring a hole directly into Maggie's skull as the lyrics began.

Everyone knew the words. They all had heard the song a million times. Everyone mouthed along, getting caught up in it as words like "love" and "forever" and "until the end of time" found their way to each and every one of them. Josh wasn't on a beach, or at the top of a Ferris wheel, or chasing Maggie through a park on the top of a red rock cliff somewhere in Sedona, Arizona. But this was better. This was real. He stared at Maggie, in the moment.

It was sweet; but it was also in the middle of a staff meeting. Then again, it wasn't her staff meeting anymore, since she had just given her notice. Still, it was awkward. She looked up to Josh, widening her eyes as if to say *please get on with this*. He waited until the sweeping vocals and the affecting harmonies reached a crescendo.

He stepped to the Bluetooth speaker, turning down the volume. "I would have preferred to play that song for you somewhere else," he said, eyeing Brian's pig-sty of an office, "but since you refused to return my calls, you gave me no choice. I had to come here." He eyed the bullpen outside. "But I do like the open office space," he said, nodding approvingly. Brian, of course, seized on the compliment, raising his eyebrows as if to tell his ungrateful staff that the open office strategy *was* a good thing.

"You know why I didn't call you back. What's the use?" she said, stoic. "You already made up your mind. You made a choice. And that choice wasn't me." Robyn patted her knee, now firmly planted in the role of best-friend-in-meeting supporter.

"I did make up my mind," he replied, "but not in the way you think. You never let me finish before you stormed off. *Yes*, I took a meeting. Diana had already set it up for me and I didn't want to disappoint her. But I walked into that meeting already knowing what you *don't* know. That no matter what, I wasn't going to take that job. Not after meeting you. Not after witnessing the signs. Not after falling for you. Fate, Maggie. We've been crossing paths for most of our life, but we're just realizing it now. How could I ever walk away from that?

From you? I got the official call from the ESA this morning. And I gave them my official answer. I said no."

She stared at him. Everyone else stared at *her*.

"And I'm not just talking about one picture," Josh said, pulling out the paper that Mel had given him the previous evening. He dropped it into Maggie's lap. "Go ahead," he said. "Open it."

She looked around the room, then back down at the piece of paper. It was a list of a few hundred names. "The Lion's Club Community Honoree Luncheon," Josh announced. "Dallas, Texas. May 2002. I was there."

Maggie's eyes widened, scanning the list. Her finger slid down over the names, until she got into the alphabetical M's. There was her name in plain sight.

"Niagara Falls. Dallas, Texas. I'll bet you if we really thought about it, we'd realize we'd crossed paths during spring break in Mexico," he laid out. "There's a reason we keep crossing paths. There's a reason we keep running into each other. There's a reason we never found that perfect person in our lives until now." Josh swallowed. He believed it; it was just nerve-wracking to say. Tina entered his head and he swatted her away. He wasn't going to let her impact his happiness any longer. He would embrace the Tina of it all, and dive into that metaphorical bowl of popcorn with reckless abandon.

"We're soulmates," he said, moving closer to her. "We belong together. From tonight until the end of time."

Robyn's eyes were watering. Alyssa leaned in, on the edge of her seat. Carly and the stringer monkey unknowingly reached out and held each other's hands.

Everyone turned to Maggie, including Brian, who was now seemingly invested in the drama unfolding before him. Maggie didn't jump up and embrace Josh like the movies said she should. She stared down at the paper and the names, taking it all in. Sure, had this been *Jerry Maguire*, she might have thrown up some sign language about completing each other or shed a completely noticeable, perfectly symmetrical tear. But this was real life, where a small, insignificant response could impact one's entire future in an entirely significant way. Was she really ready to do that?

"You're not convinced," Josh said.

Maggie stared at him. "Not totally, no."

"I anticipated this," he shot back, "because you're generally pig-headed." He held up his finger, moving to the double doors of the office. "One second, please." Everyone watched him go.

"He's coming back, right?" Brian asked. "Because if not, I'd really like to get back—"

"Oh, he's coming back," Maggie replied, fatigued.

Josh kicked back open the double doors. In his hands he held Maggie's Nikon SP. The one her father had given her at the age of eight. The one she had cherished all those years. The one she had lost during the move to Los Angeles, and which had been sold to a pawn shop in Hollywood, which Bruce Anderson had purchased and donated to the California Science Center for their Technology Through the Ages exhibit. The one that Josh had asked the Chair Emeritus to give him, after laying out the story about two souls finding each other after being lost to each other for so much time.

Josh carefully placed it in Maggie's lap. She picked it up, stunned, opening the case and running her fingers over the message inside. She was uncharacteristically devoid of words, or opinions, or plucky pop-culture barbs. "How did you … ?" she stammered.

Josh smiled, then shrugged. "I think it's time we stopped asking so many questions and just went with it, don't you think?"

Maggie stared at the camera. The message inside. Around the room at her co-workers. Back at the open-plan bullpen. Robyn and Alyssa looked at her, eyes pleading. She nodded, then burst up and into Josh's arms, kissing him intensely. Josh wrapped his arms around her and pulled her in even closer as the entire room (including a reluctant Brian) stood up and clapped.

"Best meeting ever," Alyssa chimed in, as Chumley barked his approval.

"Now can we get back to our meeting?" Brian asked, rolling his eyes.

Maggie and Josh stood outside *The 818*, with the traffic whizzing by on the main thoroughfare.

She looked down at the Nikon SP, then back up at the building, then over to a smiling Josh taking it all in. She pushed her hair out of her face, then stepped in even closer to him, blocking the sun from her eyes so she could look into his.

"So, you said no."

"That's right," Josh said.

She bit her lip. Contemplating. "I just can't help thinking," Maggie began, "that this job at the ESA? It's been a dream of yours ever since you were four. I can't stand in the way of something like that. I'd never be able to forgive myself."

"And I could never stand in *your* way of the career you have here," Josh replied.

Maggie cocked her head, looking sheepish. "About that," she began. "Right before you burst into that meeting with your '80s playlist? I quit my job. So currently there's no career for you to stand in the way *of*."

"You what?"

"And I can be a food photographer anywhere. Even," she cringed, "*Paris*."

"But you hate Paris."

"I detest Paris," she one-upped. "But that was when it didn't have you in it. There's an off-chance that you might actually make it less detestable." Josh stared at Maggie, floored. "Can you still say yes?" she asked.

He could.

But the question was, should he? Hadn't his decision to say no been the reason he was now standing before Maggie? If he went back on that instinct to say no, would the universe leap up and change for the worse? He thought back to all the small decisions he had made in life; all the small decisions that those around him had made. They had all been simply based on what seemed right in the moment. In hindsight he could see the zigs and the zags in the map of life that got him here, to this moment, playing Chicago's "You're the Inspiration" on a portable Bluetooth speaker, to the girl he was fated to be with. To the woman he was with right now. But this wasn't some modern-day retelling of *Sliding Doors*. He hadn't been given the chance to see what two diverging paths in the road might have done for his life and his future. He'd simply trusted his instinct, and let the infinite pile of chips fall where they were meant to fall. And now they were leaning in his direction.

"I can," Josh replied.

"Then you should," she said, nodding with a sly smile on her face.

Twenty-Five

THE FRIES SAT ON a teal ceramic plate, nestled between three different dipping sauces exclusive to Chips, the newly rebranded buzzworthy fries-only haunt in Hollywood. There was the tangy relish-like *Piccalilli*, the mayo- and vinegar-based Salad Cream, and for those jonesin' for something spicy and American, there was the classic Honey Chipotle Ketchup. And when Kylie Gibson, the previous owner of Gibson's and the new *Terminator*-like owner of Chips, saw the photos of her flagship (if not only) food item on the menu, she was stunned by the absolute beauty of it all.

"The depth," Kylie whispered, because Maggie had continued to propagate the old wives' tale about needing silence to work, "is stunning. The composition, the lighting … bloody fantastic." She stood over Maggie's shoulder as she cycled through the images on her laptop, which sat next to a hulking new Nikon D5 and the classic camera the universe had seen fit to return to her.

"I think photos three, twelve, sixteen, and twenty-four," Maggie pointed out on the screen, cycling through the best of them, "are your best bets for the digital menus. And if the weekly mag is looking for something to go with the article, definitely four."

Maggie had hit the ground running after she had walked out on

Brian and the all-singing, all-dancing bullpen of *The 818*. The restaurateurs who had benefitted from her previous in-print compliments were quick to sign up for her services, and the ones who had garnered less than two forks took a few months to come around. But they did. After the iconic 360 degree buffalo cauliflower installation for McCaulie's and the Hollywood Cinerama Dome's twelve-story-high caramel popcorn billboard, it was clear to most of the culinary community that Maggie had a knack for capturing imagery of food that made reservation lists fill up quicker than a twelve-ounce microbrew.

As for Josh and the European Space Agency, he had said yes.

Despite the long-distance connection, and the wavering cell phone signal, Josh stammered successfully through the phone call, alerting Bertram to his life-changing decision, having given his six-month notice to Diana at the Center, with plans to move to Paris four weeks after that. He'd also be bringing his girlfriend, so they were on the lookout for a great neighborhood that could house them both. Fortunately, Bertram's tentacles reached far and wide, which would result in his college roommate Emile Laurent offering up a wonderful flat in the 15th Arrondissement, just ten minutes away from the ESA on Rue de Javel.

"*Javel*, in French," his mother would announce to Josh and Maggie at a Sunday dinner they'd both show up for willingly, "means *bleach*. I don't know about you, but renting any place on Bleach Street seems awfully questionable. Criminals use bleach to get out blood."

Josh would look at his mother in a scolding way, a facial expression that he had become astute at curating over the six months since the "You're the Inspiration" Incident, causing her to catch herself. "Or do what you want," she'd follow up. "After all, it is your life."

It was his life. It had always been. But now that it had been verbalized by the one woman who had, allegedly, "shit on his hopes and dreams," it made it feel even more real, even more satisfying.

"Hallelujah," Mel would proclaim from within the *pellucidar*, having worked with Barbara like a modern-day Professor Henry Higgins for months.

Those six months would give Josh and Maggie the opportunity to pull back the layers of their onions, and further deepen their relationship with one another.

They would spend more time together, realizing that the commonalities far out-tallied the few isolated differences. They'd discover that they were both obsessed with black licorice, hated marzipan, loved going to sleep with the sound of rain but couldn't go back to sleep once someone was responsible for the sound of urinating in a toilet. They'd uncover each other's fanaticism for bubble wrap, Tic Tacs and the '80s hair band Poison. On the few isolated occasions when Josh presented a single rose to Maggie at the start of a date over those subsequent six months, he'd ensure the flower shop left one single thorn on the stem, so he could launch into his own self-written parody of Abbott & Costello's *Who's on First*.

"Did you know?" he'd say to Maggie, revealing the rose.

"Know what?" she'd ask, playing along for the umpteenth time.

"Every rose? It has a thorn."

"Just like every night also has its dawn?" she'd ask.

"No," he'd correct her. "Just like every cowboy, you know … sings his sad, sad song."

Four weeks before leaving, they'd travel to Chicago to stay with Maggie's parents, taking them out for a night on the Chi-town and a dinner at her father's favorite haunt: the Berghoff.

Frank Mills would get the Sauerbraten, topped with sweet and sour gravy, while Maggie would enjoy the Spatzleknödel with a side of a sudden realization that she wouldn't have to write one damn thing about it. And while Jean Mills always got the Reuben on that dense house-made rye, it didn't stop Josh from ensuring he got her a basket of her own pretzel rolls, all buttered up, with the knowledge that every single one would remain untouched by the hands of one Josh Allen.

"So, when do you start?" Maggie's father had asked Josh.

"In a month," Josh announced proudly. "You know, I always

thought NASA was the be-all and end-all, but I never imagined an opportunity like this would ever be possible."

"I did," Maggie chimed in, supremely enjoying her meal.

Josh looked to her, nodding. "I gotta say, Maggie's encouragement has made all the difference. I mean, what did *I* do to deserve this? What did I do?"

"Exactly," Frank replied, still playing the role of the protective father he had been born to play.

Three weeks before leaving, Maggie would help Josh pack up his townhouse.

They would pack up the toys and the movies and the posters and the trinkets. They would pack up the clothes she deemed appropriate to keep in their now-combined future, and gave away the rest. They would stand at the top of the second floor of Josh's townhouse, with the Slattum perched at the edge, wondering if they could even get it out in one piece.

"Maybe we should ask my neighbor Antonio to help," Josh said, leaning on the Slattum, sending it over the edge and careening down the stairs. As it slid, every single joint gave way, the wooden pegs coming out as it vibrated down the stairs, reducing the one-piece upholstered bed frame into its original form of twenty-nine separate slats. Yes, it was really that easy, breaking them down.

"Do you still have the original box?" Maggie wondered.

Josh gazed out the second-floor window, catching a view of what was not the sun and not the sky. "I don't," he said, feeling a sense of satisfaction that he'd soon have different sights to gaze upon. "And I'm okay with that."

Diana slid a brand-new sushi lunch box across the conference room table to Josh.

It had a slick black ceramic base with an ornate crest on the top cover, adorning a bamboo top that opened up to reveal multiple sections inside. Josh pulled it toward him, comparing it to the one in front of Diana, and realizing it was exactly the same. He knew Diana and her proclivity for spending inordinate amounts of money on ridiculously niche items; he knew the cost of this was well beyond his expectations. He opened it up, revealing a fully prepared sushi lunch, with salmon sashimi, crab rolls, and unagi.

"Spared no expense, I see," Josh said, digging in and taking a bite of the crab roll.

"It's a special occasion," she smiled. "One of my baby birds is leaving the nest. Finally." She slid a pair of stone chopsticks across the table to Josh, wrapped in a soft black cloth. He unwrapped them, plucking a piece of the salmon into his mouth. Diana watched him, doing the same.

They'd been across tables from each other for years, and as time had passed it felt less awkward and more comfortable. So much so that Diana could now correctly identify the moments when Josh retreated into his head, thoughts racing, doubts growing.

"Don't," she said.

"Don't what?"

"Second-guess. It's too late. I've already promoted David."

He rolled his eyes. "I'm not second-guessing," he said, despite the fact that he was. "I'm just going to miss this place. After being here for as long as I have ..."

"'You can do what you have to do,'" she quoted, "'and sometimes you can do it even better than you think you can.'"

It was true. Josh nodded, taking a breath. "Who said that?" he asked, clearly used to Diana's obsession with the poetic and inspirational words of others.

"Bertram. When I met him for the first time at UCLA. A long time ago."

"Oh really," Josh said, widening his eyes.

"Well, Bertram quoting Jimmy Carter. Still," she reminisced. "A German quoting Carter? Practically unheard of. One of a kind."

Josh watched her. She noticed, snapping out of it and digging back into her lunch. "I didn't invite you here to stare," she said. "I invited you here to eat. So, eat. Then get out before I have to show any real, genuine emotion," she said, allowing a smirk to find its way through.

David was waiting outside the conference room for Josh, donning a purple shirt for the first time since he'd started at the Center. Josh's leaving had left open a slot in the organizational structure, giving David the opportunity he'd been dreaming of since his fourteenth day there. He stood, at attention, a clipboard already filled with notes and opinions; there would be no lapse in productivity under his watch, Freddie had heard him say.

"Looking sharp," Josh said, eyeing the Sauropodomorph rising high above them in the first-floor atrium. It had been one of his last significant contributions before the six months had come and gone.

David turned, regarding it as well. "She's a beaut," he agreed. "Your legacy will be tough to top. That's why I've already started brainstorming new potential exhibits. Got big shoes to fill."

Josh eyed the clipboard and the numerous notations. David held it out, pointing to one item in particular. "How does this strike you?" he said, putting his hands out in front of them as if to create a window into the exhibit's experience. "Rockets: A Blast from the Past."

"You're going to do great," Josh complimented. David was moved, his eyes starting to mist up. Josh had never seen him like this before. "Are you getting emotional because I'm leaving?" Josh asked.

"No, I'm emotional because you're finally going," he said. "I thought I was going to have to knock you out and ship you blindfolded in a wooden box to Mexico, like in *The Game*."

"Honesty, I like that," Josh laughed. Behind him, Maggie approached, noticing David's purple mesh shirt.

"I see the student has become the master," she joked.

Josh looked up at *Endeavor*.

Maggie stood next to Josh, giving him space, as she was well aware of what *Endeavor* had meant to him over all those years. A green-shirted employee stood nearby, guarding the entrance to the shuttle, as was the case during the hours that the Center was open to the public. Josh reached up, putting his palm on the underbelly of the craft, as if to say goodbye, then moved to the ladder in an attempt to get one last look inside.

The green-shirt stepped in front of him. "I'm sorry, but the shuttle isn't open to the general public."

Josh and Maggie shared a horrified look at the utterance of the phrase *"general public."* "Today's my last day," he said, leaning in to read the name tag of the worker. "*Justine*. If it wasn't for me, Josh Allen, the space shuttle *Endeavor* wouldn't even be in this facility in the first place."

Justine looked at Josh, squinting. "For your information," she said, "this spacecraft is here as the result of many people. In fact, if it wasn't for the teamwork between multiple organizations and facilities, *Endeavor* would not be here today."

Josh looked to Maggie. *Shit.* She was right. "So, you're not going to let me up?" he asked, hopeful.

"Only purple-shirts," she said, reciting the clearly defined rules.

Josh and Maggie took a step back. "End of an era," she said.

"Beginning of another," he replied.

It was 2019. Josh was just thirty-four.

Twenty-Six

IN THE BEGINNING, BEFORE Chef Maurizio Tallerico was actually able to drop the word *chef* before his name, he was just a plain old Italian Jew named Maury with a speech impediment from the Upper East Side.

Perhaps that was why, from a very young age, Maury spent more time inside with his mother Mary than out on the street playing stick ball, or riding bicycles, or flipping baseball cards for cash. It was probably why he found an affinity for thinking up new and exciting combinations of food and the spices that defined them, rather than thinking up new ways to blow up mailboxes and torment the young girls who frequented the East 72nd Street Playground on the edge of Central Park. It was most definitely why, before either of his parents could correctly spell (or *say*) the phrase "acidulation," he was cooking up a storm for family, friends, and the random Purim celebration at the Park East Synagogue.

So, it was no surprise that upon graduating Eleanor Roosevelt High School, Maury applied to the New England Culinary Institute in Vermont, changed his name to *Maurizio*, and reengineered his embarrassing speech impediment into a hybrid Italian slash French accent that supported the legend of his eccentric new name, despite continuing to confuse people regarding just what country he hailed from.

"It's like Madonna's accent," one of his fellow Institute students would accurately say, when she had been going through her British slash English slash Swedish phase.

Maury ... er Maurizio, had loved to cook ... for anyone. When he first started at the Institute, he was enthusiastically gung-ho for any and all opportunities to hone his craft and delight partygoers with his unique farm-to-table creations. It helped him to develop his skills, a startlingly fresh style, and his reputation in the circles that mattered. But by the time Maurizio had graduated from the NEI and moved to West Hollywood to further his studies and create new opportunities for his future, he was so inundated with practice that the isolated dinner party became few and far between. But the work and dedication would pay off. A mere eighteen months later, Maurizio would emerge from his culinary cocoon as the butterfly now known as *Chef* Maurizio and open the West Hollywood hot spot M, which had only become a hot spot because of one very important, very influential young writer.

That very important, very influential person was Maggie.

At the time, Maurizio was drunk off the four out of four forks, the packed houses, and the four-month-long waiting lists to get in, so it was no surprise that on that infamous opening night he had promised Maggie she could call upon him, like a Shake n' Bake Batman, when she needed him most.

"I need you," she had said, over the phone, four years later to the day.

"Give me more," he said, in a refined Italian slash French slash Scandinavian accent.

"Remember that boy I met three years ago?" she asked. "Well, we're getting married. And I need you there."

Chef Maurizio made his way around the large metal table in the center of the hotel's industrial-sized kitchen, checking the platters of exquisite appetizers that were being readied for after the ceremony. He checked on the savory goat cheese baguettes with cranberry jam, adjusted the layout of the gluten-free mini bread bowls filled with homemade butternut squash chowder, and sampled a taste of the vegetarian botanas. Everything was perfect.

Of course it was. "Chef Maurizio Tallerico is here," he'd say, his answer to any complicated conundrums. Was something over-cooked? "Chef Maurizio Tallerico is here." Were there not enough baguettes so that each guest could have two? "Chef Maurizio Taller-ico is here." Was the sun going to swallow up the earth and destroy all of humanity within a few hundred thousand years? "Sure ... but Chef Maurizio Tallerico is here."

He moved past his factory line of catering assistants and peered out the expansive wall of windows that looked out into the beautiful, tree-lined area where the ceremony was about to begin. Close to a hundred and fifty guests filled the white wooden chairs, arranged in two equal sections that faced the bridesmaids and groomsmen, shaded by a fantastic oak tree that hung low over the proceedings. At the front of it all, standing and waiting patiently, was Josh.

He shared a look with his groomsmen. There was Damon, his best man, his father Mel, Maggie's brother Teddy, and JPL intern/ nemesis Spencer McCurdy, who had clearly become a colleague and friend of Josh's since he had started his new career at the European Space Agency. Josh gazed back down the aisle, still awaiting Maggie's entrance, then turned to look across the aisle at her bridesmaids, all impatiently standing happily. There was Cameron, who had refash-ioned Maggie's choice for a bridesmaid's dress into something far more punk rock; Alyssa, who she had become far closer with now that she didn't have to see her every day; and Robyn, who looked out into the crowd to share a look with her mother Diana, sitting completely enamored with her date and not-so-newfound partner, Bertram Söhm.

As Josh looked out across the sea of familiar faces, he couldn't help but think about how he had gotten here. How, if his mother had not squashed his hopes and dreams, he may not have landed at the Center. How if he hadn't landed there, he would have never met Diana, who was the primary catalyst of the ESA job with Bertram. Had his childhood been without consequence, and happier and more fulfilling, would he have settled for some other woman he'd met over the years? Would he have even built up such a wall of emotional defenses, afraid to make the wrong choice with his future partner, if his life had been less complicated?

Yet at the same time, Diana and Bertram might not have come back together had he not been in her life. Damon and Lisa, who sat in the front row ribbing Josh silently, would never have met if it wasn't for Josh inviting him to stay with him in Burbank that one time. And had Mel never decided to take that job in California, none of the events would have ever happened at all. The same could be said for Maggie and her life: Cameron working for Trey, that night in The Fisherman and the Whale, failing miserably at photography, and so much more. Had Josh not worked for Diana, and Maggie not worked with Robyn, would they have even met that day at the Western Auto Body shop?

It could make your head spin if you spent too much time thinking about it.

Yet there were moments, after Josh had come home from work at the Agency or Maggie had finished a string of menu layouts or advertising campaigns, where they'd find themselves out at a café or sitting on the balcony of their Parisian flat, when they would talk about it. While they had no real window into the future, they could look back with reckless abandon, drawing out the timelines and pointing out the tiny decisions the people in their lives had made, wondering where they'd be had those decisions never been made in the first place. *The small stuff*, as they'd come to refer to the choices that had brought them together, was wild to look at but mind-numbing to analyze.

Josh's head was spinning, but not for long, as Maggie and her father appeared at the back of the aisle, framed between two hulking trees. She was absolutely stunning, in an elegant white dress. She rolled her eyes at Josh as they waited for their cue. See, while Maggie had decided on the catering and the location and the flower center-pieces and so much more, Josh had only one thing he felt passionate about. One thing he needed to control. It was the cue. The *music* cue. The soundtrack to Maggie walking down that aisle, standing up beside him, and committing to a lifetime together.

The speakers clicked in, then the sound of lilting orchestra strings piped in and around the captive audience. It was familiar. It was nostalgic. It was composed by none other than John Williams. It was "The Flying Sequence" from *Superman: The Movie.*

Josh smiled, nodding to Damon, who rolled his eyes at the cinematicness of it all. The two gazed down the aisle as Maggie and her father began the slow walk toward Josh and the officiant. Maggie threw out her arms like she was flying at a particularly inspiring moment in the music, sharing a smile with friends in the audience, including the rest of *The 818* team, including a surprisingly put-together Brian Epstein.

"You were dressed like a Civil War soldier," Maggie said, drawing laughs from the crowd.

She stood in front of the audience, reading her vows from her cell phone screen, enjoying the crowd's response as she continued to lampoon her husband-to-be. "At first, I thought you were a Civil War fanatic, which would have been bad. But then you told me you were only dressed that way because your mother made you … and that was far more disturbing." Maggie shared a look with Barbara in the front row, clearly OK with the ribbing and more concerned with getting the credit, pointing to herself so the audience would know it was her.

"And while we don't remember meeting each other the second time and my recollection of the moment may be slathered in a residual alcoholic haze, other witnesses at the scene of the crime have attested to the fact that you were wearing yellow fluorescent flip-flops and a gaudy pink tank top. Yes, I know it was a long time ago, but those combinations were never in style. Not even in the eighties."

Maggie shared a look with witness Damon, before looking back down at her screen and scrolling to the next portion of her speech. "And the third time I met you, you were drinking hot water out of a plastic cup and wearing a purple mesh shirt. Yes, I know ..." she turned to the Science Center crew in the peanut gallery, "*regulation.* But still. Not a look that inspires romantic thoughts or hot fantasies ... sorry, Mom and Dad."

Josh raised his hands to the crowd as if to apologize for his decades of uninspired fashion statements, then motioned to his refined, designer-made tuxedo.

"Point being?" she continued, turning to Josh with an affectionate look, "I must absolutely love you because I'm up here now, proclaiming my undying dedication to you ... despite your historical inability to dress for the moment, or life in general. Aw, *hell.* It's true. I *do.*" She turned serious, leaning in. "I never believed in soulmates until I met you. I couldn't believe it when I did. Every day I wake up, I thank your lucky stars that it's our reality." She lifted her phone, then dropped it like a mic. She scrambled to pick it up, laughing. "The ... *end,*" she said, then reached out and gave Josh a pat on his chest, as it was his turn.

He pulled out a piece of paper, unfolding it like his forefathers had once done during the dark times of economic and technological infancy. He cleared his throat, then turned toward the audience before facing Maggie.

"I was an attractive five-year-old," he began. "Like TV's Gary Coleman attractive," he continued, laughing. "Now I didn't know this, or I would have so obviously leveraged it to secure double snacks and extra nap time, but as is often the case with the minds of young children, I was more focused on something else entirely. Namely, a girl. Now, let me tell you, this girl, whose name shall remain shrouded in secrecy, was a pretty cool girl. She wasn't like the other kindergarten gals that scoured the four-square court for their future husbands. She was normal. Well-adjusted. She even shared her Cheetos with me, which if you know the market value in kindergarten for a bag of those things, you know she was extremely generous. Now, while I never admitted it publicly, I had a thing for her. I wanted to take things to the next level, but I was also afraid to do so. Anyway, one day we were at the movies seeing *Big*, which if any of you out there haven't seen it, you really need to, as it should be undoubtedly in everyone's Top 10 … And I shared my popcorn with her. It set off a chain of events that resulted in her expressing her feelings for me the very next day. Which scared me. So much so that I moved to a different desk, and never looked back."

Josh scanned the crowd, then turned back to Maggie. "For years, for decades, that moment was always in the back of my head. It conditioned me to turn my back when things got tough, or complicated, or bordered on potential romance. In a good way, it kept me on the market until I met you. But then, had you not been *you*, I probably would have moved to a different desk and given up the Cheetos. But you kept me honest. You called me out. And you gave me the courage to take that leap … the one I didn't take so many years back. And I'm glad I did, and that it was with you." Maggie swooned, grabbing Josh's hand.

He pointed out into the sea of people. "If it wasn't for Tina Willis, who messed me up for everybody but Maggie, none of us would be here today." Everyone turned. Tina Willis, sitting with her husband and eight-year-old daughter, smiled up to Josh, waving. The crowd muttered under their breath, absolutely taken with the surprise. Barbara leaned into Mel; she had been out of the loop as well.

"To Tina!" Maggie yelled from the front.

"To Tina!" everyone yelled back in unison.

The band was playing a cover of The Eagles' "Hotel California."

Newlyweds Josh and Maggie made their rounds, hitting each of the tables that had been set up on an adjacent part of the hotel's property, arranged up against the covered open bar, near the polished wooden dance floor and a grassy knoll where guests were socializing, having drinks, and catching up. They stood at the back of *The 818 table*, arranging themselves to take a group picture with all the usual suspects. When the photographer was finished, Brian got up and approached Maggie.

He reached out with open arms, hugging her. "Congratulations … on everything," he said. "I've seen some of your stuff, and can I just say …" He paused. Maggie cocked her head, waiting. "… I don't get it. I mean, is that a lucrative career? Taking pictures of food?"

Maggie smiled. Old habits die hard. She leaned into Brian, whispering into his ear. His face went slack, his eyes wide. "*That much?*" he said. "I don't believe it."

"Believe it," Josh chimed in, as they left him slumping down in his seat.

Mel and Barbara stood up from the table, introducing Josh and Maggie to the rest of their dinner crew.

"And you remember Tim Reingart," Mel announced, pointing to an older, yet charismatic man in his late sixties. "My boss from ValleyCon," he reminded Josh.

"Tim," Josh recalled, "thank you so much for coming."

"I wouldn't miss it for the world," Tim smiled. "You used to come around the office when you were just in high school. I'm sure you remember my daughter, Ellie?" he said, referring to the blonde woman to his side. She stood up, reaching out to shake his hand.

"I remember a seventeen-year-old Ellie," Josh said, laughing.

"She's thirty-eight now," she joked, referring to herself. "With an eight-year-old off doing god knows what," she said, turning to point to her son, tromping after a little girl who was stealing olives covertly from the bar.

"Oh, I believe he's causing chaos with *my* eight-year-old," chimed in Tina, who was sitting at the table with her husband Kevin. "That's Laney," she said, pointing as Laney led Ellie's son through the throngs of partygoers.

Ellie caught her son's eye, waving him over. He reluctantly turned away from Tina's daughter and came to the table. Laney, no longer having her admirer in tow, gave chase until both were standing in front of Josh and Maggie.

"Say hi to Josh and Maggie," Ellie said. "Say *thank you* for such a wonderful party."

Her son mumbled a response. "How many people did you invite to your wedding?" he asked.

"About two hundred," Josh said, matter-of-fact.

"That's a *lot* of people," her son replied.

Josh thought about it for a second, looked to Maggie, then back to the boy.

"It takes a village," he said, believing that with all his heart.

Thirty-One Years
(and Two Hours Later)

IT WAS NIGHTTIME. And everyone was gone.

Josh sat in a rickety old chair, the observatory structure lit up from within, a shaft of light protruding from the top of the dome and into the night sky. Josh took a sip of wine, then approached the open door to the structure.

He looked up at it, took a breath, and let it out. There were people he'd wished could be here. But sometimes, not everything worked out the way you wanted. Sometimes the universe had other plans. Ironically, tonight, Josh had his own plans for the universe.

He stepped inside, closing the door, and climbed the stairs.

Maggie looked at her watch.

The self-driving taxi moved smoothly through the streets of Sèvres, turning off the D407 and taking Rue Brancas toward Rue du Clos Anet. As it did, she stared out the moon roof of the vehicle, taking in the night sky. It was glorious and clear, sparkling with the light of a million stars. She smiled, knowing that if it made her happy, there was someone else who would be happier even still.

Especially today.

She unfolded her cell phone, extending it to the size of a small mirror, then turned on the backlight so she could get a good look at herself. Inside, she still felt thirty-three, but the reflection in the mirror contradicted those feelings with the reality of a sixty-three-year-old face. But it wasn't all bad news. Maggie looked happy, content, even fulfilled. Her eyes, bright and alive, checked every corner of her face—her lips, eyes, nose. Satisfied, she folded the phone back up and collected her gear as the drive to the house appeared through the taxi's front windows.

"Right here's fine," she spoke aloud, which the A.I. inside the taxi recognized. It pulled into the driveway, disengaging the locks, and opened the doors with a hiss.

Maggie closed the front door behind her.

She placed her metallic suitcase on the floor in the foyer, letting the wheels carry it to the edge of the stairs. Then she picked up her other two gear bags, slung them around her shoulders and continued on inside, past a wall of framed photos, showcasing her and Josh in their earlier days. On their first trip to Paris. On Josh's first day at the European Space Agency. The two of them painting walls in their Paris flat. Out at cafés. Touring the Louvre. There were pictures of Maggie taking pictures of food, opening her own artistic space, then transitioning to an even bigger one. There were photos from magazines, beautiful shots of gourmet dishes, and even a profile of Maggie in *Modern Photography*.

There were pictures of Maggie, pregnant. Shots of her and Josh with their daughter, Paige. Kindergarten, elementary, junior high, and high school. A picture of prom and high school graduation. The wall of photos spanned thirty years together, with the most recent ones showing the sixty-something versions of Josh and Maggie still together, and still in love.

At the end of the wall, a small ornate table sat under the light of a stained-glass lamp. Multiple pictures sat in an arranged semi-circle. One was the drunken selfie they'd taken at Mister Taco that infamous night, with Sombrero Frog and Salsa Frog behind them. Another housed a Polaroid of Josh, as a kid, on the It's a Small World ride at Disney World; another of Maggie perched atop Mulholland Drive with fireworks shooting off in the background. And there was the ornate frame that had, a long time ago, held the stock photo of the Lewis family; it was now replaced with the photo from Niagara Falls in all its glory with Maggie mugging for the camera while Josh looked sheepishly away.

Maggie entered a door at the end of the hallway, flipping on the lights to reveal a hi-tech darkroom. She placed her gear bags on the metallic table at the center of the room, opening the first to reveal a futuristic digital camera, which she put off to the side. Then she opened the second one, revealing the Nikon SP in all its glory.

She eyed it, brushing off the dust it had accumulated during the trip to London, getting into the nooks and crannies, restoring it to its always pristine condition. She had lost it once, and ever since she vowed to take care of it like a second child. Now that her father was gone, it meant more to her than ever before.

Josh pressed the rotation buttons at the base of the telescope, rotating the mechanism 45 degrees and bringing the Orion Nebula into focus. He leaned down excitedly, peering through the eyepiece, stunned at the clarity as the rotation reached its desired coordinates.

"Kind of an eyesore," a voice teased from behind him.

Josh turned, spotting Maggie hovering at the open door to the observatory, arms hanging from the top of the doorjamb in a confident, playful way. "Once we laid down the foundation there was no turning back," he said, grinning. "This eyesore is here to taunt you until the end of time."

Maggie crossed the threshold to Josh, and they kissed, then embraced. "How was London?" he asked, wondering about her latest week-long photography seminar that she had been teaching now for years. After a decade of building a reputation as the preeminent food photographer, and another decade of opening up her own shop, she'd turned to lecturing and teaching others, in the hopes that she could lend the kind of direction to her students that she'd wished she'd had in the early years. Had Josh not taken the job at the European Space Agency and fallen into teaching in his later years, Maggie may never have explored the opportunity for herself. She loved the act of giving back and making a difference with the next generation of artistic troubadours.

"Aside from a few who I wanted to slap upside the head, a wholly productive seminar," she joked, now home and present and wanting to give Josh's accomplishment the time it deserved. "Show me," she said, pointing to the telescope. "Show me what you see."

Josh made room so she could look into the eyepiece. "The Orion Nebula," he said, matter-of-fact. Maggie leaned down, squinting, adjusting her head until she remained still. Josh watched her, took her all in, ecstatic that she was as passionate about it as he was. She gasped as she took in the full view of the heavens.

"It's so clear. So beautiful," she said. Josh stood tall, proud, giving the structure's insides a once-over. He reached out for Maggie's hand, pulling her outside and into the backyard, where he led her to the two rickety chairs. There was an open bottle of wine and two glasses at the ready. He poured for both of them.

"Sorry I missed the unveiling," Maggie said, taking a sip. "Heathrow was a mess."

"It's fine," Josh replied. "You're here now."

They looked up at the observatory, standing tall in the middle of the backyard. The sounds of crickets buzzed around them, an unseen blanket of noise.

"It's going to kill our chances of ever selling this place," she said. "We're stuck now, buddy. House poor, with nowhere else to go."

"I can be okay with that," he said, smiling, "as long as you're here with me."

"Can I get back to you on that one?" she joked.

"Yes, you can," he replied, holding up his glass and clinking it against hers.

Josh lay still in the oversized bed, watching his chest rise and fall as the breeze from the open window turned the curtains into living, dancing beings. He stared out at the sky, a crisp blue hue, providing a home for the bright yellow of the rising sun. He turned onto his side, coming face to face with a still-slumbering Maggie, examining her face while she slept. He squinted at her beauty, trying to remember a time when she wasn't there.

But she had always been there.

Over the years, the puzzle pieces had materialized and come into focus. They had crossed paths more times than they had even remembered. But with time came realization. And with realization came proof.

There was more proof than anyone could have ever asked for.

There was the time Josh's parents had taken a six-year-old him to Walt Disney World, where he had found himself on the classic It's A Small World ride. His father had documented the visit, taking numerous pictures, including one from the front of the boat, looking back into the candy-colored landscapes. Behind them, there would be yet another boat, populated by another family, that just happened to include a four-year-old Maggie Mills.

They had stood in line next to each other minutes before the ride.

There was the time Maggie's father took the seventeen-year-old her to UCLA as part of her college tour. They'd be on their way to the UCLA Store, past Boelter Hall, the Science and Engineering Library and the UCLA Planetarium, where Astronomy 127, Stellar Atmospheres, Interiors, and Evolution would just be letting out. Josh, arms full of books and head in the clouds, would bump right into Maggie, dumping his scientific booty all over the ground.

She would help him pick up the books with her father watching on with suspicion, catching each other's eyes for a split second, then returning to their paths of the day. Josh would watch her go, hanging onto a feeling that he'd seen her before.

There was the Fourth of July in 2011, when Maggie and Cameron would forgo the usual fireworks celebration in Malibu, and hoof it up to the top of Mulholland Drive, ascending the roadside hills that looked out onto the San Fernando Valley. Cameron was sel-fie-obsessed that night, snapping dozens of pictures of the two of them, with the crackling lights hovering in the sky behind them.

There would be a shot with Josh in the background, laughing with one of the many women over the years whose name he couldn't even remember now, just like Maggie had trouble remembering the faceless men she'd dated over all those years.

It hadn't been Tina's fault. Or Gabriel's fault. Or his mother's fault. Or her father's fault. There was one very specific reason the two of them had never found that perfect relationship, or had long-term partners who they felt were "the ones." It was simple. And obvious. And when the puzzle pieces came together and the pictures revealed themselves, there was only one answer to it all.

They had been simply waiting for each other. And it had taken time, like most good things did. Besides, the universe often engi-neered fate at its own pace, on its own terms.

You couldn't argue with that even if you tried.

Maggie was standing by the front door when Josh lumbered down the stairs. He was wearing sneakers, a pair of sweatpants, and an old ratty t-shirt. She was far more fashionable, wearing form-fitting leggings, a tank top, and cross-training shoes.

"Chop chop," she barked.

"Yeah, yeah," he replied.

Their bicycles were already at the ready, parked on the cobble-stone path just outside the front door, retro in look and style. Maggie straddled the cruiser, connecting her phone to a pair of speakers in the basket up front. Josh got atop his, shared a look with Maggie, then they pedaled slowly until they reached the edge of their prop-erty and the main thoroughfare.

Maggie tapped an icon on the screen of her phone. The opening drum beats of Toto's "Africa" began playing. It was their go sign; she hit the pedals, as did Josh, picking up speed as they passed by the suburban neighborhood of Sèvres, its inhabitants still gearing up for a new day.

Maggie sang. Loudly. Incorrectly. "… *There's nothing that a hungry man or orca diver do.*" It echoed throughout the neighborhood. Josh laughed. After all these years, some things never changed. She looked at him, wanting his approval of her questionable rendition of the song. He piloted the bicycle, holding on with one hand, giving her a thumbs-up with the other. She smiled. Life was good.

"*Arrête de chanter!*" a voice shouted from a window along the street, desperately demanding that they stop singing. Maggie and Josh regarded it with surprise. Then amusement, as a chorus of disgruntled neighbors joined in.

This wasn't a fluke. This wasn't new. This had been going on for years.

And it wasn't like *Beauty and the Beast* at all.

Epilogue

I WAS JUST EIGHT years old when I met Laney Willis for the first time.

She was eight years old, too, she'd tell me, although I'd been born in February while she'd been born in August. She was afraid of spiders, loved crickets, hated cats, but loved dogs. Guinea pigs, well, you couldn't even mention the things. She liked to dress up, but also had to be comfortable; she had already taken off the ribbon around her dress because it hampered her ability to run at full speed. As for weddings, she just plain thought they were silly because "if you already love someone, why do you hafta dress up?"

She was cool for a fellow third-grader, I remember thinking, watching her swipe black olives from the bartender's stash when he wasn't looking, then shoving them in a glass like a chipmunk preparing for winter. I followed her around, weaving in and out of the well-dressed guests, until she finally turned on me and demanded to know who I was and what my intentions were. "You're stealing olives," I said, ever the good Samaritan of the libation-curation sub-culture.

"I'll share," she said with her piercing, confident eyes, as if sharing would dissuade me from turning her in. Well, *it did*. I nodded, because what else could I do, and she held out the glass so I could take a few for myself. "I love olives," she said, "especially the black ones … because they taste like metal."

Other eight-year-olds might have found it strange. Or weird. Or just plain crazy. But I found it cute. Disarming. Even endearing.

I was in, hook, line, and sinker.

When I was twelve, I landed in the hospital with a broken leg.

Had my best friend's father not worked at a lumber mill, a job he had only taken after losing one as a plumber's assistant, we would have never had the resources to build the bike ramp in the first place. And had we not chosen Shop as our seventh-grade elective at school, which had only happened after Coding had filled up due to popular demand, we would have never had the skills to get it built. And had the street not been closed for sewer repair that day, we would not have had the street free to ourselves, nor would it have allowed us to test the ramp, as we did, by jumping over multiple bags of garbage. At which point, of course, I would go careening sideways, landing on my leg, and breaking it in three places.

Had the local hospital down the street not been closed due to a water main bursting, my mother would have never taken me to the one at the edge of town. And had we not gone to the one at the edge of town, we would have never sat down in the waiting room, only to find ourselves sitting opposite a very familiar face.

It was Laney Willis and her mom.

Over the years, it became comical, bordering on strange.

I'd run into her at sixteen at an ice cream shop, and nineteen at a bar during winter break. We'd cross paths at eighteen at a graduation party, despite never remembering it happening, and at twenty-four while at the DMV. At twenty-five I'd see her from afar at the Hollywood Bowl, and at twenty-seven she'd see me passing her by on the freeway in the carpool lane with an attractive woman by my side. We'd run into each other, or just miss each other, or see each other when the other didn't, over and over again, as if the universe had seen fit to make it so.

Each moment would exist, not randomly, or by chance, but as a result of the small stuff. The tiny, insignificant decisions that the people around us were making, unknowingly putting us in a position to finally meet in a meaningful way.

Which had all begun at the wedding of Josh Allen and Maggie Mills.

Since their story had been the beginning of our story, I knew it frontwards and backwards, sideways and upside-down. I'd heard the stories, memorized the details, and repeated the anecdotes for years. One thing became clear throughout it all. If not for the small stuff that brought them together, Laney and I would have never had the opportunity ourselves.

When I was thirty-two, we'd find ourselves in the same elevator, at the same time, going to the same floor.

At first, as most people do, we stood on our respective sides of the elevator, attempting to busy ourselves with noise on our portable data devices. She'd look at her watch as I looked at my schedule on the augmented reality glasses I'd worn, barely paying attention to the grinding sound of the elevator as it labored to carry two reasonably light human beings from the lobby to the sixth floor. The building had once housed an online publication called *The 818*, that in hindsight was mostly known for its stellar restaurant reviews. But that's something I knew, and something that you knew too.

When the elevator grinded to a halt, it shouldn't have been a surprise. Because when you've got an Otis HydroFit from '08 in a building that should have been future-fitted in the thirties or forties, it's clearly the fault of the passengers willing to take a ride in one when it finally gives up the ghost and grinds to a halt in between floors. *As it did.*

Laney turned, nervous. "Did the elevator just …?"

I eyed her. She was familiar. There was something I recognized about her. I watched as she opened the ancient phone compartment built into the wall of the elevator to find that the phone receiver had been ripped out entirely.

"It did," I said, referring to the missing receiver, "and that's clearly not a good sign, either."

The not-so-good sign was replaced by a better sign: the two of us, having hovered at the periphery of each other's lives for years, had finally found ourselves in the same place, at the same time, with no distractions. There was no one else to put a pause on the moment, to drag us away, to keep us apart. For once in our lives, the distractions faded into the background, and the timing was right for us to simply focus on one another.

"*It's you,*" she said.

Had my grandfather never offered a job to Mel Allen, he would have never moved to California or worked at ValleyCon. Had he never worked at ValleyCon, I would have never been invited to his son's wedding. Had her mother not been in the same kindergarten class as Josh Allen, she would have never shared a desk (*and popcorn*) with him, thus impacting Josh in such a way that she, too, would be invited to his wedding. If either of those two things had not happened, the two of us would never have met. But that had just been the beginning. There were choices and decisions she had made over the years that brought her to Texas, then Colorado, then back to L.A. She had dated these men, broken up with those men, then found herself focusing on just herself for some time. She had changed careers twice, then finally landed on the one she was pursuing now, which had brought her to this building, on this day, for a job interview.

The same job interview that I had shown up for, too.

Was it fate? Was it chance? Was it the infinite universe, making finite choices for a finite life? The pathways were twisting, intersecting, and converging, all behind the scenes. If you looked back, they were clear as day, right there out in the open. Tied intimately to the village of people on the periphery of our lives, whose tiny insignificant decisions had a significance we only recognized after the majority of the work had been done.

So, then why? Why them? Why us?

Sometimes it was better to leave well enough alone, and not ask the big questions. Sometimes good things happened and you just had to accept them. Sometimes when your hopes and dreams became a reality, it was better to stop worrying about how'd they come to pass or who had tried to stand in the way, and just embrace one's present reality while you could.

It was a small thing, but what the heck. Sometimes it was the small stuff that made all the difference.

Acknowledgments

Thanks to my wife. To my kids. To my dog. For your undying love, support and enthusiasm. Also, thanks for letting me talk your ear off about every tiny, little insignificant moment I chose to put in this book and then thank you (kids) for letting me replace your bedtime stories with "suspicious" sounding ones that were really just scenes from upcoming chapters I wanted to test on my own personal focus group. I may have done some developmental damage to you, but by the time you figure out where this deep-seated baggage came from, I'll be long gone.

To my mother and father, my sisters and brothers (some in-laws, some not) and extended family members, all of whom were able to blindly support me in my endeavors because they don't live with me. If they did, this whole schtick might get old, so thankfully they don't. Also: some of them read multiple versions of this book, some read half of one, and some simply marveled at how many pages it was without reading it at all … but I still love you all the same no matter your level of investment or sweat equity.

Major props to my editor, Kate Ankofski, who helped me shape and hone *The Small Stuff* with her sharp, insightful and constructive feedback. You know you've got a stellar book editor when you look forward to receiving notes, so … chalk that up for what it is. The book is better for Kate's involvement in it.

Then there's artist extraordinaire, Max Dalton, who lent his enormous talent to the front and back cover of this book. Not only was he up for the challenge, but working with him was an easy, inspiring and satisfying journey. Had I dreamed of the perfect cover for my debut fiction novel, it wouldn't have come anywhere close to what he delivered.

And who could forget Hadleigh House and its three principals – Anna Biehn, Allison Mann, and Alisha Perkins? Not me. Their approach to this creative partnership, with an emphasis on collaboration and communication, is more than I could have imagined. Their advice and counsel throughout the entire process has been invaluable and appreciated immensely.

I'd also like to thank Nia Vardalos, Ann Garvin, David Yoon, Luke Geddes, Melissa Maerz, Suzy Krause, Elizabeth Gonzalez James, DM Sinclair, Gary Goldstein, Fabian Marquez, and an extremely awesome Cameron Crowe, whose own writing and generous creative feedback on some of my past projects kept the engine running even when it was low on gas.

Finally, and in the spirit of this book, *The Small Stuff* would never have come to be if it wasn't for my grandparents' dog Inky, my childhood hamster dying from pneumonia, my parents' choice to move from the East Coast to Northern California, my mother's misguided decision to hire me to work in her bookstore, the Pleasant Hill dome theater, asking that redhead at summer camp to "go steady," getting a 99/100 on my driver's license written test, moving to Los Angeles to work on a film about a blind woman directed by a British auteur, going through that red light on Beverly Boulevard that one day after work, agreeing to dress up in 70s attire for that party at Miyagi's on the Sunset Strip, working as a producer on a reality TV show shooting south of the border, meeting the Muppets, taking a gig in the Pacific Northwest at one of two technological behemoths, burning my tongue on faulty Sour Patch Kids … and about a million other tiny, insignificant moments, that I probably don't even remember experiencing but I should definitely acknowledge.

So … thank you, insignificant moments of my life.

Thank you very much.

About the Author

Paul Davidson is an author and producer who has spent years working in Hollywood, as well as the maddeningly hilarious world of tech behemoths.

He lampooned Corporate America in his first book *Consumer Joe* (Random House) and imagined what the world would have been like if historical figures had been able to blog in *The Lost Blogs* (Hachette). His writing has been featured in *Wired*, the *Los Angeles Times* and *Mental Floss*. *The Small Stuff* is his first fiction novel.

Paul lives in Los Angeles with his wife, two daughters, and their dog Samson.

Find him at www.pauldavidson.net.

CPSIA information can be obtained
at www.ICGtesting.com
Printed in the USA
LVHW040035290422
717483LV00007B/989

9 781735 773872